THE
BLACK
MADONNA

**Center Point
Large Print**

Also by Davis Bunn
and available from Center Point Large Print:

Full Circle
Gold of Kings

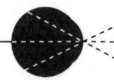

**This Large Print Book carries the
Seal of Approval of N.A.V.H.**

THE
BLACK
MADONNA

DAVIS BUNN

CENTER POINT PUBLISHING
THORNDIKE, MAINE

This Center Point Large Print edition
is published in the year 2010 by arrangement with
Howard Books, a division of Simon & Schuster, Inc.

The text of this Large Print edition is unabridged.
In other aspects, this book may vary
from the original edition.
Printed in the United States of America
on permanent paper.
Set in 16-point Times New Roman type.

ISBN: 978-1-60285-884-8

Library of Congress Cataloging-in-Publication Data

Bunn, T. Davis, 1952-
  The Black Madonna / Davis Bunn.
    p. cm.
  ISBN 978-1-60285-884-8 (lib. bdg. : alk. paper)
  1. Americans—Middle East—Fiction. 2. Antique dealers—Fiction. 3. Relics—Fiction.
  4. Large type books. I. Title.
  PS3552.U4718B57 2010b
  813'.54—dc22

                                                    2010020962

This book is dedicated to
Nicholas and Sheila Wood,
whose support and good humor
enrich our projects and our lives

ONE

FROM THE CREST OF THE Herodium dig, Harry Bennett could look out and see three wars.

The isolated, cone-shaped hill rose two thousand feet over the Judean Desert. Herodium, the palace-fortress built by Herod the Great, had been erected on the site of his victory against the Parthians in 40 BCE. Herod had then served as king of Judea under his Roman masters, but he had been utterly despised by the Judeans. When Herod's sons were finally vanquished, Herodium had been evacuated. Over the centuries, the city became a legend, its location a myth.

Modern excavations had begun in the sixties, only to be interrupted by wars and intifadas and disputes over jurisdiction. Harry Bennett was part of a group excavating the original palace fortress. The current project was supervised by a woman professor from the Sorbonne. She had fought for six years to gain the license, and nothing so minor as somebody else's war was going to stop her work.

The volunteers came from a dozen nations, to dig and learn and bury themselves in history. Most were in their twenties and tried to keep up a brave face despite the rumbles of conflict and the brutal heat. The day Harry arrived at Herodium, three

Scandinavian backpackers had perished hiking above the Ein Gedi National Forest. With water in their packs. Just felled by the ferocious heat.

And here Harry was, huddled under the relentless glare of that same deadly sun, using his trowel and his brush to scrape two thousand years of crud off a stone.

Officially Harry and the other volunteers were restricted to the dig and their hilltop camp. With Hamas missiles streaking the nighttime sky, none of the other unpaid staff were much interested in testing their boundaries. But twice each week the Sorbonne professor traveled to Jerusalem and delivered her finds to the ministry. When she departed that particular afternoon, Harry signaled to the Palestinian operating the forklift. Ten minutes later, they set off in Hassan's decrepit pickup.

The angry wind blasting through his open window tasted of sand as dry as volcanic ash. Hassan followed the pitted track down an incline so steep Harry gripped the roof and propped one boot on the dashboard. He tried to ignore the swooping drop to his right by studying the horizon, which only heightened his sense of descending into danger. North and east rose the Golan hills and sixty years of struggle with Syria. Straight north was the Lebanese border, home to the Hezbollah hordes. To the southwest lay Gaza, provider of their nightly firework displays.

All West Bank digs were required to employ a certain number of locals. Hassan was one of the few who arrived on time, did an honest day's work, and showed a keen interest in every new discovery. On Harry's first day at the site, he had put the man down for a grave robber and a smuggler.

The West Bank was the richest area for artifacts in all Judea. There were thousands of sites, many dating from the Iron Age, others from the Roman era, and more still from Byzantium. Many sites remained undiscovered by archeologists but were well known to generations of Palestinians, who fiercely guarded their troves and passed the locations down from generation to generation.

Hassan's former job wouldn't have sat well with the Israeli authorities. But people like Hassan took the long view. Eventually things would settle down, and when they did, Hassan would return to his real trade. In the meantime, Hassan hid his profession from the Israeli authorities, lay low, and remained open to a little persuasion. In Harry's case, that amounted to a thousand dollars.

They arrived in Hebron three hours later. The city crawled up the slopes of two hills and sprawled across a dull desert bowl. Entering Hebron around sunset, in the company of a Palestinian smuggler, was an act of total lunacy.

Harry Bennett wouldn't have had it any other way.

Clustered on hilltops to the north of the old

city rose the UN buildings, the university, and a huddle of government high-rises built with international relief funding. Other hills were dominated by Jewish settlements. These were rimmed by fences and wire and watchtowers that gleamed in the descending light. The rest of Hebron was just your basic war zone.

Sunset painted Hebron the color of old rust. The city held the tightly sullen feel of a pot that had boiled for centuries. Even the newer structures looked run-down. Most walls were pockmarked with bullet holes and decorated with generations of graffiti. Harry saw kids everywhere. They bore such tight expressions they resembled old people in miniature. Looking into their eyes made Harry's chest hurt.

The streets were calm, the traffic light. Which was good, because it allowed them to make it to the city center early. It was also bad, because the Israel Defense Forces soldiers had nothing better to do than watch Hassan's truck. Two IDF soldiers manning a reinforced guard station tracked the pickup with a fifty-caliber machine gun.

Hassan said, "This idea is not so good, maybe."

Harry nodded slowly. He smelled it too, the biting funk of cordite not yet lit. But he would trust his driver. "You say go, we go."

Hassan's gaze flitted over to Harry. "You pay?"

"The deal's the same. You get the other five hundred when we're done."

Hassan wiped his face with a corner of his checkered head-kerchief. "We stay."

Harry halfway wished the man's nerve would fail and he would turn his rattling truck around. "Better to come in twice than not go home at all."

"You know danger?"

"Some."

"I think maybe more than some. I think you see much action."

"That was then and this is now," Harry replied. "You're my man on the ground here. I'm relying on your eyes and ears. I can't tell what's real and what's just your normal garden-variety funk."

Hassan skirted a pothole large enough to swallow the neighboring Israeli tank. "Say again, please."

"Let's assume for a second that you and I can do business together."

Hassan pointed at Harry's shirt pocket holding the five bills—the rest of his fee. "This is not business?"

"I'd call it a first step. Say your man shows up like you promised. Say he's got the goods and the buy goes well. What happens next?"

"If the first buy goes well, you trust me for more."

"Right. But I need someone who can sniff out traps and see through walls. There's so much danger around here, my senses are on overload."

The man actually smiled. "Welcome to Hebron."

"I didn't go to all this trouble for just one item, no matter how fine this guy's treasure might be. I need you to tell me if we're safe or if we should pull out and return another time."

Hassan did not speak again until he parked the truck and led Harry into a café on Hebron's main square. "What you like?"

"You mean, other than getting out of here with my skin intact? A mint tea would go down well."

Hassan placed the order and settled into the rickety chair across from Harry. "There are many Americans like you?"

"I'm one of a kind."

"Yes. I think you speak truth." Hassan rose to his feet. "Drink your tea. I go ask what is happening."

All Harry could do was sit there and watch the only man he knew in Hebron just walk away. From his spot by the bullet-ridden wall, isolated among the patrons at other tables who carefully did not look his way, Harry felt as though he had a bull's-eye painted on his forehead. Even the kid who brought his tea and plate of unleavened bread looked scared. Harry stirred in a spoonful of gray, unrefined sugar and lifted the tulip-shaped glass by its rim. All he could taste was the flavor of death.

AFTER SUNSET, THE HEBRON AIR cooled at a grudging pace. Harry watched as the city square filled with people and traffic and shadows. The café became crowded with people who avoided looking Harry's way. Across the plaza, the Tomb of the Patriarchs shone pearl white. Beside the cave complex stood the Mosque of Abraham, a mammoth structure dating back seven hundred years.

The caves had been bought by the patriarch Abraham for four hundred coins, such an astronomical sum that the previous owner had offered to throw in the entire valley. But Abraham had insisted upon overpaying so that his rightful ownership would never be questioned. He had wanted the caves as his family's burial site because supposedly they were also where Adam and Eve had been laid to rest. Besides Abraham himself, the caves also held the remains of his wife, Sarah, along with Rebecca, Isaac, and Jacob.

The guy who made his way toward Harry's table resembled an Arab version of the Pillsbury Doughboy. The man waddled as he walked. His legs splayed slightly from the knees down. His round face was topped by flattened greasy curls that glistened in the rancid lights of the café. He walked up, slumped into the chair across the table from Harry, and demanded, "You have money?"

Harry kept his gaze on the square and the crawling traffic. "Where's Hassan?"

"Hassan is not my business. He is your business. You must answer my question. You have money?"

Harry was about to let the guy have it when he spotted Hassan returning across the plaza. When he reached the café's perimeter, Hassan seated himself at an empty table, facing outward toward the plaza, placing himself between Harry and any incoming threat. Harry relaxed slightly. It was always a pleasure doing business with a pro.

Harry said, "Let's take this from the top. I'm—"

"I know who you are. Harry Bennett seeks treasure all over the world. You see? We meet because I check you out."

"What's your name?"

"Wadi Haddad."

"Wadi, like the word for oasis?"

"Yes, is same." He wore a rumpled linen jacket, its armpits wet and darkened with sweat. He reached in a pocket and came up with a pack of filterless Gitanes. "You want?"

"Never learned to use them, thanks."

Wadi Haddad lit the cigarette with a gold lighter. The stench of black tobacco encircled the table. "I have much interesting items. Very nice."

"I didn't come to Hebron for nice, Mr. Haddad. I came for exceptional. You understand that word?"

"Exceptional is also very expensive."

"One of a kind," Harry went on. "Unique. Extremely old. And I have always been partial to gold."

Wadi Haddad revealed a lizard's tongue, far

14

too narrow for his globular face. It flitted in and out several times, tasting the air. "How much money you have?"

"Not a cent with me."

"Then I also have nothing. Business is finished." But Wadi Haddad did not move.

"Here's how it's going to work," said Harry. "You show me the item. I photograph it."

"No. Photographs absolutely not to happen."

"I show the photographs to my clients. If they like, they transfer the money to an escrow account at the Bank of Jordan in Amman. You understand, escrow?"

"I know."

"Good. Then you bring the item to Jerusalem and we make the exchange."

"Not Jerusalem. Too much police everyplace."

"Okay, Mr. Haddad. Where would you prefer?"

"Petra."

"Too small. I like bright lights, big city."

"Then Amman."

Which had been Harry's choice all along. Even so, he pretended to give that some thought. "Okay, Amman. Hotel InterContinental. You got an account at the Bank of Jordan?"

"I make one happen."

"Then we're ready to roll. All we need is the merchandise."

"No photographs."

"Then no business. Sorry, Charlie."

"My name is Wadi."

"Whatever. I don't shoot, I don't buy."

"Photographs cost you a thousand dollars."

Suddenly Harry was very tired of this two-step. "Fine. But I take the thousand from the final purchase price. And don't even think of arguing."

Wadi Haddad did not rise so much as bounce from the seat. "Okay, we go. Not your man." He nodded toward Hassan. "Just you."

"Be right with you." Harry walked to Hassan's table and squatted down beside the man's chair. "You find anything?"

"Hebron is one tense city. People very worried."

"Yeah, I caught that too." Harry liked how the guy never stopped searching the shadows. "Where'd you see action, Hassan?"

"Nowhere. I see nothing, I do nothing. In the West Bank there is only IDF and terrorists."

"Wadi's taking me to check out the merchandise. He says I've got to do this alone. You think maybe you could watch my back?"

"Is good." Hassan held to a catlike stillness. "I see something, I whistle. I can whistle very loud."

Harry rose to his feet, patted the guy's shoulder, and said, "You just earned yourself another five bills."

WADI HADDAD MOVED SURPRISINGLY FAST on his splayed legs. He led Harry deep into the

16

old city. The West Bank crisis was etched into every Hebron street, every bullet-ridden wall, every building topped by an IDF bunker. The streets were either dimly lit or not at all. But walking behind the wheezing Haddad, Harry had no trouble picking his way through the rubble. Behind him, the mosque and the cave complex shone like beacons. And up ahead loomed the wall.

The barrier separating the Jewish sector from Hebron's old city was thirty feet high and topped with razor wire. Searchlights from the guard towers and nearby IDF bunkers serrated the night. The wall gleamed like a massive concrete lantern.

Somewhere in the distance a truck backfired. Wadi Haddad froze. A searchlight illuminated the man's trembling jowls. Harry said, "You're not from here."

"My mother's family only. I live sometimes Damascus, sometimes Aqaba."

Aqaba was Jordan's portal to the Red Sea, a haven for tourists and smugglers' dhows. "Must be nice."

Wadi Haddad started off once more, Harry following close. But when Haddad entered a dark, narrow alley, Harry dug in his heels. "Hold up there."

"What's the matter, treasure man?"

The buildings to either side reached across to

form a crumbling arch. The windows fronting the street were both barred and dark. The alley was black. Harry had spent a lifetime avoiding alleys like this. Then he saw a cigarette tip gleam. "That your buddy down there?"

"Is guard, yes. In Hebron, many guards."

"Ask him to step out where I can see him."

Wadi didn't like it, but he did as Harry said. The man emerged and flipped on a flashlight. In the dim rays reflected from the walls, Harry could see a face like a parrot, with too-narrow features sliding back from a truly enormous nose. The man's eyes were set very close together and gleamed with the erratic light of an easy killer.

"Ask him to light up that alley for us."

The man smirked at Harry's nerves but did not wait for Wadi's translation. The flashlight showed an empty lane that ended about eighty feet back with double metal doors. "What's behind the doors, Wadi?"

"Where we go. My mother's cousin's house."

Harry motioned to the man holding the light. "Lead on, friend."

The guard spoke for the first time. "You have guns?"

Harry lifted his shirt and turned around. "Make business, not war. That's my motto."

"He can search you?"

"Sure thing." Harry gestured at the doors. "Inside."

18

THE DOORS RATTLED IN ALARM as the guard pushed them open. Wadi called out and, on hearing no response, stepped into a neglected courtyard with Harry close behind. The dusty compound appeared empty. A pair of plastic chairs sprawled by a rusty outdoor table, their upended legs jutting like broken teeth. From inside the house a dog barked. In the distance Harry both heard and felt the grinding tremor of an IDF tank on road patrol.

Wadi led Harry to a flat-roofed side building of unfinished concrete blocks and opened a door with flaking paint. The interior was an astonishment. The front room was a well-appointed display chamber about twelve feet square. Two walls were stuccoed a light peach. A third wall was covered by a frieze of mythical birds carved from what Harry suspected was olive wood. The fourth wall held a narrow steel door with a central combination lock.

"Looks like I found the guy I've been looking for," Harry said.

Wadi held out his hand. "Thousand dollars."

Harry was about to insist he see the item first, then decided there was no reason to get off on the wrong sandal.

Wadi counted in the Arab fashion, folding the bills over and peeling the oily edges with his thumb and forefinger. He slipped the money into his pocket and motioned with his chin to the guard.

The steel door swung open on greased hinges. The guard stepped inside and emerged with a black velvet stand shaped like a woman's neck. What was draped on the stand took Harry's breath away.

The concept of women's ornamentation was as old as civilization itself. The earliest forms were fashioned as temple offerings and were considered to have magical properties. Many ancient cultures revered such jewelry for its talismanic power either to ward off evil or bring good health and prosperity.

In the very earliest days of Christianity, new believers drawn from Hellenistic temple cults often brought with them such ideas about the powers of jewelry. The necklace dated from the second century AD. The chain was a series of gold tubes, each stamped with a Christian design. It ended in an emerald the size of Harry's thumb. The gemstone had been sanded flat and carved with the Chi-Rho symbol.

Without asking, Wadi handed Harry a pair of white gloves and a jeweler's loupe. Closer inspection only confirmed Harry's first impression. This was a museum-quality piece.

The problem was, Harry could not identify it as a fake. Which was troubling, because Harry knew for a fact the item was not genuine.

Harry Bennett had nothing against a little smuggling. He would certainly not have helped anyone track down another treasure dog.

Counterfeiters, though, were a different breed of lice.

After nearly three years of roiling conflict, the Israeli Antiquities Authority had basically lost control of smuggling in the West Bank. In the past, the IAA had nabbed about ninety thieves each year for pilfering tombs, ruined cities, palaces, and forts. Since the latest political troubles began, however, arrests had slumped to almost nothing. The IAA knew without question that the worst culprits were getting away. The international arts market was being flooded with ancient Hebrew treasure. What was more, a growing number of these items were bogus. Extremely well crafted, their workmanship often able to fool museum directors and other supposed experts, but phony just the same.

The Israeli government had needed somebody with Harry Bennett's credentials, known throughout the world as a dedicated treasure dog. Somebody capable of infiltrating the system and identifying the source of the fake artifacts.

Only when Harry looked up did he realize he had been holding his breath. He handed the loupe and gloves back to Wadi and unsnapped the case of his pocket camera. "Okay if I shoot a few?"

21

Wadi smirked as he pulled the cigarettes from his pocket. The man knew a buyer's lust when he saw it. "Sure, sure, many as you like. You want tea?"

DICKERING OVER PRICE TOOK UNTIL well after midnight. Even so, when Harry stepped through the compound's steel door, the city remained noisily alive. Such was the manner of every Middle Eastern city Harry had ever visited, and it was one of the reasons why he relished the Arab world. These lands were full of pirates and their love of dark hours.

Wadi Haddad wore his sourest done-in-by-the-deal frown. "You give me no profit. My daughters starve."

Harry clamped down on his first thought, which was that this guy definitely hadn't missed a lot of meals. "Phone you in four days, right?"

"Four, maybe five. These days the border is very tight."

"Then maybe you ought to bring out the other items you're holding here for sale."

"You buy more?"

"If they're as fine as what you just showed me, sure, I think I can find buyers."

"Not same price," Wadi complained. "Too much hard bargain."

Harry was about to say what he thought of Wadi's poor-boy tactic when, from the distance, he heard a shrill whistle pierce the night.

The guard stood at the alley's mouth, searching in all directions. Wadi remained intent upon business, sucking on his cigarette and grumbling through the smoke as he walked past where Harry stood tense and rooted to the dusty earth. "Next time your price plus thirty percent. You pay or I go find—"

Harry leaned forward and gripped Wadi's shoulder and pulled him back. He slammed Wadi onto the alley wall, placing himself between the trader and the road. Wadi's breath whooshed out in a fetid cloud. His eyes registered surprise and rising protest. But Harry kept him pinned where he was.

Then the world of Hebron roared in rage and flames.

TWO

PALM BEACH REVEALED A NEW fashion statement that season. Storm Syrrell called it Bankruptcy Bleak.

Ever since the Madoff scandal had struck Palm Beach like a medieval plague, conservative suits and muted tones had been in vogue. Which was why Storm wore her bleakest outfit to the bankruptcy auction.

Storm actually had no business attending that day's event. She was still arguing with her aunt as she crossed the causeway and headed north.

Storm told Claudia, "All I'll do is offer the vultures another carcass to swoop over."

"Pass out a few cards. See if anyone is hiring."

"Like I'm packing the perfect résumé for hard times. Girl for hire, good at only one thing. Pretending to run an arts and treasures business."

"There is no one on earth who is less of a pretender than you."

"Which is why I've managed to run Syrrell's Palm Beach into the ground. Twice. This after burying the founder of our fine company. Not to mention sending my own father to jail."

Claudia went silent. Storm's aunt had never fully recovered from the previous season's strain. Claudia had walked the family antiques business through bankruptcy, discovered her father had been murdered, and then was kidnapped by her own brother. Storm's elegant aunt tended to become somewhat frayed around the edges whenever confronted by those memories.

Storm blinked through the sheen of Florida sunshine on her windshield and said as an apology, "I had another conversation with our banker this morning."

"I overheard your side of that little chat, remember?"

"He is not advancing us any more credit."

"I assumed as much, given the way you hammered down the receiver and then blistered the ceiling."

"I don't know if we can manage—" A click on her earpiece freed her from needing to finish that thought. "I've got another call."

"It's not your fault, Storm."

The fact that her own head said the same thing, only to be drowned out by the wash of repeated guilt, left Storm greeting the new caller with a choked hello.

Which, given it was the banker who was threatening to cut off their financial air, would on any other day have been good for a laugh. "Gerald Geldorf here, Ms. Syrrell. I thought you should know a significant deposit just arrived in your account."

Storm had been promising as much for six months, hoping against all economic logic for a moneyed buyer to take some of their dusty wares off her hands. But a frantic search of her mental inventory did not reveal any such genie.

"Hello? Are you there, Ms. Syrrell?"

She cleared her throat. "Which deposit would that be, Mr. Geldorf?"

"Four hundred thousand dollars."

"Say again, please."

He did so. "May I take some of these funds to write down your overdraft?"

"I'll have to get back to you on that."

"I must remind you, Ms. Syrrell, your company is currently operating in very dangerous territory, and unless there is a swift balancing of your corporate books, we may be forced to—"

Whoever chose that moment to phone her deserved a commission, if only she could afford to offer one. "Sorry, Mr. Geldorf. Another call is coming in."

"I will be expecting your response, Ms. Syrrell. Today."

She cradled the phone, hunted for a decent breath, then hit the button for the new call. "This is Storm Syrrell."

A male voice said, "I assume that you have received the deposit of funds."

"Who is speaking, please?"

"I am faxing through instructions for you to bid on my behalf. An oil by Pokhitonov is coming up in today's auction. Do you know the name?"

"Of course, but—"

"I want you to obtain it."

Storm pulled up to a stoplight and checked the phone's readout. The incoming call showed a British prefix. She asked, "Is there any reason I should not know your name?"

"Unless you are successful today, Ms. Syrrell, the only thing you will need to know about me is the account to which you must return my money."

THE REGION OF MANALAPAN WAS, in Storm's opinion, about as seriously strange as rich people would ever want to get. The peninsula below

South Palm Beach was eleven miles long and eleven hundred feet wide, but had a maximum elevation of ten inches. One decent blow and the island would vanish beneath the storm surge.

Storm Syrrell figured the inhabitants were so rich, they assumed they could order hurricanes north.

In the midst of the worst economic downturn since the Great Depression, the last remaining strip of Manalapan sand went on the market. Nineteen hundred feet wide, eleven hundred deep.

Fourteen million dollars.

Storm's destination that day was a palace that occupied Manalapan's southern tip. She parked outside the gates for a quick getaway, showed her ID to the security, accepted her catalogue and bidding paddle, passed through a foyer of Jerusalem granite, and entered a parlor that could have swallowed the Miami Dolphins' stadium. Despite having seen her share of interiors on the block, this place was good for a gawk.

Not even Manalapan's superrich had managed to escape the Madoff plague. Bernard Madoff had wintered in Palm Beach. His clientele had included many of Palm Beach's finest. There were some streets on Palm Beach Island where every family faced bankruptcy, every multimillion-dollar home awaited the auctioneer's hammer, every bank account was wiped clean. The locals called these areas Bernievilles, after the Depression-era Hoovervilles that had infested U.S. cities.

Needless to say, it was not ideal timing for a lady to establish herself in the Palm Beach antiques and treasures trade.

As Storm slipped through the vultures clustered at the back of the room, someone softly called her name. She waved without seeing who it was. They might smile, they might wish her well. But her financial woes had the same effect as an arterial wound.

She found a seat, checked her catalogue, and saw the Pokhitonov oil would not come up for at least another hour. Then a man slipped into the adjacent chair and whispered, "I've been trying to contact you. Might I say, my dear, that is a most becoming outfit."

"Until this spring, the only time I wore it was for Sean's funeral."

"Then it fits the season." Jacob Rausch lifted his paddle, bidding on a pair of Rodin marbles. "I am truly sorry to hear of your troubles. You deserve better. As does Syrrell's."

Jacob Rausch's family was considered nobility within the New York antiques trade. Rausch was in his early fifties and was known for his polished manners and his Savile Row suits. His expression of sympathy might have been genuine. But for the right commission he would have eaten his own young.

28

Storm replied, "Don't believe every rumor you hear."

Jacob waited while the auctioneer went through his introductory spiel over a late Impressionist oil, then said, "I have made it my business to obtain the facts about Syrrell's. How long can you survive, a week? Certainly not a month."

"Longer."

Jacob Rausch offered a smile as welcoming as a polished blade. "I doubt that very much. While I admire you for settling Sean's outstanding debts, your timing could not have been worse. You can only live on consignments and the goodwill of your grandfather's allies for so long. The economy is in dire straits, the general market has dried up, you do not have a strong enough client list of your own to survive. Syrrell's is going under."

Having her own conviction delivered by an outsider, and in such a courtly manner, only twisted the knife. "Thanks for your concern, Jacob. But I have—"

"Do me the courtesy of hearing my offer." He raised his paddle. Again. Shook his head at the next counterbid. Then said, "My son is coming along well. I've decided he should establish a new base in Palm Beach. I want to buy you out. Your shop's entire contents, your lease, your name. The works."

"That is not an offer. It's a death sentence."

When her phone chirped, Storm checked a readout she could not actually see and rose unsteadily to her feet. "I have to take this."

Jacob Rausch chased her away with, "It's time you faced facts. Syrrell's is finished. At least this way Sean's name will live on."

Storm crossed the foyer, passed the bodyguards, and reentered the brilliantly humid day. The phone's readout said the call came from Claudia. Storm said, "Give me a minute." She paced the brick forecourt, searching for an easy breath, then lifted the phone and reported, "I just got savaged by Jacob Rausch."

Claudia listened in silence as Storm related the offer, then said, "I hear Jacob's just gotten married again. For the fifth time. His bride is twenty-two. Which is probably why he wants his son out of the way. Reduce the in-house competition."

"That's your response?"

"What were you expecting—for me to tell you to do it? I stopped singing that tune over a year ago."

"So why did you call?" asked Storm.

"I am holding a very mysterious fax. Ordering you to purchase an oil by a Russian whose name I don't recognize."

"I know," replied Storm. "I've spoken to the buyer. And our bank." She rubbed the aching wound over her heart. "But one new client doesn't make for a turnaround."

"It's a start." When Storm did not respond, Claudia pressed her. "Go in there and win us a commission. We can discuss funeral arrangements when you get back."

TODAY'S SECURITY OFFICERS HAD BEEN supplied by the auctioneers. Storm had met them at other stops along the bankruptcy trail. A number of Palm Beach's finest had clung to solvency through the high season, hoping against hope for a white-knight buyer who would permit them to depart with their dignity and credit ratings intact. But the season had never really gotten off the ground, and cash buyers remained absent. Hope drained as fast as the temperatures spiked. The auctioneers had never been busier. Their security possessed a well-honed talent for spotting their next client. They treated Storm with a courtesy normally reserved for the bereaved's immediate clan.

In order to avoid another confrontation with the genteel hangman, Storm selected a row where hers was the only unoccupied chair. She pretended to inspect her catalogue as a Klimt was placed on the stand beside the auctioneer. Before Hurricane Madoff struck Palm Beach, such catalogues were glossy and bound and boasted highly detailed prints on their covers. Nowadays they were often little more than stapled computer printouts.

Storm lifted her paddle a few times, bidding early on the next several items, dropping out before the prices moved anywhere near closure, just establishing herself in the auctioneer's eye as a potential buyer. Despite the day's overcast mood, she felt a familiar adrenaline rush over being back in the game.

The Klimt was replaced by a lovely trio of Degas sketches, and they by a one-off Waterford crystal tiger with fiery rubies for eyes. Storm watched her painting begin its gradual procession up the side aisle. This was the game she was destined to play. The only job she had ever wanted. In the only world that ever mattered enough to push her heart to the redline. Even on a day as fractured as this.

"Item seventy-six. An intimate portrait by Ivan Pokhitonov, an important Russian realist."

A lovely young assistant wearing a starched tuxedo shirt and matching white gloves paraded the oil before the gathering, then settled it on the easel to the right of the auctioneer.

"The painting, entitled *The Red Army Soldier*, holds a provenance beyond question. Acquired by the current owner directly from the painter's son." The auctioneer tried to inject a note of significance into his windup. But he could not quite keep his gaze from drifting down the aisle to where his next item, an early Modigliani, beckoned. "An excellent example of Russia's struggle to preserve and reinvigorate their national culture."

Storm shared the auctioneer's unspoken disdain for the portrait. It possessed the rough-hewn quality of many Russian artists of that epoch. Like late-nineteenth-century writers, Russian artists had struggled to redefine their national identity. In Storm's opinion, Ivan Pavlovich Pokhitonov was remarkable only for his attempts to draw from the nation's former intense interest in Orthodox mystical religiosity. This particular portrait was supposedly of a Red Army soldier who had saved the artist's life during one of the numerous uprisings that had swept through the countryside prior to the First World War. The painting revealed a clash between the old Orthodox concept of divine protection and newer, colder Soviet attitudes. In Storm's opinion, the artist had failed to mesh the two. Yet this had not stopped the price of Pokhitonov's paintings and that of other pre-Soviet artwork from shooting into the stratosphere, propelled by Russian billionaires and their newfound patriotic fervor. All this had ended, however, when the price of Russian natural gas and oil had tumbled.

"Bidding will begin at seventy-five thousand. On my right, seventy-five. Who will offer me eighty?"

Storm held back until the painting reached what she assumed was the final stage of bidding at two hundred and ten thousand dollars. Bidding hung there for what to Storm felt like an electric eternity. Finally one of the original bidders, a female dealer from Boston with a fullback's jaw and orange hair, gave her white-knuckled assent.

"I am bid two fifteen by the lady here in the second row. Who will give me two twenty? No one? Two fifteen, going once. Anyone willing to offer me two twenty for this fine example of—"

Storm raised her paddle.

"Two hundred and twenty thousand, a new bidder to my right. Who will offer two twenty-five?"

The woman jerked in surprise but caught herself in the process of turning around. She nodded as much as her rigid muscles permitted.

"Back to you, madame, at two twenty-five. Am I offered two thirty?"

This time, when Storm raised her paddle, she felt eyes around the room begin to shift in her direction.

"Two thirty from the lady to my right. Two forty. Anyone? Come now. The price of Russian oil is bound to lift out of the cellar sooner rather than later. Consider this an investment in your company's future. Thank you, madame. Bidding stands at two forty." The auctioneer lifted his gavel at Storm. "Back to you at two fifty. Who will offer me two eighty?"

The woman's hesitation granted Storm a chance for some lightning calculations. At two hundred and fifty thousand, her 6 percent commission amounted to fifteen thousand dollars. Not nearly enough to erase their overdraft, but it would halt the banker's daily tirades, at least for—

"Two eighty from another new bidder at the back of the room. Who will offer me three?"

Storm fitted in her Bluetooth earpiece and hit the phone's redial button.

The mystery buyer had clearly been waiting for her call, for he answered on the first ring. "Where do we stand?"

"Bidding is at three hundred thousand and rising in twenty-five-thousand increments." She lifted her paddle once more. "It is yours at three fifty. But not for long."

"Who are we up against?"

"All of the original bidders have dropped out." Storm turned in her seat. The man lifting his paddle in opposition shot her a furious look. Storm said into her phone, "It's down to you and Rausch."

"The old man?"

"No. The son." Storm lifted her paddle. "We've just hit four hundred thousand."

"Who else is bidding?"

"No one. Sir, as your representative I feel I must tell you that given the current state of this market, four hundred thousand dollars for a Pokhitonov portrait may not be the best use of your—"

"Never mind that. Keep bidding."

Storm touched a button on her phone and said, "I am now recording this conversation."

"Good. Now follow my instructions and acquire that oil."

"Sir, I need to have a limit."

"Whatever it takes to keep Jacob Rausch from winning this article." Her client's accent had grown stronger. "Where are we now?"

The auctioneer's voice had lifted a full octave with the excitement of having a bidding war over this most unexpected of items. "I am at five hundred thousand. Who will offer me five fifty?"

"Keep bidding," said the voice in her ear.

The auctioneer used his gavel to gesture his acceptance of Storm's bid and said to Rausch, "Back to you, sir, at five fifty. Who will offer me six?"

Lifting her paddle had become a struggle against Storm's own natural instincts. "You understand, sir, that if you do not make good on the full purchase price, you will be out both the auctioneer's eight percent commission and my own six percent?"

"Of course I understand. Do I sound like a novice to you?"

"I merely wish to make the point perfectly clear, sir." And to have a recording of his confirmation. Storm lifted her paddle. "We are now at seven hundred and fifty thousand dollars."

"Anyone else bidding against me besides Rausch?"

"To be honest, sir, no one in this market would be wise—"

"Answer the question."

"No, sir." She kept her voice at the proper level for someone who had a keenly attentive audience. "Rausch has just bid eight hundred thousand."

"Stop this nonsense. Go to a million."

"Very good, sir." Storm did not so much stand as soar upward. "I offer one million dollars."

Even the auctioneer was taken aback. He touched his hair, adjusted his bow tie, smoothed a lapel, and cleared his throat. "Very good, madame. One million dollars to you. Sir, at the back, do you care to respond? No? Anyone else? Item seventy-six, a portrait by Pokhitonov, going once for one million dollars. Going twice. Anyone? Sold to the lady on my right for one million dollars."

Storm seated herself to a soft wash of applause and excited chatter. Such moments had become rare. These days, most dramas surrounded high-value items going for pennies. The man next to her beamed, as though delighted with the bidding insanity. Storm took a long breath, willing herself to stop shaking.

The voice in her earpiece shouted, *"Well?"*

"Sir, the painting is yours for one million dollars."

"I will immediately forward the funds to your bank. Do not leave today without that painting in your possession. Do you hear what I am saying, Ms. Syrrell? You *must* take that painting with you."

"Very good, sir. Might I please remind you to include our commission with your—"

The phone went dead.

THREE

STORM'S BANKER REPORTED, "THE FUNDS were transferred into your account from the New York branch of Credit Suisse."

"Is there any reason I should be worried about that?"

"Not from our end. I have spoken with our legal team. Everything is aboveboard. The proper notification has already been sent to Treasury. Are you intending to export the painting?"

"I have no idea."

"So long as we leave a clear paper trail and your taxes are paid on time, there should be no problem." Gerald Geldorf's attitude had undergone a drastic transformation. Gone was the pressure, the condemnation, the anxiety. In its place was a man intent on making things happen. "Money is money."

"Tell me again how much he transferred."

"One million, two hundred thousand dollars." If Gerald Geldorf found anything odd about a client who could not believe her own good fortune, he did not show it.

Storm did a quick calculation. The auction house's 8 percent commission was added on top of the item's price. That and her own commission brought the total to one mil one forty. "The client overpaid," she said. "I need you to set up an escrow account for the extra sixty."

"Certainly, Ms. Syrrell."

The prospect of a mystery client who did not bother with such details as sixty thousand dollars left Storm weak at the knees. "I may be drawing out expenses."

"As far as my bank is concerned, the escrow is there for you to use at your discretion."

"I'll be taking the painting with me as I leave the estate this evening. I need to deposit it in our safety-deposit vault."

"A bank official will be here to assist you whenever you complete your acquisition, Ms. Syrrell. Day or night."

"And the funds are ready to be transferred to the auctioneer's account?"

"As soon as I receive your confirmation, Ms. Syrrell. We are standing by."

"My very own yes-man."

"Is there anything else, Ms. Syrrell?"

"Try to find out whose account made that funds transfer. If you learn anything, call me on this number."

Storm shut her phone and remained standing outside the estate's main gates. She would have liked a moment to bask in the unaccustomed light of having the banker off her case and on her side. But a cloud by the name of Jacob Rausch chose that moment to insert itself between Storm and the sun.

Rausch demanded, "Who is your client?"

"You know I can't tell you that."

"You don't have one. You knew I was intent upon purchasing the item." Even Rausch's fury held an elegant sheen. "You used this for revenge."

"Sorry, Jacob. Those are Manhattan tactics. In case you hadn't noticed, we're standing in Manalapan."

"I'll do you a favor. Give me the painting and I'll offer half a percent commission and not a penny more."

"And I'm telling you, I have a client."

"You're lying. You just spent your little business into bankruptcy for sheer vengeance against me. I will take pleasure in grinding you and your paltry firm into the dust where it belongs. My offer for Syrrell's is hereby revoked."

Storm responded with her sweetest smile. "What offer would that be?"

Rausch wheeled about and almost collided with Claudia. "Kindly move out of my way."

Claudia watched him stride away, then asked, "Who put a roach in his sandwich?"

Suddenly even the clammy April afternoon tasted sweet. "That would be me."

IT BECAME AN AFTERNOON FOR weaving dreams. Claudia arranged the details regarding the purchase while Storm returned to the auction and assumed the role her grandfather had once dominated. She worked the room, giving out every card she had, smiling at little jokes she did not even bother to hear. Eyes followed her everywhere. A visit to the coffee table meant fielding a series of quick intros from dealers desperate to make the acquaintance of that rarest of breeds, a dealer with money to burn.

As the final lots came up for bidding, a late-afternoon storm swept across the waterway. The rotunda-style windows behind the auctioneer's dais revealed a violent display of wind and lightning and walls of rain. Storm pretended not to detect a note of foreboding when the thunder drowned out the bidding.

The auctioneers had turned the butler's pantry into a payment office. Storm found Claudia standing in one corner, frowning down at their acquisition. Claudia remained somewhat hollowed by the previous year's ordeal. Her refined features carried new shadows, and there were times when it seemed to Storm that her stylish clothes were all that kept the lady intact.

Claudia greeted Storm with a quietly murmured, "This oil isn't worth a million dollars."

"No."

"Maybe half that. On an extremely good day. At the top of a superheated market."

Storm recalled words from another time. "If the dream seems too good to be true, it probably is."

"Sean used to say that."

"I know."

Storm arranged a loan of two security guards and one of the auctioneer's vans, then phoned the bank to reconfirm their after-hours delivery. As they watched the oil being loaded, Claudia said, "I did a little checking after you phoned. Pokhitonov's son hid this painting through Stalin's years of chaos. It was the last of his father's oils that he sold. He claimed its spirit protected the family from harm. Every other citizen of their village wound up in a Siberian gulag."

"Here's what I think happened. Either Rausch himself or the money he's representing did the dirty on our mystery buyer. Our guy wants it because they want it. Price means less than his chance to savor the taste of revenge."

"Where does that leave us?"

"You mean, other than holding a sixty-thousand-dollar lifeline?" Storm waved to the van's driver and unlocked her car. She was suddenly eager to leave behind the strangeness that was Manalapan. "I have no idea."

FOUR

A S SOON AS STORM HAD stowed the painting in the bank vault, she phoned her mystery buyer. The man definitely did not possess a New York accent. Storm was thinking possibly French, but with some kind of colonial overtone. Probably someplace hot. Swampy and snake-infested. Dreadful enough to breed this mystery guy's bad attitude.

"I assume you have somewhere extremely safe to keep my oil."

"The basement vault of Worth Bank."

"I suppose that will do."

"Exactly who are you?"

"My name is Raphael Danton."

"Spell that, please."

He did so. The man sounded vaguely dissatisfied, as though he had half hoped she would fail. "I have another assignment for you."

"Are you French?"

"Are you paying attention?"

"Is there some reason why I shouldn't know—"

"I have received word that the Amethyst Clock will soon come up for sale."

With any other client, she would have couched her response a bit more diplomatically. "That's pretty amazing. Seeing as how the item couldn't possibly exist."

"The clock will not come onto the public market."

"Think about what you're saying. The Amethyst Clock is a legend about a device that stops time. The forgers would be ridiculed. Not to mention be arrested for the crime of stupidity."

Raphael Danton did not give any indication he heard her at all. "I want you to buy it for me. I will pay any price."

"You're wasting your money. And my time."

"Nonetheless, I want you to act on my behalf."

"Sir, maybe I didn't make myself clear. There is no clock to find."

"I say there is."

"Mr. Danton—"

"Name your price, Ms. Syrrell."

"Excuse me?"

"Obviously you are concerned about my wasting your oh-so-valuable time. Fine. I will make it worth your while. Tell me what retainer you require to justify depriving your numerous other clients of your precious counsel."

His words burned harshly enough to color both her tone and the amount. "A hundred thousand dollars."

"Very well. One moment. The money is now transferred. A British Airways flight leaves Miami for London Gatwick in four hours. Your ticket has been purchased."

"Wait, I—"

"Hurry, Ms. Syrrell. Make that flight. Danton out."

STORM WAITED UNTIL SHE HAD arrived at the Miami airport and checked in before returning Emma Webb's call. When her friend answered, Storm related the day's events, then said, "I packed in precisely twelve seconds. For London. I'll probably wind up there with three left shoes and a dress I haven't worn since my high school prom."

Emma Webb, recently of Interpol, was now chief of her own investigative task force within the Department of Homeland Security. "Girl, with a hundred thousand dollars in the bank, you can afford to shop."

"You haven't seen my overdraft. Not to mention overdue rent. Bills. Melted credit cards. Unsold goods gathering dust in my front window."

"Storm, you have got to stop blaming yourself for the global recession."

"Not the whole thing. Just my little corner."

"Where are you now?"

"You're going to love this."

"Tell me."

"Miami airport. A leather sofa in BA's first-class lounge. Crystal glass at my elbow. My feet are on a burl table I wouldn't mind having on display in the shop. Every thirty seconds or so a servant comes by with nibbles on a silver platter. The ticket my mystery buyer arranged cost more than my car."

"What was his name again?"

"Raphael Danton." She rubbed one stockinged foot with the other. "I should have told him I wouldn't travel for less than a million."

"Hold on, let me see if we've got a file on the man." After a pause, Emma said, "Whoa."

"What?"

"This guy is hot. Not to mention rich. And he's single. There must be something seriously wrong here. I'm thinking some secret wasting disease."

"His attitude is about the worst I've come across."

"Honey, a rich single hunk isn't allowed to have a personality. It's the law."

"He's really a hunk?"

"Let me put it this way. When Brad Pitt and Angelina Jolie's kid grows up, he's going to look like armadillo roadkill beside your new client."

"Why does Homeland Security have a file on him?"

"Probably because he's so hot. I can imagine some lonely chief investigator spotting this guy in line somewhere and ordering her crew to find his home address."

"Is he French?"

"Swiss. Raphael Danton, born in Geneva,

thirty-two years old, father died when he was two, stepfather a biggie scientist in the pharmaceutical industry. Get this, the guy actually won a Nobel Prize."

"My client?"

"No, fool. His stepfather. Okay, Danton currently resides in London. He owns a company called LEM, incorporated in Switzerland, no indication here of what it does. Which is strange in the extreme. He was an officer in the Swiss army, then headed to Africa. Won a big-game license for a two-hundred-thousand-acre game preserve in northern Congo. When the country's government went south, he . . ."

"He what?"

"Our boy went over to the dark side. Ran guns to the rebels."

"So I'm buying oils with an arms smuggler's money. Sweet."

"It gets worse. Danton fought on the side that didn't win. Which classes him as a mercenary, which is why we are reading this file." Emma was all business now. "What does he want you to do for him now?"

"Locate a myth called the Amethyst Clock."

"A myth how, exactly?"

"The thing is supposed to freeze time for anyone who possesses it." The hostess chose that moment to signal Storm. "Sorry, Emma, they've called my flight."

47

"Watch your back with this guy. And call me the first chance you get. And, Storm?"

"Yes?"

"While you're at it, try to enjoy yourself, okay?"

EMMA WEBB HANDED THE PHONE to the technician. She leaned back in the ergonomic chair she would have liked to steal for her own office. She stared at a blank side wall as she let go of her smile. Emma wished she could go scour her skin with a wire brush.

Homeland Security had taken over a campus-style compound in the ghetto called Northeast Washington. The site had once housed the Coast Guard Academy and remained a tiny island of green and trees and orderly sidewalks and rectangular seventies-style buildings set in the heart of the nation's premier drug frontier. The campus was both paranoid and intensely secretive. Four years after it was first conceived, Homeland Security remained bitterly segmented along its original divisions. Orders to share information among branches remained nothing more than departmental memos. Which was why Emma knew better than to ask the names of the two dark-suited men standing by the conference room's opposite wall.

One of the men was Latino, the other African-American. A tribute to diversification in

America's intelligence services. Both shared the stony expressions of people who worried they might have infiltrated enemy territory. From the cut of their suits, which was somewhat more stylish than was normal around Homeland, and the steel-tight way they scoped the room, Emma was thinking CIA.

Emma's immediate superior, Tip MacFarland, was seated three chairs down the table to her right. Tip was a rumbling pachyderm in a rumpled suit. He tested the weight limit of his chair, shifting around so he could prop one size-fourteen hoof on a desk and lean against the wall opposite Emma, and said to the two men, "So there I was, doing my job, saving America from the latest threat we hope nobody will ever know about. And I get a call from the director's office. Which, I've got to tell you, gets my attention. On account of how I'm so far down the totem pole I assume the director's office couldn't find me with a guide dog and a map."

The African-American checked his watch and said, "Sir, we should check in."

MacFarland ignored the interruption. "The director orders me, *orders* me, to give all due respect and assistance to two visitors he does not even bother to name. Naturally I stand at attention and place my hand on my heart and promise I'll do just that." Tip MacFarland's voice rumbled along as though he had nowhere to go and nothing to do. Which, Emma knew, was the only warning Tip MacFarland gave before opening the bomb doors and locking on target. "So as per your request, I bring in one of my top operatives and direct her to place calls that make no sense to me at all. Do they make any sense to you, Agent Webb?"

Emma just sat and rocked and fumed.

"See, up to this point, I thought we were all working on the same team. In my book, teammates take time out to explain what's happening."

The Latino reached forward and plucked the file from Emma's grasp. "Thank you for your assistance, Agent Webb."

"Is my friend in danger?"

"Our local operatives are under orders to maintain close surveillance."

"That so does not answer my question," Emma snapped.

The Latino's response was cut off by the fifth person in the room, a technician seated at the table's far end. He looked up from his laptop and reported, "Sir, I can confirm the package was delivered and is operational."

Which only made Emma hotter. "Is your man telling us he's just turned Storm's phone into a bug?"

"Electronic surveillance is necessary for Ms. Syrrell's own safety."

"Oh, and keeping Storm alive is suddenly your

number-one priority, is that what you're saying?"

MacFarland said, "Last time I checked, we were required to obtain a warrant to tap an American's cell phone."

"Not in matters of national security."

Emma Webb huffed, "You guys are totally loony tunes if you think Storm Syrrell is a threat."

MacFarland demanded, "What does your highly sanitized file on this Danton guy not tell us?"

"Sir, your director did not see any need to ask such questions of us."

"Our director is five buildings away. Which, as far as you're concerned, might as well be Albania."

They exchanged glances, then the African-American said grudgingly, "If Danton is operating on his own, we have no interest in this at all."

"So who does he represent?"

"That," the Latino said, "is what we are trying to find out."

Emma asked, "How did you identify Storm Syrrell?" When they did not respond, she guessed, "You've been tracking Raphael Danton's calls. When he contacted Storm, you traced her back to me and had your boss call ours."

The Latino said, "You are hereby ordered to initiate no further contact with Ms. Syrrell until we green-light you."

"You expect me to leave my friend dangling on the end of your line?" Emma shook her head. "I don't think so."

Tip said, "You don't know who Danton is working for. But whoever it is, you're certain they've got watchers in place?"

The African-American said, "This is so much bigger than you imagine."

Tip MacFarland snorted. "Hey, I wish I could tell you how impressed I am with that news flash."

The Latino added, "No contacts, no research, no casual questions dropped around by your friends in the field."

Her boss shot Emma a warning look. She smoldered in silence.

The African-American said, "We'll be in touch."

"And when might that be?"

"When it suits us."

Tip MacFarland snorted. "Don't let us keep you gentlemen from catching your crosstown bus."

Emma watched the pair gather up their technician and depart. And waited.

Tip MacFarland had been Emma's boss at Treasury intel. When Emma had returned from her last foray with Storm and Harry Bennett, Tip had invited her to join his team as head of a Homeland Security task force. Tip MacFarland was smart, dedicated, and an experienced

Washington infighter. He rose from his chair and said, "Let's walk."

He waited until they were strolling beneath towering elms that lined the campus sidewalks to ask, "What's the status of your current projects?"

Emma replied, "Boiling along nicely."

"You have confidence in your number two?"

"Total."

He stopped her with a subtle gesture, which turned into an inspection of his thumbnail. "Any idea what that item was your friend mentioned?"

"The Amethyst Clock? No. But if Storm calls it a myth, we can take it to the bank. She knows her stuff."

"Somebody has got to consider it vital if they're paying her a hundred thou and flying her first-class across the Atlantic."

"That pair neglected to order us to stay away from the clock. I'll check it out."

MacFarland continued to inspect his thumbnail. "I imagine the director will insist we give the Langley brigade forty-eight hours to come clean."

Emma did not try to keep the whine from her voice. "Two days is an eternity to leave Storm dangling in the CIA's wind tunnel."

"You ever heard of this Danton?"

"No."

"We need to check our system, but my guess is we'll come up blank. Let me handle that part. I don't want your shadow passing in front of their sights."

"Give me a break, Tip. I can't just sit and hold my breath for two days."

"I don't expect you to. As far as the system is concerned, you're at your desk, working your crew, fighting the good fight. Do you trust your crew to hold up that fable?"

"Absolutely."

"Leave your ID with your number two; have her slot you in and out of the building's security. Go see Jimmy over in Documents. Have him work you up a new ID. Tell him the orders come from me and you can't show up on any in-house protocol."

She could have hugged the man. And not just from relief over Storm. Emma had not been in the field since the previous spring. Washington was gradually becoming just another over-crowded prison. "Thanks, Tip."

"Save it, girl." He did not share her excitement. "My gut is telling me this could grow into something seriously poisonous. For all of us."

FIVE

STORM'S LIMO DRIVER STOOD WAITING just beyond Heathrow's customs controls. The guy folded his little sign and actually doffed his hat before taking her luggage. He spoke cheerfully about the weather, which was awful, as he shepherded her through the terminal. Their destination was a Rolls the color of old money. The driver waited as she eased into the butter-soft seat, then pointed out the silver carafe of coffee, the burled-walnut table she could fold down to hold her Limoges china cup, the damask napkin to wipe the royal fingertips, the sterling cutlery, the smoked-salmon sandwiches, the television, the ironed newspapers, the half bottle of champagne in the sweating silver ice bucket. At eight o'clock in the morning.

The Rolls was a soothing unguent applied to London's morning rush hour. Storm did not bother to ask where they were going, nor did she much care. Jet lag remained a faint shimmer upon the rainswept horizon. She knew she needed to focus on what lay ahead. But she had never been to London before and was not going to let a little danger spoil the show.

Their destination proved to be the Mayfair branch of Coutts. The bank had been in business for over three hundred years. The royal family banked with Coutts. Coutts only accepted clients with over a million pounds in liquid assets. Not even the worst recession in three generations could fracture the bank's haughty demeanor.

The bank's door was opened by a junior staffer in striped trousers and a formal cutaway jacket whose manner was as starched as his shirt. When she gave her name, Storm was ushered into a rear conference room.

Her first thought upon spotting her new client was, Don Rafael. As in, Spanish conquistador. Minus the silver filigree, but with the coldhearted brutality required to conquer a more primitive world.

Raphael Danton possessed eyes of cobalt ice, a frigid blue one shade off midnight. Chiseled features, high cheekbones, cleft chin, tan the shade of Baltic amber. With a voice and accent to match. "My sources neglected to mention you were beautiful, Ms. Syrrell."

Had the comment been offered with anything other than complete disdain, Storm might have beamed. As it was, she found it easy to offer aloofness in return. "What sources might those be?"

Raphael Danton closed the file he had been studying and rose from the chair at the conference table's far end. He carried his cup to the silver coffee service on the sideboard. "Will you take something?"

"Thanks, but I had all I needed on the way into London." She walked around the table and took a seat. The walls were wainscoted in vintage South American silk wood, now almost extinct. The paintings were all of clippers under full sail, probably privateers financed by the bank's more rapacious investors. The chandelier was more gold than crystal. Storm waited until Danton settled back at the head of the table to say, "If you used the same sources who claim the Amethyst Clock is real, I'm amazed they found me at all."

Something flickered deep in his gaze. "You are wallowing in so many fine offers these days you can afford to scoff at me?"

Seven hours' sleep at thirty thousand feet left her feeling smooth as the limo's leather. "There's no profit in scoffing, Mr. Danton. I'm just trying to move us through the fog of misdirection. You don't believe the clock exists any more than I do."

He sipped his coffee, checked a watch of woven gold, and said nothing.

"Just like you know the Pokhitonov portrait is not worth a million dollars," she continued. "But revenge is. You're after whoever Jacob Rausch represents. Rausch's client thinks the Amethyst Clock exists, so you want it." Storm offered him two open palms. "See? I've just moved us a hundred miles closer to the truth."

Raphael Danton's grimace was the first not-handsome part about him that she had seen. Not ugly, though. This guy could have stuck out his tongue, crossed his eyes, and blown spit bubbles at the ceiling and still stopped female traffic. But his frown released a tiny sliver of whatever oozed beneath that cool surface.

He said, "So you think you can handle the truth."

Then it hit her. Danton was angry. At *her*.

Danton took her silence as assent. "My company is LEM. LEM stands for Lifestyle Enhancement Managers. We are a luxury concierge service. I assume you have heard of such?"

"Sorry. That's a new one." This guy isn't just miffed, she thought. He is livid. But why? Had he expected her to fail at the auction? Then why fly her over when she succeeded?

"My group has clients in eighteen countries. There is nowhere on earth we do not operate. And no service we will not offer, so long as it does not breach the laws of the country in question. Anything from hiring a private yacht on six hours' notice to handling all financial correspondence for a retired executive. No service is too large or too small. Our clients like to call us wish fulfillers."

Storm realized what it was. Raphael Danton liked to hold all the cards.

Why had he chosen her? Simple. Because she was desperate. Danton did not want her hungry. He wanted her *scared*. A guy able to offer her this level of luxury was also a guy willing to take it away. He had rescued her from the precipice, and he expected her to grovel. Instead, she was giving him lip.

Storm said quietly, "I see."

"I have no interest in a second-rate oil by Ivan

Pokhitonov. But my client does. The same client who insists that the Amethyst Clock both exists and is coming up for sale. Your task is to track this clock down and buy it."

"What if I prove the clock is a fake?"

"Do so with the item in your possession, Ms. Syrrell."

"You will collect your commission on a fraud?"

"I will do what my client requests."

Storm nodded slowly. It was all coming clear. The world was full of dealers on the edge who would pawn off a fake as the real thing. What Danton wanted was a dealer whose reputation was beyond question. So that when they hunted down a clock they both knew was a total scam, the seller would treat the offer as real. The question was, of course, why either Danton or his mystery client was so eager to buy an obvious fake.

"There is an auction in Marbella starting at nine tomorrow morning. I want you on this afternoon's flight from Heathrow." Danton pulled an envelope from the file and slid it across the polished table. "Your flight, hotel, and a description of the four items I hereby order you to acquire."

STORM HAD NO IDEA WHAT she'd expected to find in Spain. But it certainly would not have been this.

Of course, she was so zapped out on the six-hour time change and the two flights and the missed night and the luxury and the money, it was entirely possible she was staring at a mirage.

But she didn't think so. Over her cell phone she said to Claudia, "Say that again."

"Your new banker pal, Gerald Geldorf, called to say there was another deposit of two million dollars this afternoon." Claudia gave that a beat, then asked, "Where are you?"

"Marbella." Storm stared out her window at a Mediterranean sunset. "Or maybe heaven. I'm not sure."

"Didn't you go to London?"

"That was three limos ago."

Her hotel was a former Moorish castle perched on a rock promontory jutting into the Med like a rust-colored tooth. The ancient stone breakwater was rimmed by a road and topped by a pedestrian walkway. The seafront promenade was as packed as the road. Streetlights formed a glowing yellow necklace along the shorefront. Old women dressed in black were accompanied by entire families. Trysting lovers lined the wall. Children raced about waving balloons and ice cream. Their speech and soft footfalls were as musical as the waves frothing the shoreline.

To her right stretched tourist mania. Hundreds of villas and apartment towers and hotels, all colored in Disneyesque pastels. The structures filled every square inch of level space and crawled up the sloping hillsides. Hundreds of pools sparkled in the sunset like illuminated dominoes.

Storm said, "I need everything you can dig up on the Amethyst Clock."

"Is this some kind of joke?"

"Yes. Of the two-million-dollar variety. And while you're checking, let it slip that we're in the market to make an acquisition."

"We'll be the laughingstock of every dealer in the Western Hemisphere."

"And what are we now?"

"Storm . . ."

"What?"

Claudia sighed away her protests. Then she said, "A legal aide at Baxter and Bow called. She has documents that require your attention. She requested your current address."

Baxter and Bow was the Palm Beach law firm where Emma Webb had been inserted while keeping surveillance on Storm's grandfather. Storm read the hotel's address off the notepad by the phone, wondering why Emma had not called her directly. "Did they say what it was about?"

"Only that it was a matter of utmost urgency and confidentiality. Is something wrong?"

Storm hesitated, then replied, "Call them back as soon as we hang up. Tell them I'll only be here for a couple more days."

SIX

THE MAIN READING ROOM OF the Library of Congress was a cathedral to books and knowledge. The high-ceilinged chamber was rimmed by shelves and stained glass. Emma Webb sat in the only alcove where cell phones were permitted. She told Tip MacFarland, "Storm was right. This Amethyst Clock business is bogus from start to finish."

"Given the interest shown by the Langley brigade, I'm not certain we should be talking about this on an open line."

"And I'm telling you there is nothing for them to find." Emma checked her notes. "Three hundred years ago, the best clocks in the world were made in London and were called chronometers. For two centuries, ships' captains used them to calculate their latitudinal position. The best cost as much as a palace and were often encased in gold and precious stones. One of them came up recently for auction at Christie's and sold for eleven million dollars."

"Doesn't sound bogus to me."

"Here's where we take a ninety-degree turn from reality. In the seventeen hundreds, Catherine the Great asked her cousin the king of England to let her send a royal clockmaker to study with London's finest chronographer. This was a very big deal. Possession of an accurate chronograph meant the difference between a ship arriving at its destination and disaster. I've read reports of pirates attacking British ships when they were empty and the ship's crew was on easy duty, just to take their clock. Their manufacture took as much as two years and was tied into alchemy and mysticism. The king refused the request, of course. Then Catherine threatened to shut England out of the Siberian fur trade. That is how vital they considered the issue."

"So where does the myth fit in?"

"Because of what is claimed to have happened next. The clockmaker Catherine sent studied with the chronographer in London for nine years. During this time he managed to complete the clock Catherine wanted. And then he died."

"In London?"

"Right. He never made it back. But his son did. Not to Russia, however. See, this clockmaker wasn't Russian at all. He was Polish. And while he served the Empress Catherine, his son was a fierce Polish patriot." She stopped. "I need to give you a little history lesson. It explains where this myth came from."

"Fire away."

"Catherine is called 'Great' because she almost doubled Russia's size. Her conquests included a deal with the Prussians and Austro-Hungarians to split Poland into three parts and swallow the country whole. But Poland did not rest easy in her chains. There was a constant struggle by insurgents, which drew strength from the Polish Catholic Church. The Polish people paid a huge toll in horrible persecution for their loyalty to a country that didn't exist anymore. The Russian rulers were infamous for their cruelty."

"Where does the legend fit in?"

"This clockmaker's son arrived in Kraków and took the chronograph intended for Catherine to some monk, a man revered as a saint even while he was still alive. And let me tell you, this chronograph was supposed to have really been something."

"Fit for an empress."

"The clockmaker had hollowed out a solid block of amethyst, the largest stone of its kind ever found up to that point. He spent the last three years of his life creating the works, then in his final weeks he created a series of gold figurines to adorn the case."

"So the son takes the clock to this monk."

"Right. And the monk blesses the clock." Emma paused.

"And?"

"According to legend, this blessing granted the clock the power to stop time."

"Get out."

"I'm just telling you what I've found. Long as

the owner is in the same room as the clock, time stands still."

Tip gave that a beat, then said, "So this clock is blessed by a monk, acquires magical time-stopping powers, and then it vanishes. Three hundred years later, the CIA invades our turf because your friend is told to hunt it down."

"Pretty much."

"Does that make sense to you?"

"Not a bit."

"Okay. I guess we can assume that it's not actually the clock they're after. Which means your friend is probably about to face some serious heat. Where is she now?"

"Marbella, Spain."

"You know what to do. MacFarland out."

THERE WERE CERTAIN DAYS EVERY spring when Washington held a solid grip on beauty. The Mall felt like the center of the universe, a perfect strip of green lawn and reflecting pool and minty trees and buildings that proclaimed the hopes of a great nation. Even the clouds drifted in proper formation through a sky of colonial blue. There were a few such days in April, more in May, and then they tapered off as the humid heat of June took hold.

Emma descended the Library of Congress steps until she stood in the brilliant sunlight. Then she pretended to check her watch. She had another hour before she headed for Dulles to catch her flight to Spain. Emma wanted to stretch out her arms and do a little twirl, like Julie Andrews in *The Sound of Music*. But she was a federal agent, and federal agents didn't just dance down the stone steps of a federal building. Not even when she was green-lighted to trade the humdrum bureaucratic world for a trip to the Costa del Sol.

Emma pulled out her phone and checked to see if Harry Bennett had called her back in the past ninety seconds. Emma and Harry had met while searching for Sean Syrrell's killers. She was still working on precisely what best defined their relationship. The more intense her feelings became, the stronger grew her midnight fears. Even so, knowing this trip would bring her four thousand miles closer to Harry was yet another reason to break into song. Emma made do by lifting her face to the sun and breathing until her chest threatened to explode.

Then she spotted the SUVs pulling up to the curb.

The two vehicles were standard federal bomb-proof issue. Black, chunky, darkened windows. A man in a gray suit rose from the first vehicle and scoped the outer perimeter. A guard emerged from the second vehicle and opened the rear door. Pedestrians stopped and gawked, hoping some-one important would appear. Instead, a priest rose to his feet and solemnly thanked the guard. The pedestrians returned to city rhythms, walking fast, talking faster.

The first thing Emma noticed about the priest was how anxious he looked. The second was that he appeared to be taking aim straight for her.

He climbed the stairs and asked, "Agent Emma Webb?"

"Who wants to know?" It was no proper way to greet a foreign emissary, which the cleric probably was, given his ride. But there was something about the way he stood, slightly canted as though carrying a severe pain, that promised to wreck her day.

"I am Father Gregor. I serve at the Vatican's consulate."

Polish was her first guess. But she would have believed Belarusan or Ukrainian. A land that taught men the grace of formality, even their priests. A language so complex that fluency in another tongue never erased the verbal creases. "Since when does a Vatican staffer rate bullet-proof transport and security details?"

"The vehicles belong to an ally." The brilliant sunlight only heightened the man's evident worry. He was slender, a decade beyond middle age, and his hand shook slightly as he gestured toward where security still held the door. "Please, madame. Would you be so good as to grant me a few moments of your time?"

The agent holding the rear door scoped her once, a two-second blast, then returned to checking the street. The other man never even glanced her way. They were tall and slender and taut and olive-skinned. Emma started to get in Father Gregor's face, demanding to know who pulled the strings here. But the priest was already scuttling around to the opposite door, and the agent on her side had moved in as though to block incoming fire with his own body, pressing with wordless efficiency for Emma to move faster still. The instant she settled into the seat, the two cars pulled away in smooth tandem. Emma snapped, "Tell your driver to pull over."

"Madame, we feel it would perhaps be better if we continued—"

"First you tell me what this is about. Either that or you let me out at the next light."

The leather seat squeaked as the priest shifted around, clearly unable to find a proper way to deliver his message. "Agent Webb, we are taking you home."

The car's interior was compressed by the steel cage and the reinforced windows. Sound was condensed, voices flattened. Emma always felt as though she shared the air conditioner's struggle to find a decent breath.

One of the agents spoke into his wrist mike, saying the only word of Hebrew that Emma knew, *"Beseder."* Which meant okay.

Emma knew instantly the day was anything but. She fought for the air to ask, "Is it Harry?"

The priest gave a fractional nod. "Madame, I regret to inform you that Harry Bennett is dead."

"That can't be."

"It should not be, I agree. But it is."

"Harry was working on a dig. He told me he was perfectly safe."

"So the Israeli authorities assumed, Ms. Webb."

"Are you sure?"

"I am afraid so."

"How? I mean, how did . . ."

"An incendiary device."

Emma did not realize she was weeping until the priest pulled a clean handkerchief from his pocket and passed it over. "Harry was killed by a bomb? On a dig?"

"No, madame. In Hebron."

The priest related what he knew, which was not much. Emma tried to listen, but her senses had become separated from the outside world. Not even time held her any longer, for one moment they were riding along the Mall and the next they were parked beneath the springtime trees flanking her Georgetown apartment.

As soon as the car halted, the agent in the passenger seat opened his door and stepped out and waited for a man from the other vehicle to walk over and settle in. The newcomer swiveled in his seat so that he faced her as straight as he could

69

and said, "Agent Webb, I wonder if you perhaps recall our last meeting."

Trying to see the man clearly was like looking through a translucent screen. She fought for enough air to say, "No."

"Rubin Kleinmann. I had the honor of serving as Israeli ambassador to the United States. I have handed over the responsibility to my successor and am preparing to return to my country next week."

"Th-the church," she recalled, "Sean's funeral."

"The funeral of my dear friend. Just so. May I say, Agent Webb, how deeply sorry I am for your loss."

"You're certain?" Her swallow was a battle-ground trek. "Harry is . . ."

"There is no doubt. I am sorry. Agent Webb, you must please forgive me for speaking with you at such a distressing time. But the matter is most pressing. When did you last have communication with Mr. Bennett?"

She applied the now drenched handkerchief to her eyes. "Three days ago. Harry said something about driving to Hebron to check out a buy."

"Mr. Bennett was assisting us in tracking down counterfeiters of ancient artifacts operating inside the West Bank. Did he tell you of this?"

"H-he said there was no danger."

"Agent Webb, please, this is crucial. Did Harry say anything about who he was planning to meet?"

"Just that he thought he had found the source."

"Did he mention Russians?"

"What?"

"Did Mr. Bennett make any suggestion that Russians were involved in this trade? In the past they were heavily involved in the Palestinian insurrections; of course you know that."

"But all that stopped years ago."

"Yes. So we assumed as well."

"I-I don't understand. You're saying Harry got caught in West Bank crossfire?"

The priest spoke with the professional manner of one who had often dealt with the recently bereaved. "We have heard through sources that Harry Bennett was the target."

"Harry had nothing to do with Russians."

The former ambassador said, "When we first heard this rumor, we discounted it as well. Hebron has been the flashpoint for several intifadas. We assumed Mr. Bennett was simply the unintended victim of internecine conflict. But our sources have now confirmed what the Vatican heard. We have checked very thoroughly. The attackers used a bomb in an attempt to mask their operations. And the Russians were most definitely involved."

But her mind could not get past the possibility that this was all some grotesque mistake. "Harry has more lives than a dozen cats. Maybe he escaped."

"I regret to tell you that we have received

absolute confirmation of his demise." The ambassador paused dutifully and then continued. "Agent Webb, please try to understand what has happened. We hired Harry Bennett thinking that the worst he might find was a counterfeiting organization that funneled money to insurgents. Instead, he seems to have uncovered an attempt by the Russians to reinsert themselves into our region. We know they have recently made overtures to Syria and Hezbollah in Lebanon. But this is the first time we've found evidence of their operations inside the West Bank."

The priest said, "What is confusing to us, Agent Webb, is that the Palestinians themselves brought us this news. We have numerous projects within the community of Palestinian Christians, you see. An ally in Hebron came to our mission and reported that the Russians had been behind this. Why, our source did not know. But it *was* the Russians and their target *was* Mr. Bennett."

The ambassador said, "Agent Webb, can you tell us what Storm Syrrell might be working on at this time?"

The day's tumult condensed to where it crimped her very soul. "Storm is in Europe."

"Are you aware, Agent Webb, that Ms. Syrrell recently bid on and purchased a Russian oil from the postrevolutionary period?"

She blew her nose. "You're not making sense."

"I agree this is most confusing. But please try to

understand. At the same time that Mr. Bennett was tragically lost to us, Storm Syrrell arrived at an auction to bid on one particular item. The sale price was one million dollars. This is double what the painting should be worth. Possibly three times its value."

Emma reached for her door. "I have to go."

"Agent Webb, please hear us out. We fear that whatever killed Harry Bennett may also be targeting your friend Ms. Syrrell. There is the utmost urgency to our determining why the Russian government considered Mr. Bennett such a threat. We are concerned they might also go after Ms. Syrrell."

Her door handle did not work. "Let me out of this car."

The ambassador spoke to the agent behind the wheel. Instantly the man was moving. "Please, Agent Webb. Can you tell us—"

"Storm is supposed to search out something called the Amethyst Clock."

The priest said, "But that is a myth."

"Storm thinks so as well."

"What is this?" asked the ambassador.

"It is nothing; is what it is." Father Gregor appeared insulted by the news. "A legend that should have died centuries ago. A fable with no importance except that it represents a most tragic period in my nation's history."

Emma was moving before the agent fully opened her door. The ambassador leaned over farther and offered her his card. "Please, Agent Webb. Call me if there is anything further you might think of."

"Or need," Father Gregor added, pressing a second card into her hand. "We are ready to serve you, madame. And please accept—"

Emma slammed her door on the condolences and fled.

But midway up the path, she found herself turning around and hurrying back to the car. Apparently the analytical portion of her brain still functioned, even when her heart was crushed and her life over. When the agent opened the rear door, she leaned down and asked the priest, "Why you?"

"Pardon me?"

"A Polish priest just happens to receive word about a bomb in the West Bank. Why?"

The priest shared a look with the ambassador, enough for Emma to know she had this one thing right.

Father Gregor said, "There is far more at stake than a good man's tragic demise."

Not for me, Emma thought, and was forced to clear her face once more.

"No matter what Ms. Syrrell has told you, this crisis does not revolve around a mythical clock." The priest's blurred image leaned in closer. "The Black Madonna. Remember this name. If you hear it mentioned, any fragment of information at all, you must contact me, Agent Webb. Immediately."

SEVEN

HARRY BENNETT WATCHED THE LIGHT fade. An hour earlier, when he had first awoken, the window across from his bed had framed a vision of purest gold. It was as fine a welcome-back as he could have ever imagined.

His brain felt fuzzy around the edges. Every motion had a tentative feel, as though he could rip the veil of drugs apart with one wrong move. Even shifting his gaze stretched his cocoon of safety.

Desert sunsets were slippery things. Back on the Herodium dig, the sun had dropped like a big red stone. Bang and gone in what felt like ten seconds. The Herodium crew usually stopped what they were doing and watched the western hills become a rim of burnished gold, then copper, then rust, then a simple silhouette against the stars. The heat faded more slowly. But by the time everybody had showered and gathered for dinner, the night winds carried a chill that would have seemed impossible a couple of hours earlier. Harry never thought he would look back on Herodium with fondness. But just then, being able to recall anything at all made for an extremely fine moment.

A nurse passed through the hall turning on the lights and shutting the windows. At least Harry thought she was a nurse. She wore a colored scarf over her dark hair and a tattered blue surgeon's shirt over blue jeans and house slippers. She checked on several patients as she passed their beds. Harry's field of vision gradually expanded to where he could take in the long chamber where he lay. Beds lined both walls, and every one that Harry could see was occupied. The nurse shut the window against the night breeze, crossed the aisle, and spoke to the kid in the bed beside Harry. The nurse stroked the forehead of the silent boy, then she noticed that Harry's eyes were open.

She walked over and spoke to him. Harry thought for a moment that the drugs kept him from understanding. Then he realized she had addressed him in Arabic.

The nurse spoke again. Harry remained silent. It was not a conscious decision. He felt as though he needed to get his head fully around whatever it was that had landed him here. Wherever here was.

Then a pair of policemen appeared behind the nurse. They wore dark blue uniforms with Arabic lettering sewn in gold on their sleeves and above their shirt pockets. The nurse plucked a tattered ID from the white metal table beside Harry's bed and handed it to them. The policemen studied it, inspected the bandages covering Harry's forehead and cheek, then handed back the ID. As the nurse stowed it away, Harry recognized the ID as belonging to the parrot-faced guard he had last seen outside the alley.

Harry decided if the policemen and the nurse all thought he looked like that guy, he must be in as bad shape as he felt.

His thirst was so fierce Harry couldn't let the nurse go. So he slowly ungummed his mouth. The nurse got the message and lifted a cup and fitted the plastic straw into his mouth. Harry sucked and moaned and sucked until the straw hit air.

One of the cops spoke to him in Arabic. Harry followed the guy with his eyes but made no move to speak. Not yet, he decided. He had, after all, been wandering a Hebron street well after midnight in search of illicit gold. Which was bound to rank fairly low on the Palestinians' list of decent jobs.

Not to mention the fact that he was a professional salvager. Who just happened to be in Hebron secretly helping the Israelis track down counterfeiters.

The other cop chimed in with the first one. Harry followed the exchange with his eyes, thinking, Thanks just the same, but I think I'll sit this one out.

Then he made the mistake of trying to cough.

Harry had never imagined so many different parts of him could shriek all at once.

The problem was, now that he had started, he

couldn't stop. And every cough only racked his poor body further, wrenching out more pain.

The nurse hustled the two cops away. Harry would have begged her for something to ease his situation, only just then he couldn't find the air to breathe, much less speak. Which turned out to be for the best. The nurse rushed back over, this time holding an old-timey glass syringe with metal loops like trigger guards for her fingers and an oversized ring for her thumb. Harry noticed all this because he watched the needle find his vein like a starving man inspecting a slab of prime rib.

The drug flooded his system like ice. He could actually feel it swoosh through his veins, a huge rush that just plucked him up and carried him away.

EIGHT

THE SPANISH AUCTION WAS PROVING to be a rolling three-day circus. None of the first day's items had interested Storm. But there were worse places for a girl to have a day off than Marbella, even if she did share the old city with a million beer-swilling Brits. She did a little shopping, then retreated to poolside. But an early night did little to prepare her for Emma's surprise arrival with world-wrecking news.

"Are you sure he's gone?"

"As sure as I can be with nothing to go on." Emma paused long enough to reapply her handkerchief. "Nobody can tell me a thing."

Storm was making do with Kleenex. She had gone through the little packet in her purse and was now working on Emma's. The space around her chair was littered with damp white blotches. "Did you speak with the archeologist in charge?"

Something about the question caused Emma's eyes to leak more. "Twice."

"What did she say?"

"You don't want to know."

"Tell me, Emma."

Her neck was so taut that Storm could watch her pulse. "They can't identify enough remains to bury."

That silenced Storm for a time. "How can they be sure?"

"They tracked Harry into Hebron. The last time we spoke, he said he was on the trail of a master counterfeiter." Emma blew her nose. "I could wring his neck for taking such risks."

"But if they haven't actually found—"

"Let's not forget the mystery guests who demolished my last afternoon in Washington."

Marbella's main theater was filling for the auction's second day. Storm and Emma occupied a pair of chairs at the back of the foyer. New arrivals broke and swirled about them like dark-suited fish avoiding some tragic shoal. Storm said, "If they haven't identified Harry it means he could still be alive."

Emma gave her the look of a woman afraid to hope. "I've been trying to tell myself that very same thing for a day and a half."

Storm needed both hands to pry herself out of the seat. "It's time for us to go be corporate."

Emma rose in stages. "I'm not sure how much good I can be."

"I can't handle this alone. Not now." Storm gave her face another wipe, pushed back her hair, and said, "Let's do this so we can get out of here."

Storm knew she looked a wreck and didn't care. The cloak of mourning was evident enough to silence all conversation as they passed through the crowd. The other attendees glanced over and then swiftly turned away, as though Mediterranean etiquette said it was impolite to watch two women fall apart.

The four men and one woman surrounding Aaron Rausch fled as though Storm and Emma's sorrow were contagious. Jacob Rausch's father, however, was made of sterner stuff. "My son will be most displeased to learn you are here, Ms. Syrrell."

Storm ignored the rebuff and said, "This is Emma Webb. Emma is a senior agent with Homeland Security. Emma, show the man your badge."

The sight of Emma's leather case, combined

with the women's stricken features, left the New York antiques trader very pliant indeed. He made no protest as Storm pulled him to the stairwell leading to the closed upper balcony. "What is the matter?"

"I can't tell you." Not and keep hold of what control she had left.

Emma added, "Our current crisis does not directly affect you or your company."

Though in his seventies, Aaron Rausch possessed a certain ravaged handsomeness. His hair was swept back into a mane of silver froth, his clothes impeccable. Where his son Jacob Rausch was New York slick, Aaron Rausch revealed a courtly eastern European veneer. "Forgive me, Ms. Syrrell, but if you can tell me nothing and you have a crisis that does not affect me, then why are we speaking?"

"I want to offer you a take-it-or-leave-it bargain."

"Every deal contains a certain amount of what my son likes to call wiggle room."

"Not this one." Storm pulled from her purse Raphael Danton's list of the four items she was to acquire. She passed it over. "Not if you want to acquire any of these. I have been granted an unlimited budget and instructions to pay whatever is necessary to obtain them."

He handed back the paper and tried for disinterest. "And your offer is?"

"My guess is, you're planning to bid on all four items," Storm said. "Maybe you came with the same orders as I did. Buy them all for whatever it takes. So it's in the best interests of both our clients if we reach a compromise."

"I'll take the first two."

The items were listed in order of descending estimated value. "First and third or second and fourth, that's your choice."

His gaze flickered over and back. "Second and fourth."

"Done." Storm stowed the sheet away. "See how easy that was?"

"Now if you ladies will—"

"Wait, Aaron, please. We're not done yet. I told you. My client *doesn't care* how much it costs. For all I know, he *wants* to bid you up, just to have the pleasure of winning no matter *what* you offer."

"You're bluffing."

"That's what your son thought and look where it got him. I want information, Aaron. That's why we're having this conversation. Tell me why this particular auction is so important."

"I can't speak for you and your associate. But I represent genuine buyers who—"

Storm stepped forward, revealing how close she was to the edge. "I'm going to offer truth in exchange for truth. I have a new client, one so wealthy the price of the items I've been sent to acquire does not matter. I do not know my client's name. I am dealing with agents who take pleasure in mystery. I want to know what's going on."

"How on earth could you expect me to tell you that?"

She clenched herself tight enough to stay calm as she said, "Because my best friend has been killed, and I'm worried it was because of something tied to this auction."

"That is why Homeland Security is involved?"

Emma replied for her. "Maybe. We're not certain what the parameters are. Or the dangers."

"You can't expect me to divulge confidential information."

"Anything you can offer is more than I have right now." Storm fished in her purse. "Do you have a tissue?"

"I'm sorry—"

"Here." Emma slipped a fresh Kleenex into Storm's hand.

"Perhaps you ladies might care to sit down?"

"I'm okay here."

"The auction. Well." He shot his cuffs. Patted his silver-fox sideburns. Gathered his dignity. "This sale is under the auspices of the Spanish anticorruption judiciary. For the past ten years, the Costa del Sol has seen the biggest real estate boom in Europe's history. When the bubble burst, the authorities discovered an underlying web of African dictators and Russian mafia who had used the boom to launder money. Licenses were granted to construction projects that have overwhelmed local services and wrecked southern Spain's last remaining pristine wilderness. The auction yesterday was of assets seized from corrupt Spanish officials who were bribed huge amounts to look the other way."

"And today?"

"Now it is the Russians' turn." His gesture took in their location, Marbella's Teatro Municipale. "This theater is across the street from the bank used to store the seized assets. And other than the football stadium, it's the largest venue they could find. They are expecting a standing-room crowd. I must warn you, bidding will be fierce, regardless of what arrangement you and I—"

"What happens tomorrow?"

"The Africans. The worst of them was Nguema Mbasogo, president of Equatorial Guinea. Supposedly he and his minions hid almost a quarter of a billion dollars around this area. Then there's Sudanese oil money, Nigerian kidnappers, Zaire diamond merchants. This region has attracted a truly vile lot."

Emma said, "Tell us about the Russians."

"Their mobs operate throughout Europe, mostly prostitution and drugs." He looked from one woman to the other. "Is that what this is about?"

"I told you, Aaron. I don't know. Is there any tie to the West Bank?"

The dealer showed surprise for the first time. "Not that I am aware of."

The auctioneer chose that moment to walk across the stage, tap on the mike, and welcome the gathered throng in both Spanish and English. Aaron said, "I suggest you ladies find seats unless you prefer to stand all day."

"Wait. What can you tell me about the Amethyst Clock?"

"Only that it is a legend with no credence whatsoever." He stepped away. "I am very sorry for your loss."

Emma waited for the dealer to make his way back to the center of the theater, shaking hands and giving a politician's wave as he went. "He knows something."

Storm tracked Aaron's progress. "I think so too."

"He tried to hide it. But when you mentioned the clock, he jerked like he'd been shot."

STORM WOKE TO THE MELODY of a foreign land drifting through her balcony doors. Sunlight frosted the lace curtains. She smelled fresh-baked bread. Out to sea, a boat chugged a deep-throated cadence while gulls sang in frantic harmony. The miniature chandelier dangling from the high ceiling gleamed a cheerful hello. For a few easy breaths, Storm felt as though she actually held the prospect of hope.

Then her cell phone rang. And as she reached

to the side table, she saw Emma watching her from the other bed. There in the other woman's hollowed gaze was everything Storm had managed to forget. At least for a moment.

"Hello."

"It's Aaron Rausch, Ms. Syrrell. I hope I'm not disturbing you."

"What time is it?"

"Just after seven. Don't tell me I woke you."

"No." She slipped her feet to the floor and tried to locate her business voice. "What can I do for you, Mr. Rausch?"

"I am downstairs. I was hoping we might have a word before the auction begins."

"Give me fifteen minutes." Storm shut the phone, turned to Emma, and asked, "How long have you been awake?"

"Wrong question." Emma spoke to the ceiling. "To wake up implies having been asleep."

"Rausch wants to meet."

"I might as well tag along." Emma tossed her covers aside. "I'm sure not doing any good here."

Emma did not speak again until they were waiting for the elevator. "I can't get over everything I've done wrong."

Storm started to say how this was probably a normal part of grief, but the look on her friend's face dissolved the words before they emerged.

Emma stared at the closed doors and said, "You know about my folks."

86

"Yes." Emma's father was a dentist, her mother a Washington socialite. They had disliked Harry Bennett almost as much as they did their daughter's profession. Harry had met them once and begged Emma never to make him go again.

The elevator pinged. The doors slid open to reveal a half-dozen faces. Emma did not move. Storm wasn't certain her friend saw them at all. They remained where they were.

When the doors shut again, Emma said, "I've known for months that Harry and I needed to move on. Stop loving each other from six thousand miles apart. Give our relationship a chance to grow. Then I'd circle back to what I grew up with. And find another good reason to let things stay like they were. Now it's all too late."

Storm waited until Emma had regained control, then took hold of her friend's arm. "Maybe we should take the stairs."

THE SIGHT OF THE TWO women appearing together did not please the elderly dealer. "I was hoping to have a private moment with Ms. Syrrell."

"Until we discover exactly what is behind all this," Emma replied, "Storm and I are joined at the hip."

Rausch inspected her carefully. "You think the death of your friend is tied to these items we're bidding on?"

"That's an excellent question, Mr. Rausch. Here's one back at you. Who precisely are you working for?"

To Storm's surprise, the dealer did not rebuke Emma for an improper query. Instead, he turned to Storm and said, "My son Jacob was most displeased to hear you were at the auction yesterday."

"I'm so glad to hear it."

"Last week I told him he was making a mistake, seeking to acquire your business. He assured me that you were on the verge of going under." The gentleman looked as elegant as he had the previous evening, down to the silk handkerchief in his jacket pocket and the fresh rose in his lapel. "My son dislikes being proven wrong."

"He wasn't wrong," Storm replied. "I got a last-minute break."

"Honesty. What an original approach." He gestured to the sunlit café. "Might I offer you ladies a coffee?"

The stone terrace was rimmed by Venetian urns and iron latticework. Their table, shaded by a broad, square parasol, was set close enough to the edge for Storm to feel the Mediterranean's chill. Their waiter wore a dark suit and bow tie. The china was Limoges. Aaron Rausch saw to their needs with the elegant ease of a man born to spend two hundred dollars on a breakfast he did not want. "No doubt my son would disapprove of our meeting like this as well. Even so, I am tempted to offer my own share of honesty. But first, I need to ask you a question. Who are you representing?"

"I told you yesterday. I have no idea." Storm hesitated, then admitted, "My deal came through Raphael Danton."

"I know of him, though we have never met. He has risen to the top of a new industry that caters to the whims of the ultrarich. Most of his competition, I suspect, will vanish with the rest of the moneyed froth. But Danton is reputed to offer value for money, and his client list is legendary." Aaron Rausch toasted her with his coffee. "I congratulate you on your eleventh-hour prize."

"He hired me because I was desperate. I get the distinct impression that Danton likes his staff to live in a state of permanent terror."

"Then he will be disappointed. You have far too much of your grandfather's nature ever to bend. You would shatter into a billion pieces first. Which is what I told my son." Aaron Rausch made a process of folding his napkin. "Very well. The answer to your question is, I represent a new client, one for whom we have never worked before."

"A Russian," Emma said.

"An extremely rich, powerful, and ruthless Russian. And that is all I am legally able to tell you."

Emma asked, "Does he have ties to the Russian secret service?"

"What an astonishing question. However could I know such a thing, since all I am hired to do is acquire artwork?"

"So he does."

"Were I to hazard a guess, I would say anyone this powerful must certainly have connections at the highest level of Russian society. These days, the line between the government and the new corporate oligarchy is so blurred as to be nonexistent."

Perhaps it was the piercingly clear Mediterranean light. Or the fact that Storm's sorrow was so pungent as to strip away even this man's veils. "My guess is, you didn't stop by this morning because of any deal we made yesterday or some vague desire to help us out. You're here because you're worried. Terrified is probably a better word, isn't it, Aaron? This guy you're working for isn't just a new source of business and profit. You're frightened he might actually bring you and your house down. You don't know why you're scared. But you're enough of a pro to know that sometimes you have to go with your gut. And right now, your gut is saying, run."

He did not want to respond. But his discreet calm slipped as he moved in and said softly, "I have never covered our back so carefully. My lawyers are growing rich from my fears over this one client."

"Why did you flinch when Storm asked you yesterday about the Amethyst Clock?" asked Emma.

"My client is convinced that it exists."

"A clock that stops time," Storm said.

"I have told him that such myths circulate around our profession. Most have to do with curses, though not all. But this . . ."

"He won't listen to you?"

"He is *obsessed* with locating this clock. And now you show up, representing another buyer who also believes in its existence."

"More than believes," Storm replied. "I'm being paid a hundred thousand dollars up front, to be taken from my commission, when I locate this item and acquire it. Not if. When."

Aaron Rausch leaned back in his seat. Storm half expected the man to warn her about competing with him and his realm of contacts and his power in the industry. Instead, he turned and spoke to the sea and the lapping waves. "My father fled Odessa and the pogroms during the chaos surrounding the Communist revolution. He fought his way up from pushing a rag cart to owning a Park Avenue establishment. When I was very young, he told me stories about those dark times when the Angel of Death swept over his beloved city on the Black Sea. His own parents were butchered by Cossacks. He escaped only because his uncle, a rabbi, had a dream. In that dream, he saw a horde of wolves pour from the bowels of the earth, with fire in their nostrils and teeth like bloody swords. My grandfather scoffed at the rabbi's dream. But it terrified my father, who was only eleven at the time. My grandfather was a wealthy merchant and would not leave everything he had spent a lifetime building up. But my father's fear was so great, his parents decided to let him go with the rabbi. My father's last image of Odessa, as they fled across the sea in a fisherman's dinghy, was of flames devouring the city while the people screamed and the Cossacks howled like demented wolves."

A sudden gust of wind caught the terrace's square parasols and flapped them hard, like a fleet of sails changing course. "My father used to tell me it was vital to remember lessons of our past. How else could we prepare when our security is stripped away once again? I had not thought of this tale in years. Now, since this new client has appeared, I think of little else. My son is concerned that I may be . . ."

"You're not wrong," Storm said.

"Two days ago I was confronted by the CIA," added Emma. "At least, I'm assuming they were from Langley. They monitored a call I made to Storm. They wanted to know the same thing you do. Who had she represented at that Palm Beach auction."

"Manalapan," Storm corrected.

"Wherever. Later that afternoon, I was swept up by a Polish priest representing the Vatican and the outgoing Israeli ambassador. They reported . . ."

Storm watched Emma's features tighten in her struggle for control. Storm finished, "They said Harry Bennett had been murdered. They think his death is somehow tied to all this."

"Forgive me. I don't understand. Why is the Israeli ambassador involved?"

When Emma found it difficult to continue, Storm went on. "Harry was killed in Hebron. He was there working on some project for the Israelis."

Emma's words sounded strangled. "Harry was helping to track down a ring of counterfeiters. The ambassador was concerned that the Russians might somehow be using the counterfeiters to reinsert themselves into the region."

"I hope you ladies will believe me when I say I know nothing of this whatsoever."

"Would you tell us if you did?"

"You have my word." He glanced at his watch and waved for the waiter. "I must go acquire items for clients who do not frighten me like this Russian. Then I shall speak with my son. Who will once again tell me that I am worrying over nothing. And while he scoffs, I will hear the wolves howling and see the flames devouring our life's work."

NINE

HARRY ENDURED ANOTHER TWO SESSIONS with the Palestinian cops. He had no idea how much time had elapsed, because he was basically awake long enough only to eat a little and get another injection and give the cops his blank stare, then he was gone again. The hospital staff swiftly grew accustomed to Harry's silence and continued to address him in Arabic. As long as his face remained bandaged, Harry hoped he could hold to the safety of anonymity.

His ward held about three dozen beds. The clinic was both decrepit and spotlessly clean. The equipment was mostly from another era, metal beds and rickety chairs and poor lighting and cracked flooring. The smells were pungent and reminded Harry of prison.

The fourth time he awoke, the cops didn't return. He could move more easily and was able to reach for the cup unaided. But he choked trying to drink laying flat. A woman seated beside the next bed spoke to him. When Harry responded by coughing again, she used the hand crank to raise him up.

Harry nodded his thanks. The woman wore the traditional colored scarf and black overgarment. She carried a sorrow that was all her own. Harry assumed the kid she tended was maybe ten or eleven years old. This time of day, most of the ward's beds were surrounded by multiple family members, who fed and soothed and pleaded whenever one of the harried hospital staff came within range.

Harry fell asleep sitting up and awoke to find the pain had eased. He decided it was time to try to rise from his bed. Which required dislodging several implements from various veins and regions that were never meant to hold such probes. By the time he had finished unplugging himself, an attendant hovered at his elbow. The guy supported Harry as he tried to stand. Several of the family members surrounding nearby beds offered encouragement. When he made it unsteadily to his pins, he did a little royal wave and earned himself a round of applause. He made it across the hall to the restroom, but by the time he got back to his bed he was ready for another numbing dose. He drifted away to the sound of Arabic murmured with tragic love.

When Harry next swam back up to wakefulness, the ward was dark. The whimpers and the half-muttered dreams and the closeness of strangers reminded him of other wards where he'd wasted too many days. Only this time, the window didn't have bars. Harry spent a while wondering if he could ever escape from who he'd once been. Then finally he drifted away again.

Harry dreamed about being lost in the Hebron

night. He ran and ran but always wound up right back in the same maw of that dark alley. The drug held him down, caging him. He heard the night beast breathing, lurking in the shadows across the Hebron street. The beast drew a breath so massive his own lungs became trapped in the airless vacuum of a closing tomb. Then once again the explosion ripped the world apart.

Harry opened his eyes. He took an unsteady breath and shoved away the cordite funk. His thirst was all-consuming. He rolled slightly in the bed and reached for the side table. The glass was beaded with sweat and glowed softly in the morning sun. He carefully gripped the glass and brought it back, every move in slow motion. His pain was perhaps a little better this morning, but he could still detect its muted growl.

The hour after he woke was endless. There was no emergency button by these hospital beds. Harry knew the nurse wouldn't make her rounds yet because he couldn't smell the coffee, and she always arrived a few minutes before breakfast. The ward's scarred walls did not hold a clock. The previous morning Harry had seen how other men had watched the sun crawl across the floor, marking the minutes in grim anticipation. Harry had heard them sigh their relief when the metal cart rattled its way down the outside corridor. He would just have to wait with the others.

Harry drained his glass and retraced his gradual

hand movements back over to the side table. Which was when he noticed the kid.

The boy in the next bed was mostly skin and bones, scarcely half a pound above being a runt. He had the refined features and the ancient eyes of someone much older. Right now, the kid looked terrified. His lips were drawn back from his teeth and he panted as he watched the ward's empty doorway.

A faint noise echoed down the outer hallway, growing like the roar of a cresting wave. Harry heard several men arguing with a nurse, with the doctor's voice somewhere in the mix. Several other bedridden men swiveled concerned gazes from the doorway to the kid and back. Harry recognized the been-there, done-that expressions of guys in the know.

Then the kid whimpered.

Harry didn't need a translator to understand that sound. He also knew he shouldn't add himself to the mix. His own situation was beyond precarious. But he couldn't just lie there and let it happen.

Harry flipped back the covers and pushed himself erect. His body shrieked a massive protest as he shuffled to the next bed. Harry pulled back the kid's covers, revealing bandage that covered the boy's entire abdomen. The kid gave another whimper, this one with words. Harry bent down and slid his arms under the kid, who gripped Harry around the neck.

Harry figured this next maneuver would push his pain beyond the redline.

He heaved and swiveled and dumped the kid in one swift motion, trying to get it all over and done before the beast struck. He almost made it. The kid spoke more words, probably asking Harry what safety there was in moving one bed closer to the entrance.

Harry couldn't have replied even if he spoke the language. The only way he had made it this far was by holding his breath. He turned back to the kid's bed and stripped off the sheets, bundled them together with the pillow, and plunked them down on the kid. He crawled back into his bed. The kid finally got it and made himself smaller still, curling into a ball that compressed the sheets to his middle. Harry used both arms to lift his right leg and drape it over the kid and the bundle. He flipped the covers back over them both. His right leg was now propped into an elevated position.

Harry opened his mouth. Breathed. And moaned as the pain attacked.

The clamor in the hallway was accompanied now by sharp footfalls. Leather soles. Cop shoes. Three blue shirts appeared in the doorway, struggling against two nurses and the doctor. A pair of men in dark suits and sunglasses and tieless white shirts paraded behind the cops, utterly disconnected from the racket. They scanned the ward.

One of them barked an Arabic bullet at the doctor.

Which was when the nurses and the doctor turned and saw the bare mattress.

Harry was not acting when he reached out a hand, the fingers rictus curled, begging for another dose of ice in a syringe.

Instantly his call was taken up by another man, followed quickly by four others. Five. Six. All of them beseeching the group, drawing the newcomers' attention away from the doctors and nurses gaping at an empty bed.

Being surrounded by people in pain did not faze the two men in suits. Which only confirmed Harry's initial impression. Their title might have been detective or secret service or special branch, but in reality they were the Palestinian version of serious trouble. One of them pulled a photograph from his pocket and did a slow scan of the room while his partner argued with the hospital staff. The guy then showed the photograph to the doctor. The doctor and the nurses only included him in their slanging match.

Finally the men signaled to the cops and retreated. The doctor followed them out, his protests gradually diminishing with the footsteps. One nurse scurried out the door. The other sat herself down on the empty bed. She leaned forward and lifted Harry's bedcovers. Harry held up one finger. Wait. He could still hear the cops arguing with the doctor.

Only when the other nurse reappeared with the rattling metal cart and took aim straight for his bed did Harry allow his hand to drop.

THE NURSE AND TWO ATTENDANTS shifted the kid back to his own bed, then treated Harry to his morning injection. The dose might have been smaller, gradually reducing his dependence on the ice canoe. Or maybe he was growing accustomed to the glacial rush. Then again, he had put his body through some serious strains, and maybe the pain was strong enough to shout down the drug's call to oblivion. Whatever the reason, that morning's injection did not put Harry under. Instead, he sort of floated away.

His eyes were slitted against light that stayed too bright even when the nurse drew the curtains. A fly settled on his forehead and tracked across his face. Harry was not bothered enough to shift and make it leave. People came and went. The light swung from east to west. The shadows changed shape. Then he must have drifted off, because the next thing he knew, he was back in the dream, fleeing through the Hebron night but always winding up trapped in that alley.

Only this time Harry stopped running.

He stood there in the dark, his chest pumping from the sheer bloody terror of knowing what came next. But waiting just the same.

Then it happened just like he knew it would.

Boom. The blast carried the same roar he felt every time the injection wore off. He opened his eyes and lay there staring at the ceiling. For once, trying to hold on to the dream rather than push the fear away.

Finally Harry blinked and rubbed his eyes and made the slow, steady reach toward the side table. Then he realized the kid's mother was holding the water glass out to him. Harry nodded his thanks and took the glass, thinking that he must look like he was coming off a three-day drunk. She waited until he was done, then she took back the cup and walked to the table by the door and refilled it from the pitcher. She returned and offered it again. Harry shook his head, figuring he had a temporary pass to stare openly. The lady was too lovely to carry an expression that sad.

She spoke to him, and once again Harry was astonished at just how musical Arabic could sound. When Harry shook his head in response, she opened a voluminous purse and pulled out a pad and pen. Harry shook his head a second time. She stowed the items away, clearly embarrassed for him, assuming he could not read or write.

Moving in careful stages, Harry pushed away his bedcovers and slid his legs around so that his back was to the kid. The man in the bed to Harry's left nodded a greeting. As did the guy beyond him. Their silent welcome to the fold helped Harry stow away his pain and shove himself to his feet.

He shuffled down the ward's central aisle, through the main doors, and across the corridor. The washroom was as old and decrepit and spotlessly clean as the rest of the place. The doctor was making his rounds when Harry shuffled back to his bed. Both the doctor and the nurse greeted him solemnly as he passed. As did the patient they were working on. And the family who were gathered around the patient's bed.

When it was Harry and the kid's turn, the nurse rolled over a trio of portable screens. The wheels squeaked and rattled across the uneven linoleum. The nurse fitted them about Harry and the kid's beds, as though his act had somehow bonded them in the best medical sense.

The doctor worked on the kid first. He peeled back the bandage to reveal a long diagonal scar with a line of neat stitches. There was quite a lot of seepage around the kid's wound, from getting tossed out of bed, Harry figured. The kid showed no distress, even when the doctor started probing. Probably thinking of the alternative.

The doctor gave the mother some serious instructions, which were gravely accepted. The doctor then turned to Harry and spoke. From the motions of the doctor's hands, Harry assumed that he was going to peel away the bandages on Harry's face and neck and shoulder. And that it was going to hurt.

With the bandages gone, the doctor's fingers felt cool through the latex gloves. He inspected Harry thoroughly, giving careful attention to his right cheek and ear and neck. The doctor moved farther down, going over the taped ribs and his bruised stomach. Then he spoke and gestured. Harry got the message that he wanted to leave the bandages off Harry's face and let the wounds breathe. He showed Harry a tube and then applied the salve, talking all the while. The ointment felt soothing going on.

When the doctor placed the tube in Harry's bedside table drawer, he spotted the Palestinian ID.

He looked at Harry and then back to the parrot guy's photo. Harry caught his breath.

The doctor slipped the ID back inside and shut the drawer. He patted the top of the table. Nodded to Harry. And walked away.

Only then did Harry realize the woman and the kid had seen it all.

When the nurse started to move the screens away, the woman turned to her and said something. The nurse glanced at Harry and nodded, leaving the screens in place.

Harry waited until the doctor started talking to the guy in the next bed. Then he leaned toward the woman and spoke the first word he had uttered since the blast.

"Help."

• • •

THE ARAB WOMAN REMAINED SEATED on the side of her son's bed opposite from Harry. "You are British?"

"American."

She pointed discreetly at the drawer to his side table. "You are not this man."

"No."

The woman's name was Miriam. Her injured son was Fareed. Miriam had waited until the lunch hour and the surrounding clamor to speak with him. The privacy screens remained an unexpected bonus. Harry had no idea how much Fareed understood, for the kid did not speak. He also did not miss a thing.

"Why are you hiding?" Miriam asked.

"To stay safe."

"You think here is safe?" She glanced at her son. "You must be in very much danger."

"Maybe."

"You think but you do not know?"

Harry asked, "Do you know about the bomb that sent me here?"

"All Hebron knows."

"How many people died in that blast?"

"Only one man." She caught his flicker of sur-prise. "You were the, what is word?"

"Target." Harry eased himself up a notch. "Maybe."

Harry's lunch tray remained untouched on his

side table. The nurse appeared and scolded Harry for not eating. Miriam resumed her silent vigil, hovering over her son. When the nurse departed, Harry asked, "What happened to your boy?"

Harry was not asking out of mere politeness. Clearly the woman understood, for she said, "My husband had no work. He, how you say, thieved."

"Stole."

"He is gone now." She spoke the words as a whispered lament. "Fareed is all I have left."

Harry voiced his guess: "The boy figured he should take up where his father left off."

The woman sighed and said something that Harry figured was the Arabic equivalent of men. Then she said, "Tonight I must move my son."

Harry understood. The boy couldn't lay here and risk having the police return tomorrow. "Can I come with you?"

"How can I refuse? We owe you too much. But to have you stay with us, we will know such dangers."

"Just get me out of here."

"And do what? Leave you on the Hebron street for another bomb?"

Harry shook his head. "Where will you hide Fareed?"

A shudder coursed through her. "I must find some way to get him to my family in Jordan. He will be safe there. The hospitals are better. He can heal. Grow strong. Escape."

Harry leaned over as far as his ribs allowed. "Maybe I can help make that happen."

TEN

MIDWAY THROUGH THE MORNING AUCTION, Storm slipped into the theater lobby to check her messages. She found three from Raphael Danton. They started off irate and grew fiercer. Storm stepped onto the pillared front portico and placed the call.

Raphael Danton answered with, "I expect my charges to be *immediately* available. Around the clock."

"Let's get one thing straight. I am not now and never will be your *charge.*"

"Did it ever occur to you, Ms. Syrrell, that your attitude is the reason why your firm is on the verge of bankruptcy?"

"No, but I do wonder if you intentionally hunt for the hottest button to push."

They both took time out to exchange a few tight breaths. Finally Danton said, "You continue to amaze me."

"Was that why you felt it so vital to call three times and foam at the mouth?"

He laughed out loud. Maybe because the sound was so unexpected, Storm actually shivered.

Danton asked, "Why did you only purchase two of the auctioned items, instead of all four?"

"I made an arrangement with Aaron Rausch. He took two, I took the other two. I assume your client is going to continue to bid against Rausch's client. If you were to go to the wall this time, what happens next? Unless your client has completely unlimited pockets and his opponent is a total dodo, the opponent is going to realize what's going on. And he's going to start bidding on things he doesn't want, just to watch your client climb the ladder to nowhere."

Danton mulled that over, then demanded, "Where are you now?"

"Standing outside Marbella's municipal theater."

"I'm coming to meet with you. Be at the private gate of Málaga airport this afternoon at three. Danton out."

STORM RETURNED TO HER SEAT. She had no need to sit through another day of sales. But she was here, and this was her world, and trends were sometimes clearest when observed from the trenches. Besides which, she needed time to seethe and think.

The theater's stage was jammed with new items. The main gallery held over a thousand people, and almost every seat was taken. The interior was neo-Gothic, with gilded cherubs adorning the upper tiers, red velvet walls, and massive chandeliers. The treasures on display revealed the private lives of some powerful and secretive people. Storm did not bother to pretend at bidding. She had established her cred the previous day. She watched the drama and she thought.

Prices were off by as much as half the previous year's highs. But interest remained keen and bidding was fierce. When the auctioneer broke for lunch, they had managed to work through only a third of the day's wares.

Storm and Emma wound their way through Marbella's cobblestone streets to a small café. Outdoor tables faced a small plaza with the requisite fountain and crumbling facades. They ordered salads and coffee and juice, then watched the street theater. When Emma had finished eating, she said, "Okay if I walk through something with you?"

"Shoot."

"We've got a Russian buyer represented by your friend Aaron Rausch."

"Rausch is not my friend."

"Seemed to me he was making overtures in that direction. Anyway, Rausch's buyer has an enemy."

"Whoever is hiding behind Raphael Danton."

"Either this new guy has a thing for the exact same line of old goods, or he loathes the Russian so much he searches out whatever Rausch's guy is after. And then Danton's guy outbids him."

Storm agreed. "It has to be revenge. You didn't see the painting I bought in Florida. There can't possibly be two guys crazy enough to pay a million dollars for that oil. Not in this market."

"In that case, we need to know what Rausch's guy did to earn this level of payback."

"And how we are tied into it." Storm nodded slowly. "And why they went after Harry."

"So let's make some guesses," said Emma. "Rausch's buyer learns about this guy who's spoiling his game. He traces the purchases through you and the Swiss cutout. And he attacks."

"There are two problems with this," Storm said.

"I didn't say it was perfect."

"Number one, why go after Harry and not us?"

"I'm guessing it has to be the Amethyst Clock," Emma said. "Harry was hunting counterfeiters. You said yourself this clock can't exist. Which means they had to find somebody to make one up."

"That still leaves problem number two. The timing. Harry could never have been dug out overnight. The Israelis took him because Harry Bennett has never worked for anybody but Harry Bennett. He is the ultimate treasure dog."

Emma struggled to repress the grief that flayed her features. Then she said, "Even so, they tracked him down."

"More or less the same day Danton sends me after that oil." Storm shook her head. "We're missing something here. Something big enough to destroy us both."

THE HOSPITAL WARD TOOK THE afternoon siesta seriously. Miriam left with most of the other visitors. Harry waited until the loudest sounds were snores from neighboring beds. He swung his feet to the floor and rose to a seated position. The drawer to his little metal table squeaked as he pulled it open. There beside the parrot guy's ID was Miriam's phone.

Harry picked up the phone and nodded to Fareed. The kid watched him with an old man's ability to offer trust and suspicion in one unblinking gaze.

The trek to the end of the outer hallway left Harry trembling hard. He breathed eternal gratitude at the sight of an empty bench beside the exit. Harry eased himself down, and when his strength finally returned, he opened the cell phone.

Harry had to smile at how just dialing Emma's number was enough to cause his heart to zing.

The phone rang a half-dozen times, then Emma's voice told him to leave a message. No soft hello, no identification as to who she was. Just a cold, professional tone and a few words shot out like verbal bullets. Even so, Harry found himself unable to respond.

His entire body clenched up so tight the tears were squeezed from his eyes. He opened his mouth but could not find the air to speak. Instead, the effort only crystallized the earlier sensations. How far he had come, yet how close he was to where he had begun. How trapped, and how liberated. How hopeful, and how very, very afraid. And how he had done nothing to deserve the woman who asked him to leave a message and the time that he called.

He shut the phone and waited for the emotions to ease off. He watched the sunlight and the world beyond the hospital's exit. When he felt he could draw a halfway steady breath, he dialed the number again.

He almost broke down again just saying the words, "Emma, it's me."

ELEVEN

THE SUN WAS A RED globe over the Málaga harbor when the taxi sped Storm and Emma to the airport. Emma kept her gaze on a pair of container vessels and a tanker anchored a mile or so out, waiting for harbor tugs and their turns at berth. With the still air and the afternoon sun, the ships appeared to float in a molten vat. Emma needed Storm's company almost as much as she needed space. They had not spoken since they had left the auction. Even so, she had never felt closer to her friend.

Highway air, laden with diesel fumes and regret, pushed through the taxi's open window. Emma felt buffeted by all the arguments she had used to convince herself that her relationship with Harry had been fine the way it was. Love from six thousand miles away was safe. She could maintain her boundaries, focus on the next step up the Washington ladder. But now that the chance for real love was gone, Emma was flayed by old ghosts. In truth, she had kept Harry at arm's length because she had never come to terms with who she was. And now she probably never would. Sorrow threatened to shred her soul.

The taxi deposited them by the smaller of Málaga's two terminals. The airport seemed asleep. The palms between them and the silent passenger terminal were motionless. The rank of taxis seemed frozen. A lone single-engine Cessna trundled toward an otherwise empty runway.

The original terminal was now reserved for private planes. The structure was a distinctly Mediterranean mix of Art Deco and municipal concrete. Emma and Storm had the main hall almost to themselves. They walked across the tiled floor to a café. An older woman in diamonds and mauve silk was the café's only other customer. Behind the service counter, a pair of attendants talked in the quiet manner of people who had exhausted every topic of real interest long ago. Emma and Storm chose seats partially isolated by potted plants. Emma pulled out her phone. Storm went to the counter and returned with coffees. She set one down on the table by Emma's purse, then settled into the next chair. "I don't know how you're keeping it together."

"I'm not." Emma sipped from the cup, tasted nothing. "I can't stop thinking about that mythical clock. You know what I'd give to have something that reversed time?"

"It's not supposed to turn back the hour. What's done is done."

"Oh, so you're the expert now?"

Storm drank her coffee and did not respond.

Emma said, "Maybe it does both. They just haven't figured that part out yet."

Storm gave that a second, then said, "I feel so guilty."

"Why?"

"The whole way out here, I keep thinking about the sound of Raphael Danton's laugh."

"I've spent years training in unarmed combat, use of restraints, you name it," Emma replied. "You need some advice on how to tackle this guy, let me know."

"Forget it. You haven't met Mr. Attitude."

"But you made him laugh. Maybe beneath that icy exterior beats a heart of granite." Emma set down her cup. "I need to check in."

She keyed for her voice mail, then hesitated. She needed to get this done. But she couldn't move past the fact that there was no one who really mattered at the other end. No man hungering for the sound of her voice. Just the emptiness of never hearing Harry's voice again.

When she reached out, Storm's hand was there waiting for her. The one reassurance that meant anything at all.

Emma dialed the access code.

And her world fell apart.

TWELVE

T O HIS CREDIT, TIP MACFARLAND did not interrupt Emma's muddled report via cell phone. He had been Emma's first supervisor after she completed her training. He had stood with her through the worst of the previous year's tempest. He was with her now. "You're certain it was Bennett?"

"I couldn't get this one wrong, Tip."

"It's a question I have to ask, on account of how this whole thing just keeps building by the minute."

Emma felt like both laughing and shrieking. Not to mention tucking down one wing and doing a circuit of the Málaga airport. "Tell me."

"Let me make sure I understand," Tip continued. "The Israeli ambassador and the Polish priest were both off target. Your treasure guy survived the bomb blast. And now he's being spirited from Hebron by some new friends he made in the hospital. He's headed for Jordan. He doesn't have papers. He's looking for a free pass across the tightest border in the known universe."

"That pretty much sums up things at my end."

"I've got to tell you, there are days when I wonder if you're worth the trouble."

Laughing should not have caused the tears to flow once more, but it did. "Storm is trying to raise the ambassador to see if he can help."

"Who is Harry Bennett running from?"

"He didn't say."

"Okay. Let's set this aside for a second. I was with the director when you checked in. We haven't heard a peep from our buddies at the CIA. My guess is, they still don't have a clue about who Danton is working for."

Emma could almost see the pieces of the puzzle swirl in front of her face, begging to be sorted into a coherent picture. But right now all she could think of was Harry's message. The silence, the breathing, the sound of what she thought was probably a sob. Followed by his second message. The hoarse voice, the tumbling broken words she had needed to listen to six times, then give the phone to Storm just to have another person confirm what Emma really had heard.

Emma realized Tip was still speaking and could only say, "Sorry, I'm not tracking."

"Think about it. Unless the CIA's sniffer dogs

are asleep, which I doubt, by now they know your whereabouts. So why aren't we receiving incoming fire about your traveling against orders?"

"They meant for me to rush over and be with her. That was their plan all along." Emma glanced over to where Storm paced and argued into the phone. "They set us up."

"Looks that way to me."

"Why didn't they just request our help?"

"I just asked the director the very same thing. His response was, 'Those guys at Langley define twisted.' Needless to say, our director's opinion doesn't need to go any further."

"I don't see it. They went to all this trouble for a reason."

"I agree. Your job is to find out why. MacFarland out."

WHEN EMMA SHUT HER PHONE, Storm related her conversation with the Israeli diplomat. The former ambassador had heard her out and promised to get back to her as swiftly as possible. Storm's voice sounded as tight as Emma's gut. There was nothing they could do until either the ambassador or Harry called back. When Emma finished relating her conversation with Tip, Storm said, "So, the CIA is on our tail. I haven't seen anybody watching us."

"You won't."

"Have you?"

"I don't need to."

"Are you sure they're there?"

"They'll have the local intel on alert, probably staffers on the consular payroll. They piggy-backed onto your cell phone's transmission when we first talked about this trip and inserted software that bugs your phone and pinpoints your location." When Storm started to pull the battery from her phone, Emma said, "It's too late for that. Most likely by now they've also wired you. They could have slipped into the hotel and tagged your clothes, shoes, belt, handbag, cases, the works. Then again, maybe they figure having me this close serves just as well."

"They're using us."

"That's my guess. Tip agrees."

"I feel dirty."

"It's what they do." She pointed out the window. "Heads up. This could be your man."

A silver teardrop fell from the sky. The jet landed so swiftly the eye kept moving forward and had to backtrack. Storm said, "What is *that?*"

"Very light jet, or VLJ. Looks to me like an Eclipse. Carbon fiber body. Williams engines. Fastest of its kind. The Ferrari of the skies." Emma noticed the way Storm was watching her. "What?"

"Nothing."

"I'm a girl who likes her toys. So shoot me."

She watched the jet whine its way toward them. The door opened and the stairs slipped down. When the man appeared, all Emma could say was, "Whoa."

Storm crossed her arms.

"This guy is rich? And single?"

Storm tightened her grip on her purse as Raphael Danton crossed the tarmac, climbed the stairs, and entered the terminal. Even the two ladies behind the counter stopped their conversation.

He wore a suede jacket the color of sand that probably cost more than Emma's entire wardrobe. A gold watch blinked on his tanned wrist. His eyes were more copper than brown. His jaw was straight from a movie by Cecil B. DeMille. Wavy hair to match his eyes. Long and strong body. Gorgeous tan.

Emma flushed. Ten seconds earlier she had been frantic with worry over Harry. Now she was a teenager wanting to put this guy's poster on her wall.

Storm's voice was flat as pounded tin. "This is Emma Webb."

The man's eyes were not cold so much as disinterested. "She is your lover?"

Emma had to grin. She would not have believed it was possible to have somebody clear her head that fast. "I'm Storm's friend. Let me know if you need help defining that word."

"How utterly delightful," Danton replied. "Two bad attitudes for the price of one."

Emma found herself taking the same grip on her purse as Storm. "You're talking to *me* about *attitude?*"

Storm, however, was obviously used to the guy's charm. "Emma needs to travel with us."

"That is not happening."

Storm moved so fast she actually backed the guy up a step. "Did you hear me ask a question? No, you did not."

"Perhaps I should remind you that I am the employer and you are the employee. I can fire you—"

"Emma Webb is with Homeland Security. We need you to fly us to Israel."

"Jordan," Emma corrected.

Storm waved that aside as unimportant. "We need to leave now."

Raphael Danton's laugh rang like a gunshot through the empty terminal. Storm was right. Even his laugh was good-looking.

"You are truly an astonishment," he said.

"Did you hear what I said?"

"You tell me your friend is with Homeland. But this is Spain, and your friend's jurisdiction ended four thousand miles ago." Danton slipped the Vuitton case from his shoulder and set it on the floor by his feet. "But please, do explain to me why I should not dismiss you."

"There isn't time, Raphael. The former Israeli ambassador to the United States is trying to help us save a friend's life. I don't know what you're not telling us, and right now I don't care." Storm picked up his valise and rammed it back into his arms. "My other best friend was blown up four days ago in Hebron. The CIA claims you and whoever you represent and the guy we're bidding against are the reasons. Now, either you go fire up that jet or I borrow Emma's gun and shoot you myself."

THIRTEEN

HARRY BENNETT RODE TO THE Jordanian border in the rear of a fifties-era ambulance. Hassan had supplied the ambulance and now served as driver. Where Hassan had obtained the vehicle and his stained police uniform, Harry did not ask. The ceiling above Harry's canvas bunk was rusted through in several places. His side window was cracked. Harry was dressed in a filthy djellaba that Miriam had supplied. The bandages were wound back around much of his face. Over the bandages he wore a checked Palestinian head-kerchief. A wheelchair was jammed into the space between his bunk and Fareed's. The ambulance's air-conditioning did not work. Six jouncing hours with all the windows open to the dust and the heat had so stained his garments that their original colors were lost. Every time Harry drank from the metal bottle jangling against his bunk, all he tasted was the road.

Somewhere to the north was the new four-lane highway. Since the last intifada, however, the Israelis did not let Palestinians use the highways unless they held special passes. Highway traffic was mostly restricted to settlers and the army and tourists seeking a relatively safe glimpse of the West Bank. The Palestinians used roads that could only be described as abysmal.

The Allenby Bridge was the West Bank's only border crossing into Jordan. It stood adjacent to a military compound, where open-sided metal structures offered shade for several hundred vehicles, including an array of battle tanks. Dozens of ochre buildings baked in the heat. Prison-style watchtowers marched into the distance.

For seventy-five dollars, a professional escort shepherded individuals and their belongings from both the Israeli and the Jordanian sides. For these privileged few, the crossing took a matter of minutes. For everyone else, the ordeal lasted hours, sometimes days. Luggage and purses and even wallets were stripped away and piled onto handcarts that vanished through a separate entrance. The individual was searched and passed on to the Jordanians. Perhaps the travelers found their luggage waiting for them on the other side.

Nobody who could afford the seventy-five dollars endured the free option more than once.

By the time their ambulance joined the line of trucks and overburdened cars, Fareed's last dose of pain medicine was wearing off. Harry's own aches magnified in the heat and the dust. But he was free, he was alive, and he was headed for Jordan in the company of friends. Harry did not complain.

Up ahead, a dozen or so flagpoles rose from the russet clouds that hugged the road. The flags hung limp and defeated. The border station itself was lost to the glowering day. The line of waiting vehicles was not moving. All of the engines were shut off.

The ambulance slid in behind a truck filled with bleating goats. Hassan cut the engine, slipped from the car, and stretched so hard his bones popped. Miriam swiveled in her seat and spoke to the boy lying in the bunk across from Harry. Fareed responded with a sharp intake of breath. Harry knew the sound all too well. The boy was intent on keeping the pain clenched inside. Miriam had been given syringes containing two injections by their doctor. But it was a long journey to the hospital in Amman. If Miriam knocked him out now, the border patrol would only wake him up again.

Miriam stroked Fareed's sweaty forehead, then stepped out of the ambulance. She and Hassan crossed the road and joined a group clustered about a kebab stand. They talked for what to Harry seemed like hours. The ambulance felt like an oven set on broil. Every now and then, Fareed took a tight, whimpering breath. Harry could hear the drone of voices and the hiss of grilling meat. The goats crammed in the truck ahead of them complained. Nothing moved.

Footsteps trod back across the empty road. Miriam opened the rear doors. "I have food."

Harry would have thought he was too hot to eat, but his stomach declared otherwise. The chunks of lamb were doused in a sauce of yogurt, dill, onions, and coriander, and wrapped in unleavened bread. Harry finished it in three seconds flat and chased it down with a Pepsi that had obviously sat in the hot sun for days. It tasted divine.

"You would like more?"

Harry handed her the empty can. "I've eaten a five-course meal in a three-star Paris restaurant. That lamb puts it to shame."

Miriam's face was made more beautiful by her smile. "I would like to see Paris so very much."

"Then I should try to help make that happen."

She glanced at her son. "Inshallah."

When Miriam returned, Hassan came with her. He handed Harry a second meal and reported, "The border is sealed. Your fault."

Miriam said, "They are calling the Hebron bomb-

123

ing a terrorist attack. They are letting through a few vehicles. This way, they are not accused of shutting the border. The truck ahead of us has been here for an afternoon and a night and all of today."

"That's not good. Can't an ambulance just drive on ahead?"

"Here, the only law is force. If we break the line, we die." She slipped into the ambulance, fitted a straw into an open can of hot Pepsi, and held it for her son to drink. "I have plan. Please, can you pretend to have much pain?"

"No problem." Not that it would require a whole lot of playacting.

She spoke to her son, who grimaced what Harry thought might have been a smile. Miriam patted the side of Fareed's face, then slipped again from the ambulance. Hassan grinned at Harry and said, "If no luck, I whistle." The two walked toward the checkpoint.

Fareed tossed his sheet aside and drew up his shirt so as to reveal the bloodstained bandage. "My mother, she much smart woman."

Harry agreed. "And brave. And you are one amazing kid."

"You watch." The movements and the words left him panting. "She show you amaze."

When Miriam and Hassan returned, they were accompanied by so many men the rear doors became completely blocked. Miriam spoke to her son, who released a cry so plaintive the men at the back moaned in response. Harry stared at the rust-stained roof and panted like the goats.

Hassan shouted something in Arabic. Harry heard more footsteps scurry down either side of the vehicle. In theory, he disliked the idea of becoming that afternoon's entertainment. Especially when two men crawled inside the ambulance, spoke words that reeked of onion and garlic right into Harry's face, then lifted the edge of his bandage. The man grunted at the sight of Harry's pockmarked face. His mate patted Harry's shoulder and clambered out.

There followed what Harry could only call a loud confab. Every time the noise died away, Fareed would let go with another of his patented keens. Miriam added a fine accompaniment of her own, turning her words into wails that pierced the hubbub.

Then one of the men shouted something that was instantly taken up by a dozen or more other voices, and two men clambered upon the ambulance's rear fender. Miriam and Hassan scurried to their seats. Hassan fired up the engine. Two more men slammed the rear doors, while others stepped onto the ambulance's running boards. Another man climbed onto the hood, unfurled his head-kerchief, and used it as a striped flag to clear the road ahead.

The ancient ambulance was not meant to carry such a load. The engine groaned. The slightest dip caused metal to scrape dangerously against metal. No one complained. Certainly not Harry.

Through the dirt-stained side window Harry saw one driver after another clamber down from their immobile vehicles and start to complain as the ambulance drove forward. Many waved pistols overhead. Perhaps the IDF considered handguns to be acceptable self-protection, especially when one was headed out of the West Bank. Harry spotted a museum-quality Colt, several Nazi-era Rugers, a Nambu, countless Berettas, and what looked like a genuine flintlock chased in silver. The men atop their ambulance shouted back. The guy on the front fender unholstered a massive .357 and waved it overhead. The ambulance crawled forward.

All in all, it made for an interesting trip.

The IDF soldiers were out in force by the time they arrived at the border. As they approached the first of the concrete barriers, their guards slipped down, patted the ambulance's side and hood, slammed the rear doors, called back to Miriam's thanks, and vanished in the dust.

The snake-like approach to the checkpoint drew them through three tight curves, each of which brought them face-to-face with the gaping maw of a machine gun. At the final approach, Miriam turned to Harry, real fear showing on her face. "What do I say?"

It did no harm to repeat the instructions Emma

had left on the lady's phone. "Dial the number my friend left for you. Tell whoever answers that we've arrived. Give the phone to the guard."

Miriam held her phone in a two-fisted clench. "You trust this friend so much?"

"With my life."

She did not move. "With the life of my son also?"

"Dial the number."

FOURTEEN

THE COCKPIT OF RAPHAEL DANTON'S jet was decked out like an elegant yacht, with cream leather seats and burled-walnut decking. The dials were high-tech electronic readouts framed in sterling silver. The plane did not take off so much as launch. One moment they were on the ground and Danton was talking a pro's talk into the mike, and the next they were leveling out at thirty thousand feet.

Danton flew from the left-hand seat. Storm sat in the copilot's seat and ogled the Spanish coastline and the sunlit sea. The jet was minuscule. Storm had crouched to make it down the central aisle. The cockpit was a bulbous dome with oversized windows. Raphael handed her a pair of aviator glasses against the glare. The view was spectacular. For once, Storm was comfortable with the man's silent reserve. It meant she could give herself fully to enjoying the view.

When they leveled off, she slipped from her seat and opened the accordion curtain separating the cockpit from the cabin's eight seats. Emma was stretched out across two seats, defeated by exhaustion and relief. When Storm returned to the cockpit, Danton's jaw muscles were working overtime.

Storm settled back into her seat and told him everything. As she talked, Raphael Danton switched on the autopilot. An electronic button eased his seat back from the controls, and he swiveled around so he almost faced her. The engines formed a rumbling backdrop to Storm's unfolding drama. Danton's sunglasses kept his expression hidden. But at least the tension in his jawline gradually eased.

When she was done, he rose from his seat, stepped to the mini-galley tucked between the cockpit and the cabin, and asked, "Will you take coffee?"

"Please."

"I believe that is the first time you have ever used that word in my company."

"Don't get used to it."

The mug he placed in the sterling holder was chased in gold. "You astonish me."

"Yeah, well, if it's any consolation, I shock myself almost every day."

Raphael slipped back into the pilot's seat. "Are you not the least bit concerned about my power to crush your career and your firm?"

"Don't talk silliness, Raphael."

The aviator sunglasses might as well have rested on a statue. "What did you say?"

"Of course I'm scared. We're riding into the unknown to rescue a friend I thought dead. My company's survival rests on a knife's edge. My fate is in the hands of some mystery buyer with more money than sense. You're paying me a small fortune to hunt down a clock that can't possibly exist. I'm terrified."

Raphael said quietly, "No one has called me silly since my wife died."

At that moment, Storm was too hot to express any form of polite sympathy. So she made do with, "I didn't know you were married."

"I assume that means your slumbering friend prepared a dossier on me."

Storm had no answer except to sip from her mug. "This is good coffee."

"What dirty little secrets did that woman manage to dig up?"

"Her name is Emma Webb." For some reason, the sharp edge to Storm's voice caused Raphael to smile. She asked, "What's so funny?"

When he replied, the customary coldness was gone from his voice. "What did Agent Webb tell you?"

"Your father won the Nobel Prize. You were in the Swiss army, then you became a big-game hunter in Africa. And then you went over to the dark side."

"He is my stepfather." Raphael toyed with the rim of his mug. "Other than that, everything she told you is correct."

So much rode on the whim of this man, it was hard to set aside her fear and see him clearly. But he held such an air of sorrow about him, she managed to say, "I'm sorry about the loss of your wife, Raphael."

"She was French. We met in Zaire. She was with the United Nations. I lost her in the rebellion." He continued to address his words to the mug in his hands. "She was four months pregnant with our son."

Suddenly the man's cold facade made perfect sense. "And then you retreated into your cave of dark deeds."

He sipped from his mug. Studied the blue horizon. "Something tells me you carry your own load of regrets."

Storm's voice sounded fractured to her own ears. "Maybe someday I'll tell you what it's like to testify against your own father and send him to jail for sixteen years."

The confession left her throat raw. She instantly regretted having spoken at all. But Raphael set his mug in the holder and said to the sky beyond their plane, "My stepfather won the Nobel Prize for biochemistry. My biological father was a senior officer in the Swiss army and died in a mountain-climbing accident before I was born. My step-

130

father has labs at the University of Bern and in one of the pharmaceutical giants. He travels the globe, speaking with leaders and other biochemical geniuses like himself. I despise the man."

"Why?"

"My sole duty in life was to worship at his feet. He never cared for me as an individual. For years I doubted whether he saw me at all. Then I began winning athletic awards. My sport was the biathlon, a combination of cross-country skiing and shooting; perhaps you have seen the combined events in the Olympics, yes? I was on the Swiss national team for three years. Then I went to Africa."

A light began flashing, accompanied by a soft chime. Danton swiveled his chair back behind the controls. "We must land and refuel."

"Where are we?"

"Forty nautical miles from Fumicino, the main airport of Rome."

Storm watched as he retook control and aimed them for a rapidly expanding strip of concrete. She had never seen a plane's descent from the cockpit. Danton handled the jet with a professional's ease, talking with the tower, scouting for other craft, lining up behind a massive 747. The plane dropped so swiftly Storm felt her stomach rise to nudge against her heart. Raphael slipped easily into the final approach and touched down with feather-light precision.

"That was amazing."

"Yes." He taxied to a commercial hangar, waved to the attendant manning the fuel tanker, and powered down. "Things will proceed more swiftly if you do not disembark."

"I'm good." Storm rose and glanced through the curtain. "And Emma is still zonked out."

"Would you care for a sandwich?"

"I'll get it." The galley was as precisely and luxuriously fitted out as the rest of the plane. Storm remained rattled by their dual set of personal revelations. She had not spoken of her tragedy since her grandfather's death. She returned with a plastic-wrapped Limoges plate and asked, "Why did you tell me about your family?"

Danton unwrapped the plate, then sat balling up the plastic. "I am surrounded by submissive women."

"Maybe because you demand it."

He revealed his first full smile. Of course the guy had dimples.

Storm said, "Take off your shades."

"Why?" But Danton did as she asked. And revealed that the smile had touched his gaze as well. The coldness was so far gone it might as well have never existed.

Storm said, "I understand what you're saying."

"Tell me."

"You have made a profession of never letting anyone close. The more successful you are, the more you dislike the people who do as you say.

You order them to submit, to fear you, to toady up. And then you loathe them for obeying."

Her words erased the smile. His gaze hollowed. For the first time, Storm felt as though she saw the real man. Raphael said, "Back in Málaga, when you spoke about your gentleman friend, I heard the love in your voice and I saw the concern on your face."

"Harry is in love with Emma. Not me."

"I heard the love. I once had friends like that. My partner in the safari business. And my wife. After she died, I joined the mercenaries fighting against . . ."

Danton stopped. He stared out the window. But Storm knew that gaze, the sightless eyes, the vision of things beyond the here and now. She knew it all too well.

Danton said quietly, "What does it matter? They are just names. Just another bitter little war in another sad corner of Africa."

The man's expression was so raw Storm found herself willing to say, "Maybe we should just start over. Put our earlier conversations aside. We have just met on the flight from Málaga. Nothing that came before even counts."

He studied her. "Do you read all men so well?"

"Hardly any. Just the few who've walked a path as twisted as mine."

"Why do—" His phone chirped. Danton checked the readout and said, "I must take this."

Storm took it as dismissal and slipped through the curtain. Emma watched her with a sleepy expression. "Are you two playing nice?"

"You'd be amazed."

"Talk about amazing." Emma pointed at her phone. "Harry left me a message while we were airborne. They're a couple of hours from the Jordanian border. I tried to phone back. Got the same Arab woman who I hope was telling me to leave a message. He hasn't called back."

"Can I hear what he said?"

Emma actually blushed. "I guess so."

"Never mind."

"No. It's okay." She held out the phone. "You're over eighteen."

"I have no interest in listening to Harry whisper—" Storm stopped because Danton called her name. "Hold that thought."

When she returned to the cockpit, Danton said, "I need you to go to England."

"All right."

"Now."

"Fine."

"I will deliver Agent Webb to Amman. But then I must leave for Budapest. That was my office on the phone. There's been an emergency."

Emma called through the curtains, "Just get me to Jordan. I can handle things from there."

Storm kept her gaze upon Raphael. "Are you sure?"

Emma no longer sounded the least bit sleepy. "It's what I do, remember?"

Raphael said to Storm, "I would not ask you to make this trip, except that our buyer is insisting this auction in Cirencester is extremely important. Vital."

"Go," Emma said. "I'll be fine."

Raphael said, "There is a BA flight to Heathrow in two hours. I have booked you a seat. Do you have money?"

"I'm a modern girl, Raphael." She reached beneath her seat for her purse. "I'm armed with plastic."

"That may not be enough in this case." As Danton outlined what he wanted, he entered the galley and unlocked the lowest drawer. He pulled out a packet of fifty-pound notes. "Here."

"I still have excess funds from your initial payment I can draw down."

"You may not have time. Take this." He hesitated, then added, "Please."

She fished a pen and notepad from her purse. "Write out a receipt. I will sign acceptance and we're done."

He did as she requested. "I was not attempting to, well . . ."

"I know. But that was business." She stowed away the pad and pen and the money. Leaned down. Gripped the man by the neck and kissed him. "This is personal."

FIFTEEN

HARRY LAY ON A PAIR of reedy mats with blankets for cushions. The mats stank of chickens. A pair of empty cages rattled against the pickup's rear window. More mats were fastened overhead but did little to mask either the sun or the dust. The truck shimmied and moaned and belched. Harry tried to recall the last time he had traveled in less luxury and came up blank.

Hassan had arranged Harry's transport with a Jordanian trucker who was returning empty-handed from the local border market. Miriam had offered to drop him at the arranged contact point. But she and Fareed were headed for family and the fully equipped hospitals of Amman. Harry's journey took him elsewhere. Besides which, Harry's danger sense continued to work overtime. A number of people knew his destination. Phone messages had been passed over the airwaves of multiple countries. If Harry was being hunted, there was both time and opportunity for watchers to have been put in place. He wanted to show up in something that would attract no attention whatsoever. If this chicken truck didn't do the trick, nothing would.

Harry must have dozed off, because the next thing he knew the truck was climbing a road so steep his mats began sliding back toward the tailgate. Out the back of the truck, Harry watched the plains of Moab become a river of yellow dust and shimmering heat. To either side rose the Pisgah, a range of low-slung hills that formed the natural border between the Dead Sea and the fertile Jordanian lowlands. The truck slowly climbed Mount Nebo, which rose three thousand feet above the promised land.

They halted in the pilgrims' parking area, surrounded by desert pines and squawking blackbirds. The driver was a squinty-eyed farmer with a beard as scraggly as Harry's. Miriam had paid him to get Harry up to the pilgrims' site, but Miriam was gone and it was just Harry and the driver now. The driver unloaded the wheelchair, argued with its locking system, then motioned for Harry to climb down.

As the driver helped him ease off the tailgate and into the cracked leather seat, a car scrunched over the pavement beside the truck. Sunlight turned the car's windows into mirrors. But as the vehicle entered the shadow of the closest bus, Harry caught a photographic flash of two hard faces and flinty eyes. Cop eyes. Or killers'. Harry figured in his case they were probably the same thing.

The trucker proved good as his word, for he gripped the wheelchair's handles and pushed Harry up the stone path toward the pilgrims' church. Harry's enjoyment of the view was severely dented by more security types. Two men in checked head-scarves and blank shades strolled the parking lot, checking tourists as they disembarked from buses. Another pair loitered by the entrance to the stone pathway. The guards flickered tight gazes his way. But the trucker pushing his wheelchair did not falter and Harry did not speak. They passed unchallenged.

The path was lined in stone turned white by the brilliant light. Tourists and pilgrims mingled with Franciscan monks as they approached the Church of Moses. On the spot where Moses had gazed upon the promised land, a sanctuary had been erected in the second century AD. In the sixth century, the original chapel had been expanded to a basilica large enough to hold the pilgrim hordes. The original church's three east apses and their flanking chapels had recently been excavated. Back at the Herodium dig, Harry had heard the archeologists speak in hushed tones about the astonishing mosaics. In one, a shepherd stood beneath the shade of trees no one had ever seen before. In another, a man played a lute to an ostrich and a zebra and a giraffe. What the animals signified was a mystery lost to the centuries. The old baptistery contained mosaics depicting fierce hunting scenes: a shepherd fighting a lion, a soldier fighting a lioness, and two hunters on horseback defeating a bear and a wild boar. In different circumstances, Harry would have relished giving the place a careful inspection.

The path was steep enough for the driver to be panting hard by the time they arrived at the basilica's entry. Another pair of security types watched as the driver shook Harry's hand, touched his heart, and offered him a pilgrim's salaam. Harry nodded thanks he could not afford to speak and wheeled himself inside.

Harry followed a tourist procession through the main archway, then joined a group of local pilgrims as they halted in one of the ancient naves. Through an arrow-slit window he glimpsed the Dead Sea melting into a pale blue sky. When he figured he had given the tourist thing enough time, he turned his buggy around and went in search of some privacy.

A line of men stood waiting at the entrance to the restroom. As Harry pushed himself out of the wheelchair, the tourists motioned him to the front of the queue. He shuffled inside, his feet slapping in the woven leather sandals. He made it into the stall, shut and locked the door, and pulled out Miriam's parting gift. Her cell phone chirped to life and instantly signaled three messages. Harry's breath constricted to taut puffs as Emma told him her plane was making its final approach into Amman.

He jerked at the sound of strident Arab voices outside his stall. Three men argued loudly. Harry had no idea what they were saying. But the tension in their voices was invasive. He punched the redial button and knew he had no choice in the matter. None at all.

Then the call was answered by the sweetest voice in the entire universe saying, "Oh, Harry."

He had to clench his entire body up tight. Even so, he almost lost his resolve.

Almost. But not quite.

He had imagined a thousand things he wanted to say to Emma. A million. But not once did he anticipate the only two words he spoke.

When the voices rose up high enough to mask his words, Harry cupped the receiver and said, "Don't come."

SIXTEEN

EMMA WAS GLAD FOR THE curtain separating her from the cockpit, because hearing Harry actually speak to her undid her entirely.

When she had recovered somewhat, Emma stepped into the cockpit and said, "Harry's told me not to come to the meet."

"Which means he is in grave danger," replied Raphael.

"Yes."

"And you are still going."

She nodded. "I left my guns in Washington."

Raphael rose from the pilot's seat and stepped into the narrow galley. "There is a line of taxis outside the main terminal. Private limo drivers often wait by the arrivals hall café. They are triple the cost. But the limos are faster and the drivers speak better English."

Raphael unlocked the galley's lower drawer, revealing piles of various currencies and documents. He hit a latch, and a hidden compartment slid out. Inside was a pistol with a polished barrel and black matte grip. "You know this?"

"A SIG Sauer. I don't recognize the vintage."

"The SIG P210 originated in the late forties from Swiss army trials for a new military pistol." He ratcheted the breech. "Short recoil, all steel, locked breech. This is the nine-millimeter professional version. Its most remarkable feature is the slide rails machined on the inside of the frame. The entire gun, including the single-action trigger, is solid steel forgings and then hand fitted. The results are increased durability and accuracy. It is one of the world's most expensive mass-produced pistols."

"Figures." She accepted the pistol, tested the heft, felt her hand sing. She had met master swordsmen who could lift a blade and know instantly its power and vintage. For her, the thrill had always come from guns. "Fixed sights dovetailed to the frame."

"They have been calibrated to three hundred meters. If you miss, Agent Webb, it is because you missed."

"I hold an expert qualification in small arms."

"Naturally." He handed her three loaded clips. "It would be helpful if you could determine who is pestering your friend. And if the bomb attack is somehow linked to Storm's work for me."

Emma slipped the gun into her purse, along with two extra clips. Then she showed him the stone gaze she reserved for special times like this. "I really appreciate the ride and the weapon, Raphael. But if you are part of Harry's problem, I will hunt you down. Ditto if you put Storm in harm's way. There is no place on earth you can hide."

A look of sadness crossed his face. "I remember once speaking those very same words."

SEVENTEEN

STORM CARRIED THE FLAVOR OF Raphael's breath all the way to London.

She took the express train from Heathrow to Paddington station, going second class with all the other normal people. From there she caught the Cotswold Express. She entered the passage between carriages and made a series of phone calls. She knew the unseen spooks might still be tracking her, and she didn't care. She left two messages for Emma and another three on Harry's phone. It felt better than good to know Harry was back from the dead.

Storm remained standing in the passage between carriages. With the windows down the compartment was windy and noisy. But once they cleared London's outskirts, the air was laden with all the scents of an English spring. The afternoon was fairly warm, but without the heavy dampness that burdened Florida in late May. Every now and then she caught a glimpse of the river Thames. The banks were draped with willows, the water dappled by sunshine and slow-moving craft.

Her final call was to Curtis Armitage-Goode, a British dealer and longtime ally. When he heard who was on the line, he responded with equal parts joy and exasperation. "Well, all I can say is, finally. Where on earth have you been?"

"Surviving."

"Have you managed to do so?"

"Barely. Which is why I'm calling."

"What is that atrocious noise?"

"I'm on a train. Between compartments. The window's open."

"Be so good as to have a conductor guide you to first class so we can carry on a civilized conversation."

"I'm calling from here for a reason." She cupped the receiver. "I need your help in tracking down two items."

"Are they in England?"

"My source says yes." She described the first piece.

Curtis pondered a moment. "I might have a lead on that. What's your offer?"

"Standard finder's fee. Two percent."

"No, no. What is your ceiling?"

With anyone else, she would have played it cagey. Storm said carefully, "For this piece I would expect to pay a commensurate amount."

"A client with deep pockets. How splendid for us both. Where can I reach you?"

"I'm headed to Cirencester for tomorrow's auction. After that, I'm yours."

"You're in England? Why didn't you let me know you were coming?"

"First, because I didn't know myself until about five hours ago. Second, because you'd ask me questions I can't answer."

"What is your second item?"

"The Amethyst Clock."

"My dear Storm. A clock that stops time? Really."

"My client insists that it exists and that it is here."

"Do you actually hear what you are saying?"

"I will pay you five thousand pounds to make a search. Regardless of the outcome."

"I wouldn't do it for fifty. I might as well cart my reputation to the embalmers."

Storm's mouth tasted of the pyre. "Some of us don't have the luxury of a choice."

"No. Quite." Curtis cleared his throat. "I don't

suppose it would harm matters if I made a few discreet inquiries. Needless to say, if I hear anything I'll be certain to pass it along."

"Exclusively."

"What other way is there? And do take care, Storm. An item that lethal is bound to attract the worst sorts. It would be a pity to lose you. There are so few good hearts who've managed to survive."

TWO THOUSAND YEARS AGO, CIRENCESTER had been the capital of Rome's westernmost province in Britain. Most of the town dated from the fifteenth and sixteenth centuries, when its wool market had brought in medieval riches. The auction took place in the main hall of the local college, a Jacobean manor of honeyed Cotswold stone. The hall was two hundred feet long and eighty wide, and tiled in Carrera marble. The domed ceiling was painted to resemble a verdant English sunrise. The sun's rays were fashioned from gold overlay and gleamed with divine promise.

The hall was packed. The items on display were of jaw-dropping quality. Yet bidding was sparse, money tight. As Storm took her seat midway up the central aisle, the perspiring auctioneer announced, "Our next item is a necklace of eighteen-carat yellow gold laden with five emeralds totaling twenty-six carats."

As his lovely assistant paraded her way down the main aisle, the auctioneer went on. "We shall start the bidding for this one-of-a-kind piece at eleven thousand pounds. Anyone? Very well, then. I shall allow you to steal it for eight. Do I see an opening bid from the gentleman in the front there? No?"

The auctioneer wiped his face with a rumpled handkerchief, then made a mess of stowing it. The cloth draped from his pocket like a white flag. "Give me five. Anything, ladies and gentlemen. I am open to any bid."

A voice from the row behind Storm called, "I'll go three."

"I think I know where you've been doing your shopping, sir. At night with a brick." He waved his hands with the urgency of a conductor. "Do I hear four? Come now, ladies and gentlemen, I am unable to proceed to sale with only one bid. Who will offer me four thousand for this very fine example—"

"Three thousand, two hundred."

"For thirty-two hundred pounds I might as well melt it down and gild my coffin. Retail valuation of this necklace is set at fifty thousand pounds. Come now, who will give me four?" He searched desperately, shook his head, raised the clapper. "Going once, twice." He slammed down the hammer. "Sold for thirty-two hundred."

The crowd murmured its own shock as the

auctioneer muttered, "I'm slaving away up here selling hundred-pound notes for ten quid."

The next item was a contemporary sculpture of warring cubes. Storm's attention drifted to the antique timepieces lining the wall closest to her. The clocks gave off a constant rain of metallic drumbeats, counting down the hours of another mystery-laden day.

As the auctioneer began his next windup, a voice from behind Storm hissed, "This is *outrageous!*"

The auctioneer halted his introduction of the next item, an oil from the Rubens school, and searched the hall.

Jacob Rausch stalked over and loomed above Storm. "Is it your intention to poison the atmosphere of every event I attend?"

"In case you hadn't noticed, Jacob, this is a public auction."

He waved frantically for the attendant, who scurried over. "This woman is absolutely not permitted to bid on a single item. Her credit is void, her company bankrupt!"

To her surprise, Storm found herself enjoying the attention. "Wrong on both counts."

The auctioneer used his mike to inquire, "Is there a problem?"

"There most certainly is!" Jacob Rausch's hand came so close Storm felt the breeze through her hair. "This woman has no more business here than a parrot!"

Storm said, "Your father thought differently."

His face grew redder still. "Aaron had *no* business making such a bargain with you."

"It saved both our clients a small fortune." Storm turned toward the front and raised her voice. "I apologize for the gentleman's lack of manners."

Rausch yelled, "I won't stand for this!"

"No problem." Storm found exquisite pleasure in not needing to turn around. "The exit is back that way."

The prospect of a brewing battle had caused the auctioneer's demeanor to undergo a remarkable change. "Might I inquire as to which item is of interest to these parties?"

Storm did not need to check her catalogue. "Seventy-three."

"Would anyone object to my shifting the order of sale?"

Jacob Rausch's voice echoed through the lofty chamber. "I strenuously object to these entire proceedings!"

"Duly noted, sir. Now perhaps you would be so good as to resume your seat? Thank you ever so." He waved the attendant forward. "Lot seventy-three, a quite remarkable example of early Byzantine artwork known as a paten. What am I bid for this splendid item? Shall we start the bidding at twenty-five thousand pounds?"

Storm raised her paddle.

"Twenty-five thousand from the lady to my right." The auctioneer motioned to his attendant, who started a slow parade down the central aisle. "Who will offer me thirty?"

Storm fitted the phone's Bluetooth into her ear and speed-dialed Raphael's number.

He answered instantly. "Yes?"

"Jacob Rausch is here."

"Excellent."

"He threw a terrific fit when he spotted me."

"I'm sorry I missed it. Where are we?"

Storm lifted her paddle in response to Rausch's counterbid. "A hundred thousand, rising in twenty-five-thousand increments."

"Dollars?"

"Pounds." She lifted her paddle. "Do I have a ceiling?"

"Quite the contrary." Raphael Danton was clearly enjoying himself. "I want you to crush the man."

"This makes no sense whatsoever."

She was half expecting another cold rebuke. But Danton continued to surprise. "My orders are specific. It is not enough that we acquire the items. Where possible we are instructed to make the opposition suffer a most public defeat."

"So my deal with Rausch Senior—"

"Did not go over at all well. My client wanted you fired. I convinced them it would be a serious error. With considerable difficulty, I might add."

She struggled to offer "Thank you."

Danton laughed. "Difficult words to say, are they not?"

"Horrible." But she was smiling. "Like pulling nails."

Rausch must have seen her good humor, because he almost shrieked the words "Two hundred thousand pounds!"

"Did you hear Rausch's bid?"

"Yes. Go to five."

As Storm rose to her feet, she felt the audience's silence, the light shift, the world refocus. The pleasure was so intense she did not even try to hide the shiver. "I offer five hundred thousand pounds."

The auctioneer sang an exultant chorus. "Five hundred thousand pounds from the lovely lady to my right. Who will give me six?"

Storm said into her phone, "We're rising in hundred-thousand-pound increments."

"How is Rausch taking it?"

She met a gaze of pure Manhattan venom. "Not at all well."

Danton laughed once more. "Let him bid twice more, then bump it to one-five."

"As your appointed agent, it is my duty to inform you that such a bid is about as sensible as looking for life on Pluto."

"Duly noted."

She lifted her paddle. "So idiotic you should

have your client's interior decorator design a padded cell."

Danton asked, "Having fun, Ms. Syrrell?"

"I'm almost looking forward to having this done so I can remember what a good time I had. Hold on a second."

The auctioneer's aide was slowly making her way down the central aisle. Storm lifted her hand, signaling to the auctioneer that she wanted time for a closer look. The entire hall held its breath.

A paten was a sacramental plate designed to hold the holy wafers. The bone-white alabaster was carved as a six-sided flower. The design had been the seal of Byzantium's emperors for over a hundred years, from the mid-fourth to the mid-fifth centuries. At the flower's center was the image of Christ holding the Law, fashioned from what appeared to be early cloisonné enamel. The plate's outer two inches were solid gold and rimmed with pearls the size of Storm's thumbnail.

The auctioneer announced, "We are back to you at nine hundred thousand."

Storm replied, "One million, five hundred thousand pounds."

Even the auctioneer needed a moment to recover, which was hardly a surprise, since Storm had just doubled the day's total take. Then he said, "Madame has raised the bid to one million five. Do I hear a counter?"

Rausch shoved his chair into the gentleman seated behind him, who exclaimed, "I say, have a care there!"

Rausch stalked toward the exit. As he passed Storm's chair, he snarled, "You are about to discover what it means to have me for an enemy."

The auctioneer's hammer smacked the podium. The audience applauded a drama strong enough to divert them from the day's gloom. "Sold to the lady for one million, five hundred thousand pounds!"

EIGHTEEN

THE JORDANIAN LIMO DRIVER WAS only too pleased to have Emma's company. His name was Saleem, and he stank of old cigarette smoke. "These days, too many arguments over payments. Too many poor tourists. My children, they starve." But he smiled as he said it, and he drove with happy abandon.

Emma replied, "Long as we make good time."

"For a pretty lady with money, we fly. Like golden . . . what you call it?"

"Chariot."

"Yes. With wings." Worry beads polished by years of nervous hands dangled from one wrist and caught the sunlight as he patted the wheel affectionately. "Good chariot. She fly for you, pretty lady."

The car was a black Mercedes of late seventies vintage, boxy and huge. But the air conditioner hummed and the wheels ate up the miles. The road north and then west started flat and was so empty that Saleem had little use for the horn. But such habits died hard. Saleem honked at everything they passed—donkey carts using the flattened earth alongside the asphalt, silent Bedouin communities, dusty children teasing a yapping dog. Saleem wore a shiny suit that bulged over his protruding belly and a starched collarless shirt. Beyond the windshield, heat shimmered and danced. Emma asked, "How long?"

"Fifty kilometers, three hills, one town." Saleem grinned. "For you, fifteen minutes."

"Seriously."

"Yes, I am thinking you are much serious lady." Saleem's eyes danced with the glee of driving a woman in too much of a hurry to dicker over his price. "We come there plenty soon. You like music?"

"Whatever gets us there quickest."

He switched on the radio and found a station. "Most tourists, they come to Nebo, they take much time. They ask many questions. They want to know, did Moses do this, do that. I say, so sorry, he was gone when I got there."

"You're a funny man."

Saleem pointed to the radio. "This is Oom Kalthoum. You know?"

The woman did not sing so much as sob in cadence to the orchestra. "First time I ever heard her."

"She very famous. Egyptian. She asks, 'Why my love go away?'" He made moon eyes. "You come to Nebo, pray for love?"

"Something like that."

"No, I think it is another reason why you come."

Emma clutched her purse, comforted by the gun's proximity. She wondered if she dared try Harry's phone again. "I don't like questions, Saleem. They slow things down."

"Don't worry, pretty lady. I talk and drive all the time."

But he did not have the chance to pry further, for Emma's phone rang. Storm asked, "Any word?"

"Not much. Where are you?"

"England. Somewhere intensely green. Tell me what you know."

"Harry's walked into some serious trouble. He told me not to come."

"What are you going to do?"

"What do you think? I'm coming."

Storm hesitated, then asked, "Do you think Raphael is part of this?"

Emma noticed how Saleem was taking a somber interest in her side of the conversation. "That is exactly the question I've been asking.

My gut hasn't decided. But he did give me something from his little drawer."

"Money?"

"Something a lot louder. With three clips of little helpers."

"You're armed, and you're being overheard."

"Affirmative to both."

"What can I do?"

"I'll let you know."

"Call me, okay? The very instant."

When she hung up, Saleem showed her worried eyes. "I am driving into trouble?"

"My trouble, Saleem, not yours."

"No, no, this is my car, so is my trouble." As they entered the desert town of Madaba, Saleem slipped his worry beads off his wrist and began clicking them through his fingers. "My babies, they starve."

"Just get me to Nebo. I'll take care of things. You can stay in the car all safe and sound." As they approached the town's central market, a storefront window display caught Emma's eye. "Stop the car, please."

Saleem pulled into a parking space. "You are policewoman?"

"United States federal agent."

He rocked in his seat. "This very much bad."

Either she calmed the man down, or as soon as she stepped from the car, he was going to scoot. No question. And there was the small matter of getting away with Harry afterward. "I want you to listen very carefully. My entire life is dedicated to protecting the innocent."

"Innocent. Yes. Is me." Saleem's worry beads clattered loudly. "Your friend, he not hurt my country?"

"Absolutely not."

"Who is after him?"

"I'm not sure. But I think maybe Russians are involved."

Saleem moaned. "Very, very terrible."

"Yes." Emma pointed at the department store's window display. "I need one of those."

Saleem had trouble focusing. "You wish to buy *thob'ob*?"

"Whatever. Will you help me?"

As they left the car and crossed the noisy street, Saleem asked, "Your friend, what he do?"

"He's a scavenger."

Saleem squinted over the unfamiliar word. "He smuggles?"

"Sometimes. He hunts for treasure."

"Why you not say so? Smuggling good business. My uncle, my brother, my cousin. All smuggle." The thought brightened him visibly. "I think your friend make very much money to worry Russians."

Emma caught the message loud and clear. "Help us get out of this mess, Saleem, and we'll be happy to share the wealth."

His smile revealed terrible teeth. "My babies, they thank you."

INSIDE THE DEPARTMENT STORE, SALEEM took it upon himself to act as Emma's personal ambassador. Saleem explained to Emma that none of the salesladies had ever dressed a Western woman in traditional Jordanian garb. They were delighted.

Saleem named each item as Emma was kitted out. Her travel-weary suit was traded for a *thob aswad*, a bluish-black voluminous dress with broad sleeves and deep, pointed lapels. Beneath this she donned a pair of *sirwa'al*, capacious long pants that covered all but the tips of her shoes. A woolen *ishdad* was belted over the *thob*. Then came the *bisht abayeh*, a mantle of the same blue-black silk, chased about the edges with silver thread. The senior saleslady showed her how to cross the scarf's leading edges beneath her chin, then drape the ends over her shoulders so that they hung down the back. The salesladies jabbered delightedly as they guided Emma toward the mirror.

The woman who stared back at her was utterly unrecognizable.

Her driver beamed at the result. "The ladies, they say you do much honor, dressing like pilgrim for Fasaliyyeh. That is our word for Moses church."

"Thanks, Saleem." Emma pointed at a rack of oversized sunglasses, the moon-shaped globes a throwback to nineties bling. "What do you call those?"

Saleem shrugged. "Ray-Bans."

"I'll take a pair."

Saleem insisted upon carrying the bag holding her former outfit. But midway back to the car he said, "No, no, is not correct."

"What's the matter?"

"You walk like soldier. Bam, bam, your feet, they . . . how you say?"

"March."

"Yes. Too long step. Too strong." Despite his evident nerves, Saleem enjoyed himself, reshaping the Western agent into a proper Arab. "Small steps. Like lady. Yes, is better. And chin too high. Good, yes. Now you are . . . what is word?"

"A wimp."

"Proper. Yes, is proper. Good." He bowed her into the backseat. "Maybe tonight I kiss my babies."

THE FINAL TEN KILOMETERS FROM Madaba to Nebo were over a series of increasingly steep switchbacks. Their destination was clear enough, a yellow mount rising well above its neighbors. The church was of ancient Orthodox design, a low structure with a rounded top and deep-set windows, fashioned from the hill's own stone.

Saleem pulled into the massive parking lot and halted beneath a trio of desert pines. He sat staring forward, his fingers busy with the worry beads.

"Here's how it's going to play out," Emma said, hoping she was right. "A modest woman dressed in proper local fashion is going to climb the rise and find the man and bring him back. We will leave. End of story."

"There will be shootings?"

"If you hear gunfire, Saleem, you have my permission to take off."

"I think maybe you pay now."

"Some now, more when this is done." Emma handed over a brick of folded notes. "Your babies are lucky to have such a good dad."

Saleem made the money disappear. "Two men by the bus, they are not tourists."

"I see them." And two more in a slowly cruising blue Peugeot. And another pair hovering like navy-suited vultures by the walk leading to the church. "Come open my door."

Saleem slipped from the car, walked around, and held her door as she rose. All without meeting her gaze. Emma started to walk off, then turned back to say, "Just so you know, Saleem. This is what I live for."

THE CHURCH HELD THE AIR of a fortress. The interior courtyards were shielded by a high stone wall. Inside the main basilica, four narrow windows with curved tops supplied most of the light. The windows added to the sense of entering a medieval garrison. A notice in six languages stated that the Franciscans operated a monastery on the site and requested that all visitors maintain silence and decorum.

Emma devoutly hoped the blue-suited vultures had taken note of that sign.

Adrenaline etched everything she saw with brilliant clarity. Tourists floated about in pastel busloads, their guides shepherding and chattering. Monks and nuns clustered in desert garb of white and black. Local pilgrims came bearing flowers and candles, their heads covered, their gazes focused on whatever problem drew them to the Moses church on this scalding day.

Two more watchers hovered in the shadows by the sacristy's main entrance. One glance was enough for Emma to be certain they were not Russians, but locals. These men had spent a lifetime learning absolute patience. One slipped by Emma, moving to where the outer walk looked back over the empty Jordanian plains. As he passed, he glanced at her and then away. Emma took his dismissal as a sign that she and Harry just might get out of this alive. If only she could find him.

She entered the nave, slipped coins from her purse, fed the offering box, and lit a candle. She joined a group of tourists and passed slowly through the basilica. As she started toward the stairs leading to the archeological excavations, Emma felt eyes upon her. But the only watcher was a bandaged Arab who wheeled his chair toward a prayer alcove.

Emma followed the group down the winding stone stairs. The tour guide slowed at the first excavations and began a long-winded lecture that Emma could not be bothered to hear. She did a quick sweep of the other tourist groups filling the quarry, then returned upstairs.

The interior quad held a small shop, tables, and a protected area surrounding a tree planted by Pope John Paul II when he had made his own pilgrimage. Emma bought a soft drink, moved under the awning that protected the gift-book counter, and scouted. The watchers were still on duty, which meant they hadn't found Harry either.

She finished her drink and returned to the basilica. She entered a candlelit alcove filled with the fragrance of incense and lilacs. The air was cool. Emma slipped into the rear pew. A puff of wind entered the basilica with the next busload, a hot and dusty reminder of the threats that waited outside with the heat.

Emma smelled him before she saw him. The scent was almost bestial. She kept her eyes forward as the wheelchair's tires squeaked over the tiled floor. She saw a pair of woven leather sandals emerging from a djellaba so filthy she could not even name its color.

He managed to breathe the word, spoken so softly it would have sounded like an old man's sigh to anyone but her.

"Emma?"

She rose silently from her pew.

Emma gripped the wheelchair's arms and slowly swung it around. As she pushed him from the alcove, Harry reached across and grazed two fingers over her hand.

NINETEEN

THE LIGHT AS THEY EXITED was blinding. Emma focused upon the top of Harry's head and the stone walkway in front of his chair as she waited for her eyes to adjust. She was almost giddy when she realized they had passed the first pair of watchers unchallenged.

The wheelchair had a squeaky right wheel. The noise acted like an amplifier to her tension. Harry's head lolled slightly to the left so that his bandages and head-kerchief kept the exposed side of his face concealed. The walkway back to the parking lot was so steep she had to brake with both feet. Emma had a tough time getting the chair over the curb between the walk and the parking lot. The two guards observed her but made no offer to help.

There were over two dozen buses now, gaily painted giants shimmering in the afternoon heat. Emma chose the most direct course back to the car, straight through the flanking buses. When the shadows surrounded her but her vision did not clear, Emma realized she was releasing silent tears.

Harry repeated his earlier action, reaching across with his left fingers to touch her right hand. Only this time he grunted with pain and did not complete the gesture.

"Are you hurt?" Then she had to laugh. "Sorry. Silly question."

"A couple of cracked ribs. Maybe three. My face got singed, but it's getting better." A moment, then, "Emma, I just want you to know—"

"Don't. If you finish that sentence I'll break down right here and howl."

"Where are we headed?"

"There's a vintage Mercedes at the bottom of the parking lot. I hope."

"I'm not sure I can wait that long. There's a lot I need to say."

The watcher chose that moment to round the bus.

Emma should have seen it coming. They had been scouting the parking lot all day. But she had spent what felt like a lifetime waiting for the chance to be this close to Harry again. The shadows had granted her a false sense of security.

Whatever the reason, she had let her awareness slip.

The watcher's eyes were shielded by the sunglasses, and perhaps there was a hint of confusion caused by peering into the shadows. But the frown grew steadily larger as he realized what he saw—a woman in Arab garb pushing an Arab-looking man in a wheelchair, both of them speaking English with American accents.

The watcher slipped one hand under his jacket and inflated his lungs to shout.

Emma was already rushing around the wheelchair. Straight from calm tears to raging lioness in half a heartbeat. Raphael Danton's jet had nothing on her launch.

The watcher gaped at the black-garbed animal who sprang at his throat.

Emma chopped the man's neck, cutting off the unspoken alarm. Her second blow was straight to the man's solar plexus. He emitted a foul stench of stale cigarettes and old coffee and folded to his knees, his rapidly swelling throat hacking desperately for breath.

The man's partner was caught totally unawares by the sight of an attacking woman in traditional garb, and was slow on the uptake. Emma heard herself emit a feral growl, the snarl of a beast that would die before even considering defeat. The man must have heard it as well, for his face reflected genuine shock.

Emma leapt over the crouching man, her black robes flying outward like the wings of a bird of prey. She kicked down and hit the second man hard in the chest.

The man bounced so hard off the bus's hood his head cracked a light. He fell hard to the tarmac.

Only then did Emma realize she was holding the first guard's pistol.

She skittered the gun under the nearest bus. She returned to Harry, gripped the chair arms, and steered him around the prone attackers.

Saleem sat frozen, gaping at her through the open window. Emma helped Harry into the rear seat, then rapped on the roof. "Pop the trunk, Saleem."

She stowed the chair, slipped in beside Harry, and said, so calmly the voice must have belonged to another woman, "Let's go, Saleem. We're all done here."

Harry's injuries did not dim his smile one iota. "That's my girl."

TWENTY

THE DINING HALL ADJACENT TO the Cirencester auction served a full English tea all afternoon long. Storm stood beside a stained-glass family coat of arms, drank from her cup, and felt a languid fatigue as fine as that from any drug. Raphael called as she finished. The man was off on some high-powered errand in Budapest. Jacob Rausch chose that moment to saunter past, surrounded by allies who shunned her with overloud laughter. Storm refused to let them disturb her pleasure and simply turned away.

She then phoned Claudia and said, "I hope I've taken you away from something really superb."

"Absolutely. Warmed-over lunch and an *I Love Lucy* rerun."

"That won't do. I need you to tell me a mysterious stranger came into the shop, paid asking price for our most expensive item, then swept you off to the Fontainebleau in Miami for champagne."

"Excuse me. I thought I was speaking with my niece, who has been lost in some gloomy swamp for months. Obviously I was mistaken."

Storm announced, "I just earned us another ninety thousand pounds' commission." Claudia's silence was as sweet a response as she had ever known. "One hundred and forty thousand dollars. Added to the fifty-five thousand from three days ago, that gives us . . . how much?"

Claudia said, "Enough to clear almost half our debts."

"Forget clearing anything. I'm about to go back inside a panic-stricken hall and buy." Storm decided the grin she saw reflected in the window could not possibly have been any wider. "Have money, will shop."

"I'd say be careful, but I seriously doubt you'd hear me."

"Listen to this. I'm surrounded by dealers whose showrooms are jammed to the gills with items they bought when they thought prices couldn't go any lower. And now they're being offered better stuff at half what they paid."

"Sounds familiar."

"Wait, there's more. I've just watched a Victorian countess's jewelry collection go under the hammer for barely the price of the gold. Early Impressionist oils selling for prices that wouldn't have covered the sales commission last year. And the dealers here can't buy anything. They don't have the cash. Or the space. Or the buyers."

Claudia's chuckle was rich enough to bring back memories of better times. "I believe my job at this point is to tell you to go have fun."

Storm heard the chime signaling an incoming call. "Your personal shopper bids you good day." She connected to the new caller and said, "This is Storm."

"Curtis here. I have a line on your item."

"That was fast."

"No need to sit on any potential new business, not in this market. Where can I pick you up?"

"But . . ." Storm waved a hand at the unseen auction. "Can it wait until tomorrow?"

"Absolutely not. The seller is available and hinted she had been approached by another buyer."

Storm turned and searched the dining hall. Jacob Rausch was nowhere to be found. "Did she say who?"

"My dear young lady, there are certain questions that dealers on this green isle simply may not ask."

"I'll meet you on the main drive in front of Cirencester College."

"That's more like it. I'm forty-five minutes out and closing fast."

AS STORM DESCENDED THE MANOR'S front steps, people broke off their conversations and observed her passage in respectful silence. She walked down the line of cars toward the college's main avenue. The tree-shaded lane was separated from the auction hall by a broad swath of perfectly tended green. The setting sun burnished the surrounding elms with an impossible shade of mint and gold. The shadows grew to where they knitted together, soft as the whispering wind and the mockingbird's song. The highway noise was a distant hum, not much louder than the bees floating above sunset-dappled flowers.

Storm halted by the curb, took a long breath of springtime air, and opened her catalogue to the next day's schedule. There was a bone-deep satisfaction in marking the items, not to dream but to acquire.

The car that approached her was as far removed

from peril as a four-wheeled vehicle could possibly get. A boxy seventies-vintage Rolls-Royce drove slowly up the lane toward her. The car looked like a Chevy, except for its immaculate condition and distinctive grille and the winged angel adorning the hood.

The Rolls halted beside her. The driver alighted and opened the rear door. A distinctly gracious masculine voice said, "I say, madame, might I please trouble you for a moment?"

The man rising from the rear seat was properly dressed for a wealthy arts patron of advancing years. The three-piece suit looked tailored, if slightly seedy. The gold watch chain dangling across his vest sparkled in the fading light. His tie was narrow and dark, his hair mostly white. He approached Storm in a slightly awkward gait, as though his old bones had settled from sitting too long.

Storm asked, "Can I help you?"

"Oh, I most sincerely hope so." He leaned heavily upon a silver-topped cane as he approached.

Storm found it odd how the driver remained motionless by the rear door, his face averted. The old gentleman stooped so far over his cane that his face remained in shadows. "Might I ask, are you by chance Storm Syrrell?"

"How did you get my name?"

"Through a most remarkable set of coincidences, really."

As the man limped closer, a ray of setting sun illuminated the face beneath the silver mane. Storm realized the man was not old at all.

She started to back away. But the man's cane was already moving. A flick of the wrist, an easy upward strike so swift and sudden it was unlikely anyone by the manor entrance would have noticed, even if they were looking Storm's way.

The cane's silver tip caught Storm's temple with a glancing blow. Stars exploded with the pain.

Storm waved her arms, a combination of blocking another blow and trying to clear her head. But the man revealed the dexterity of a fencing master, flicking his cane up and through her hands, so fast she saw nothing until another galaxy exploded inside her head.

She started to slump, but the man caught her. He walked back toward the vehicle, holding her in such a way that to an onlooker it might have appeared that she supported him. "Oh, that is too kind."

As the open door swam into focus, Storm tried to push away. The cane rose in another swift blur, another tap. "Shush now, my dear. It will all be over soon."

Her legs were of no use anymore. The man simply tossed her inside, or so it seemed to Storm. The driver guided her fall into the carpeted footrest.

"Swiftly now," the attacker said, climbing into the rear compartment.

Storm felt the adrenaline rush of unlimited fear and desperate need, though her head was too filled with shooting agony to say precisely what was the threat. She exploded into a frenzy of desperate flailing.

But the man was ready for this as well. He jammed the outer edge of his shoe into her neck, cutting off her air. His voice remained exquisitely polite. "Remain quite still, else I shall be forced to introduce you to an entirely new level of misery."

The driver put the car into gear, turned the wheel, and hit the gas. Storm gasped, "What—"

The foot pressed harder still. "Hush, now."

The car rolled smoothly away. Storm gripped the man's ankle, but the shoe did not move. The manor's shadows passed across her face. The car continued around the drive's main turn and started back toward the entrance.

She knew the attacker probably meant everything he had said about further pain. But she had no choice. She had to try.

The man must have felt her tense, for he jabbed the cane's silver tip deep into her ribs. "I assure you, there is no profit in testing—"

His threat was cut off by an assault so violent the man's head splintered the side window.

Another vehicle hammered the right rear corner

of the Rolls, causing it to skew violently sideways. Her attacker was then rocked back the other way as they bounced over the curb and collided with what Storm assumed was one of the elms. He slumped across the rear seat and did not move.

Storm was up and clawing at the handle when the opposite rear door wrenched open and a woman's voice shrilled, "Move! Move!"

The Rolls's driver jammed down on the gas. The engine howled. Metal screeched and the car heaved. The man in the passenger seat turned and gripped the shoulder pad of Storm's suit and tried to haul her back down. But the woman in the doorway found Storm's hand and pulled. Storm heard yells and shouts and knew some of the noise was hers. All she could focus on was the door and the woman gripping her hand.

The Rolls jerked forward. The driver wrenched the wheel about, the tires spun, the car gave one final shudder and then came free.

Somehow Storm kept a grip on the woman and popped from the open door, colliding with her rescuer. They both tumbled to the ground.

Which was the moment she realized she held the attacker's silver-tipped cane.

She rose unsteadily to her feet, her vision still clouded by pain and panic. The Rolls had slowed, and a man leaned out of the passenger window. He was holding a gun.

Storm heard herself say, "I've had just about all I'm going to take!"

"Wait! Ms. Syrrell!"

Storm's sudden rage circumvented the portion of her brain that said, running toward a man raising a gun in her direction was insane.

She caught up with him just as the Rolls hit a speed bump, marring the man's aim. She applied the cane to the attacker's arm like a hammer.

The man howled and dropped the gun. The weapon hit the road and went off. The pistol shot was a blast of noise and heat.

The woman raced up just as the car stopped and the passenger door opened. She sprang at the man as he used his undamaged hand to scoop the gun off the pavement. He was caught in a moment of uncertainty over two targets and chose the woman clawing for his throat.

Storm hurriedly jabbed the cane at the back of the man's skull. The sound was that of a pool cue striking a ball. The man's gun hand wavered. Storm did not have time for the full swing she wanted, but a ten-inch arc knocked the man to his knees.

The woman kicked the pistol from his grip, sending it rattling across the pavement. She gripped the man by his lapels and rapped his head against the front fender. "Who sent you?"

Storm thought she detected a strong accent in the woman's voice, but her own rasping breath and the shouts that rang from the manor behind them interfered with her hearing.

The woman rapped the man's head against the fender a second time. His heels scrabbled across the pavement. The woman shouted in a language Storm could not understand and rapped his head yet again, this time hard enough to dent the fender.

The driver raced around the hood, snarling with fresh menace.

But before the driver came into range, a white van bounced over the curb, scraped past an elm, and halted between the woman and the driver. The man driving the van shouted and gestured violently at the woman.

She released the dazed attacker, gripped Storm's arm, and said, "You must come with us."

"Why?"

The woman was already moving for the van, dragging Storm with her. "If you stay, you die."

She climbed into the van's rear door and hauled Storm in after her. The van sped away as the driver of the Rolls dragged Storm's unconscious attacker back into the car.

In the distance a siren wailed.

TWENTY-ONE

HARRY DRIFTED THROUGH MUCH OF the four-hour drive. He came fully alert with taut little jerks, pulled to wakefulness by jabs of either fear or pain or both. The jolts were worth the trouble, for Emma was there each time. Ready to gentle him with a stroke of his arm, the softest word, a caress to the undamaged side of his face. She held his hand throughout, snug in her lap.

They returned to the main highway and headed south. Just past the Petra turnoff, Saleem halted to refill his tank. At Emma's request, Saleem purchased drawstring pants and a T-shirt decorated with the Jordanian flag. Ten miles farther on, he then pulled into a desert turnout. Harry limped into the shadows and changed clothes. His ribs hurt too much to do what he wanted, which was fling the djellaba at the stars. Harry returned to the car and resumed his hold on Emma's hand.

It was fully dark when they reached the port city of Aqaba. Harry heard Emma discuss the hotel situation with Saleem without fully coming awake. He worked their words into his dream, finding bone-deep comfort from a woman he could trust to take charge.

Saleem chose for them a hotel two blocks off the main waterfront. An Indian couple smiled them in and made cooing sounds over Harry's injured state. Emma explained that he had been in an accident and needed to rest. She claimed that his papers had been lost in the accident, along with all his clothes, and that the embassy was sending down new ones. Emma paid for three rooms in cash and offered a generous tip. The proprietor smiled his enjoyment of her tale.

When she was done, Harry gestured toward Saleem and said, "We need to have a chat with your pal."

"You look all done in."

"I've felt better. But if we hold off until tomorrow, there's a good chance Saleem will vanish with the dawn."

Emma went over and asked Saleem to join them. The portly gentleman carried himself with a nervous air. Harry said, "We need your help, and we will pay."

Saleem's fearful gaze shifted from one to the other. "I am thinking anything with you has much danger."

Harry glanced at Emma. She motioned that this was his show. Harry said, "Listen to what we need, and if you think there is any risk, then leave. And we'll pay you anyway."

"I leave, you still pay?"

"Not as much as if you help us. But I'd say you've earned a bonus whatever you decide. Emma tells me you had relatives who are smugglers. Do any of them live in Aqaba?"

Saleem's furtive glances, the nervousness, the mobile features, all vanished. "Who can say?"

"I'm asking because we're looking for a smuggler who calls this town home. His name is Wadi Haddad."

"I am not knowing this man."

"No, but your relatives might." Harry slipped the Palestinian ID from his pocket. "Have them give this to Wadi Haddad. Tell Wadi the bad guys are on his trail. They've been tracking me because they want him. Tell him what you saw yesterday at Nebo."

"And tell him about me," Emma said. "Tell him everything."

"We're the only people who can help him." Harry needed Emma's help to rise from the chair. He kept the pain from his features as he said, "The clock is ticking, Saleem. Tell that to Wadi Haddad as well. I don't know how much time we've got before they show up. But my guess is, we'd all be safer moving with the dawn."

HARRY'S ROOM WAS LARGE AND slightly seedy but immaculately clean. He took what should have been the finest shower of his entire life. He could not scrub as hard as he would have liked because of his ribs. He shaved away his stubble and grunted against the pain of lifting his arms to wash his hair. Worse than his physical discomfort, however, was the alarm bell echoing through his brain.

All his previous relationships had hit a wall about now. Every time danger had reared its head, the next words his latest lovely uttered were, "I didn't sign up for this."

The arguments that followed always ended with the same ultimatum. Either Harry chose a new line of work or their time was over. Harry's problem was, his work was his life.

Which meant he had always treated women with the same cavalier attitude as most treasure dogs. Relationships started, they broke apart, and he moved to the next hunt.

Only not this time.

Harry had known for months he'd moved far beyond his normal safety zone. But so long as Emma's work kept her in Washington, he could put off confronting the new reality. The alarms had started clanging on the drive south. Now that he was here alone and safe and clean, there was nothing left to hide behind. What the lady might say, and how he might respond, left him quaking in his sandals.

Emma arrived while he doctored his face with salve the doctors had given him. She pulled a feast from various bags and set the contents on the rusted balcony table. Chunks of roasted beef in a spicy sauce, lamb with pine nuts nestled in hummus, a fragrant Arab salad of cumin and coriander and mint, on and on the dishes came. Harry ate until his belly hurt worse than his ribs.

They sat for a time, listening to the night. Harry's balcony overlooked a bustling central market. From the street below came the electrified beat of modern Arabic music. Harry smelled charcoal and cumin and diesel and donkey in the hot nighttime wind. On the balcony above his, four backpackers chattered and smoked cigarillos laced with clove.

Then he realized that Emma had shrunk inside herself.

That was how it seemed. This strong and vibrant woman had shriveled up. The only thing big about her was her eyes.

Harry realized he wasn't the only one fighting old ghosts.

The awareness brought no comfort, however. Harry was on new terrain. None of his old habits or shields or attitudes fit this scenario. The lady needed answers. Harry had none. He had never felt as poor as right then.

He struggled to say, "Maybe I should get some rest."

Emma sighed with what Harry figured was pure relief. She gave him a hug as strong and swift as summer thunder and was gone.

Hours later the traffic finally thinned, the hotel went silent, and Harry decided it was probably worth trying to get a little sleep.

TWENTY-TWO

THE FEMALE GUARD WHO HAD rescued Storm was named Tanya. She and her partner had been tracking Storm since her arrival at the auction. Why, Tanya would not say. They drove Storm to a public restroom at the border of a village park. When they pulled up, Tanya slid open the van's rear door and stepped out. The driver motioned for Storm to stay where she was. He never spoke or ceased his constant search of the night.

The restroom was built of brick and stone and resembled the surrounding Victorian village. Tanya fed coins into the restroom door, checked inside, then signaled for Storm to come over. As soon as she stepped out of the van, it sped away.

Tanya wore a dark leather jacket over shoulders that bunched and shifted like a bodybuilder's. Her dark hair was cut so short Storm could see the woman's scalp. Her lips were a thin slit. "Inside."

"What's going on?"

"You see soon enough." She pulled Storm forward, but not unkindly. "For now, you are safe. Everything else must wait."

But when Tanya started to close her inside the concrete cubicle, Storm jammed the door open and said, "Are you Russian?"

"Polish." The woman's smile was brutally tough. "You don't like Russian?"

"I have been told they are after me."

"Yes, we think so." She jerked her chin. "Get inside where you are safe. Relax. I wait here."

Storm had no way of knowing how long she was kept inside, but it felt like a very long time. At some point during the melee her watch had broken. The hands were frozen at a quarter past six. Her phone was still in the limo of the men who had abducted her, along with her purse and ID. Now and then Tanya tapped on the door and asked if Storm was okay. Twice Storm asked what was going on. When the woman did not respond, Storm did not push it. The restroom stank of industrial cleanser, but slits above the door let in a little of the night breeze. The walls were rough concrete and tightly constructed. Storm heard the sound of an approaching car. A door slammed. A motorcycle pulled up and halted. Fear blossomed in her gut at the sound of footsteps.

There was another rap on the door. Tanya said, "Open the door."

"Who is out there with you?"

"Friends."

When Storm did as she was ordered, the woman handed her a bag. "Take off everything you are wearing. You understand when I say everything?"

"Of course, but—"

"Put it all in this bag. You keep nothing. Not even your rings. Do you have a hotel key?"

"In my pocket."

Tanya held out her hand. "Give."

Storm thought of Raphael's cash tucked into her suitcase's side pocket and hesitated.

Tanya gave another slit of a grin. "You think we wait this long to rob you?"

Storm handed over the key. "Cirencester Grand. Room one eleven."

"Remember, put everything in the bag. Then put on these clothes." Tanya pushed the door shut. "Hurry."

THE BAG CONTAINED A BLUE two-piece outfit of cotton thick as sailcloth. The pants were cinched by a drawstring. The jacket had two long flaps, like identical tongues. It took Storm a moment to realize she needed to tie one end under her left arm, then wrap the outer side around. Then she had to undo both ties because at the bottom of the bag was a T-shirt, her size, also blue. The T-shirt felt much better against her skin than the rough outer garment.

The woman rapped on the door. "We must leave."

"Almost done." On her feet went Japanese-style tabi socks with a slit between her big toe and the next, then rope-soled sandals. Storm assumed the outfit came from some studio teaching hand-to-hand combat. The knowledge left her feeling safer.

She opened the door. "I'm ready."

Tanya reached for Storm's bag. "Is everything in there?"

"Yes."

"We check for bugs, then return everything." She handed the bag to a small man with unruly hair, who grinned at Storm, then loped to a motorcycle and sped away.

Tanya directed Storm back to the van. "Where are we going?"

Tanya climbed in behind her and shut the door. "London."

"Why did you make me wait back there?"

"Our job is to keep you safe. We are taking you to someone who can answer your questions."

As they entered London's outskirts, the night clouds turned the color of old bronze. Storm thought she could smell rain through the van's open window, but the streets were dry. They passed an electric sign that flashed the time, quarter past eleven. The numbers were meaningless.

The buildings they passed grew steadily grander, the street broader. One side became lined with trees. Then a park opened up. Broad paths of what looked like sand or gravel ran beneath streetlights. The walks glowed like yellow streams. Despite the hour, Storm saw a number of joggers.

The woman noted Storm's interest. "Do you know where you are?"

"I've only been in London once, and just for three hours. Less. A limo into the city, a meeting, then back out again."

"We are driving along Hyde Park."

"I've heard of it."

"Up ahead is Hyde Park Corner and then Piccadilly. The name is for a street and a circus. The word 'circus' in Latin means circle."

Storm studied the woman seated beside her. She was calm in the manner of an unprimed grenade. "You live here?"

"Once. Not now. I studied in London. Four months." She smiled thinly at the memory. "Nice place."

They sped past a cluster of fancy hotels, then turned down a broad thoroughfare lined with what to Storm looked like Regency houses. They stopped in the middle of the block. Storm asked, "Where are we?"

"Your destination."

The house was white with a colonnaded entrance. The sash windows on the first three floors were almost as large as the front door, fully ten feet high and eight across. The houses to either side were just as grand. Storm followed Tanya from the van. The driver sped away. Storm looked down a long street flanked by centuries of power. As she climbed the manor's front stairs, the first drops of rain splashed against the portico's roof.

The woman pulled a handle set inside a brass circle. A bell jangled inside the house. The door was swiftly opened by a man in a gray morning suit. He glanced at Storm's blue smock and frowned. Tanya spoke to him sharply. The man bowed them both inside.

The entrance hall was twenty feet wide and lined in faded Persian carpets. At the back of the hall, double doors opened to an elegant dining hall. The majordomo pointed them up a grand staircase. The wall to the right of the stairwell was lined with black-and-white photographs of stern-faced men. Storm took her time going up the stairs, studying the pictures. She thought she recognized General Patton in one, wearing his trademark pearl-handled pistols and flanked by two men with handlebar mustaches. The three men stood before a burned-out Nazi tank.

The upstairs hall was lined by several rooms, all of them occupied by men who smoked and drank from crystal goblets and played cards upon felt-covered tables. They observed Storm's passage with unreadable gazes. Tanya knocked on the closed door at the end of the hall. At a voice from within, she motioned Storm inside and followed, closing the door behind her.

The room was both grand and severe. Empty walls bore shadows from tapestries. The parquet floor was inlaid with what looked like a mosaic of bone and teak. Four lumpy sofas slumbered along one wall. A meager fire smoldered in a vast marble fireplace. Tall sash windows were open to the night and the rain. A lone table stood beneath the central chandelier. Two gray-haired gentlemen watched the women enter the room.

"Ms. Syrrell, what a pleasure. Do forgive me for not rising," one of the men said. He tapped his left shin with a walking cane. "My leg."

"Where am I?"

The other man, a silver-haired priest, rose and bowed. "Welcome to Ognisko, Ms. Syrrell. The word is Polish for 'hearth' and signifies a place of safety."

"Our club was started by expatriates during the Second World War," the seated gentleman said. "Nowadays it is mostly reserved for memories the rest of the world has long put aside."

The priest added, "It remains a haven for people like ourselves."

"We still have our uses." The gentleman motioned to the chair beside his own. "Will you take refreshment, Ms. Syrrell? Tea, perhaps?"

Tanya told them, "The lady missed dinner."

"We can certainly remedy that." He waved Storm forward. "Please, dear lady. Do join us."

Storm remained where she was. "Who are you?"

"My name is Antonin Tarka. My friend of the cloth is Father Gregor."

"You met Emma in Washington?" she said, looking at the cleric.

"Indeed so, Ms. Syrrell," Father Gregor replied. "Might I ask how your friend is?"

"A lot happier than when she left you. Seeing as how you got the news about Harry completely wrong."

"A mistake for which I sincerely apologize."

She detected no danger, only the sweet fragrances of wood smoke and rain. She walked over and seated herself. "Will you tell me what's going on?"

"Gladly. That is, we will tell what we know. Which is much less than we might like." He inspected her and said, "Might I say, Ms. Syrrell, I detect a great deal of your grandfather in you. It is most reassuring, given the situation we face."

"You knew Sean?"

"We both did," the priest said.

"I considered it an honor to call him a friend," said Antonin Tarka. He looked beyond her. "Ah. Your repast. Excellent."

The gray-suited butler entered the parlor, set a silver service on a card table, and asked, "How does madame prefer her tea?"

"Milk, no sugar."

"The brown-bread sandwiches are salmon; the grain are tongue. The pots contain mustard and relish." He settled a linen napkin into her lap. "Will madame be requiring anything further?"

Storm found herself oddly comforted by their stilted formality. "This is great, thank you."

Antonin Tarka studied her carefully as she ate, then turned to Father Gregor and spoke in Polish.

Father Gregor replied in English, "Are you certain?"

"I am."

"There are great risks," Father Gregor said. "On every side."

"How else is she to fathom what has happened?" Tarka did not wait for a response before turning to Storm and saying, "The only way you can comprehend the gravity of our situation is if you will make a trip with us."

"When?"

"Tomorrow. We would leave at dawn and return late that same night."

"Where to?"

"The monastery of Jasna Gora. In Czestochowa."

"You want me to go to Poland with you?" Storm rubbed the sore point on her temple. "My passport is still in the Rolls."

Antonin Tarka brushed that aside. "We can supply you with an ID."

Storm tried to think past the thunder in her head. All she could come up with was the affection she'd heard in their voices when they spoke her grandfather's name. And the tense urgency that filled the room. "All right. I'll go."

The priest fretted. "Ms. Syrrell, it is vital that you maintain strict confidentiality with the matter."

"I am very good with secrets."

"And I, Ms. Syrrell, believe you." Antonin Tarka held himself with regal formality. His features possessed an almost brutal strength, a throwback to an era of warrior princes. Neither age nor ailment robbed the man of his power. He weighted each word as though sending his nation on crusade. "Three weeks ago, we received word through allies within the art world of a new buyer. Someone who insisted on absolute confidentiality. Someone with enormous resources. This mystery buyer was intent on purchasing artwork and artifacts reputed to have special properties. Most of the items originate in Eastern Europe."

Storm said, "The Pokhitonov oil."

"Just so. We think that perhaps, just perhaps, this oil and the two men who bid its price to such ridiculous heights are somehow tied to another mystery. One that concerns us both."

Storm looked from one somber face to the other. "The Black Madonna."

"You have heard of this?"

"Father Gregor mentioned it to Emma."

"We learned from an ally in the international arts trade of your purchase of the items in Marbella, once again bidding against a member of the Rausch clan. When Jacob Rausch appeared in Cirencester, we decided to trail him. Then you appeared yet again. Even so, we still had no direct evidence that Rausch was tied to anything more than an avid buyer of Byzantine artifacts, or whether you might be a potential ally, until we witnessed the attack."

"Lucky for me."

"Indeed so. I would ask that you be our guest here tonight, Ms. Syrrell. There are private chambers upstairs, quite comfortable though a bit dated. At least we can be certain of your safety."

"I'm sure the accommodations will be fine. But back to what we were discussing—"

"Get some rest. We will depart very early." He started to rise, and instantly Tanya was there to assist him. "It is necessary to bring you face-to-face with my homeland's latest tragedy."

TWENTY-THREE

THE NEXT MORNING, HARRY MET Emma in the Aqaba hotel lobby. They shared a Middle Eastern breakfast of olives, goat cheese, boiled eggs, flatbread, and mint tea. Afterward they followed Saleem's directions down to where Aqaba's main boulevard paralleled the shoreline. Saleem and his brother-in-law were seated in a stone plaza fronting the gulf. The ache around Harry's ribs forced him to walk at a slight crouch.

Emma asked, "Are you sure you don't want something for the pain?"

"No, thanks." Harry motioned with his chin. "Spotter at seven o'clock by the van. Maybe another on the beach by the kids' playground."

"I see them."

Saleem's brother-in-law had none of the driver's cordiality, mobile features, or flab. He was a lean blade, his cavernous cheeks covered by a burglar's growth. His gaze was flat and tight and measured them fully as Emma stopped before the table and said, "Thank you, Saleem. We are in your debt."

"No debt," the stranger said. "This is cash-only business."

Emma ignored him and addressed Saleem. "Trusting us like this means a lot."

Saleem was reduced to nervous silence by the smuggler's presence. The stranger smirked at Emma's words. "I think maybe my cousin is soft in the head."

Emma kept her gaze fastened on Saleem. "Would it be all right with you, Saleem, if we sat down?"

"Sure, sure, why not? Sit." The stranger kicked an empty chair toward Emma. "Take a load off. That is what you say, yes?"

Harry stepped forward. "Mind if I take over here?"

The stranger smirked more broadly. "What you know. The boss man speaks."

"You got that wrong, bud. The lady is the real boss. She's also the one who'll pay out if we strike a deal." Harry winced as he eased himself down. Even so, he felt a genuine pleasure in being back in the game. Dealing with a man he totally understood. "But the lady doesn't realize you're playacting. How this is just your windup to naming the price. See, she thinks you're serious. She thinks you're as nasty as you're pretending. And there's a problem with that. You keep it up, she'll probably hand you your teeth."

"You try something, I give you some serious trouble."

Harry made as if to wave flies from his face. "You and I, now, we crawled out of the same hole. You're a smuggler, and I'm your buyer. I've known you all my life. So right now, it's just you and me."

Harry waited. Between the plaza and the lazy waters of the Gulf of Aqaba was a playground in the sand. A dozen or so children played on rusty swings or built castles in the sand. Their laughter drifted in the salt-laden air.

The stranger signaled to a passing waiter. He said to Harry, "You like tea?"

"Sure thing. So would the lady."

When the waiter departed, the stranger watched as Emma pulled over a chair and seated herself. "I am Ahmed," he said.

"Harry Bennett. This is Emma Webb."

"What Saleem says is true? The lady is from American government?"

Emma set her leather portfolio on the table, badge up. The man glanced briefly, then sniffed, "Aqaba is long way from Washington."

"Tell me," Emma said.

"Your buddy Wadi Haddad will be very happy to hear that Emma is with me," Harry replied. "She's his ticket to ride. Wadi will be delighted."

"You know Wadi so good, you can tell me what he thinks?"

"About this one thing," Harry said, "absolutely."

The waiter returned with a hookah as high as the table. The pipe leading to the stained bone mouthpiece was covered by a knitted cloth that had been worn away by many hands. The waiter settled a gleaming coal carried in silver forceps on top of the brass bowl. Ahmed's bearded cheeks hollowed with the effort to get the hookah bubbling. When the smoke poured from his nostrils, he said, "So, my new friend. Tell me why Wadi Haddad needs to speak with you."

"You know or you wouldn't be here," Harry said. "Wadi and I were doing business in Hebron. There was a bomb blast. I saved Wadi's life. Emma and I are here to do it again."

"Proof," Ahmed said. "It's such a nice word."

"I don't have any."

"Then we have no business. The only people I see hurting Wadi are you and the American lady."

"If that was the case, you wouldn't have your two guards skulking around the perimeter—"

"Three." Emma corrected him, nodding her thanks as the waiter set a tulip glass of mint tea before her. "There's another guard outside the café."

"Three, six, twenty, they won't mean a thing," Harry said.

"My men are good."

"They're nothing compared to the guys who stalked me at Mount Nebo." Harry sketched out his welcome committee at the Moses church. When Harry finished, Ahmed continued to smoke and watch sailboats drift lazily across the horizon. Harry said, voicing a guess, "You already know all about these guys, don't you. They've been sniffing around. Which is why you agreed to this meet."

Ahmed toasted Emma with his glass. "Good tea, yes?"

Harry said, "You and Wadi are smugglers. You survive by being invisible. The people after us are not going to give up. Sooner or later they're going to track Wadi down. When they do, your operation will vanish like smoke in a sandstorm."

Ahmed smirked across the table. "You and the American government, such great hearts. You travel all this way to save my friend."

Harry eased back in his chair, certain now the deal was done. "What I need in return is between Wadi and me."

THEY LEFT AQABA IN TWO Suzukis, a pickup and a four-by-four, both of which had seen a world of better days. Harry sat beside Emma in the rear seat. The driver wore a Glock nine-millimeter up high under his right arm. The holster was dark with generations of sweaty treks. Ahmed nestled a Nambu machine pistol between his legs, the retractable shoulder-rest fully extended. The Suzuki's rear was jammed full of supplies, as was the pickup ahead of them. A guard sprawled by the pickup's rear gate, nestling a Mauser, his headdress fluttering in the wind.

The road to Jabal Ramm paralleled the main Amman highway for the first ten kilometers. Harry knew this because when they crested a rise he thought he spotted Saleem's Mercedes tucked in between two big trucks, powering north toward Amman. Then they turned west and entered the Hashim highlands.

They were still less than fifty kilometers from the Gulf of Aqaba, but it might as well have been a million miles. The deserts of Sawwan and Hunab were realms carved by wind and sand and time. The road traversed a canyon whose surrounding walls weaved like stone serpents and revealed a billion desert shades, all of them ochre. When the canyon ended, the road scaled switchbacks, then crested a rise that looked ironed flat. The heat weaved so violently on the horizon that it erased any separation between earth and sky. Harry nudged Emma and pointed out a camel caravan that appeared and then vanished again, lost to the shimmering heat. Then the road dipped back into shadows and orange-red valleys, and the horizon closed in from infinity to a smoothbore wall Harry could reach out and touch.

Beyond the village of Ramm, the road signs were written in Arabic only. Which really didn't matter, since Harry had no idea where they were going or how to get back. To the south rose the Jabal Ramm, a lone mountain whose yellow spine climbed to almost six thousand feet. They traversed a plain so hard and level the road simply disappeared. They followed other tracks and the occasional pile of rocks and rusted road signs. The driver dropped to fifth gear and hammered the gas right to the floor. The Suzuki possessed an A/C in theory only. The windows were all down and the wind was so dry Harry could feel the sweat sucked off his skin. An hour from Aqaba, his shirt was a patchwork of dried salt.

Emma noticed Harry's grin and demanded, "What's with you?"

Harry took her hand. "Try to tell me this isn't the life."

Ahmed shouted something to the driver, who grinned at Harry in the rearview mirror, then switched on the radio. Arabic music blasted from a broken speaker. The driver started singing along. Ahmed tapped out the beat on the Nambu.

Emma turned to Harry and said, "You realize they might just skin us for the price of our hide."

Harry's grin widened. "Welcome to my world."

TWO HOURS PASSED. THE DESERT'S intensity grew with each breath. The sun began its descent behind them. They left the plain and the road reappeared. The asphalt was cracked and rutted, as if the highway had been plowed by time. The road ahead took a sharp turn north, and a pitted track branched off south. They went south.

Harry figured they were maybe seventy klicks from the Saudi border. They trundled over road that was little more than a gravel strip. Finally the pickup ahead slowed and stopped. There was no need to pull off the road. The world was empty.

Both drivers cut off their engines. Harry eased out in sore stages. Ahmed climbed on top of the Suzuki's roof and scouted in every direction. The guard riding in the back of the pickup did the same. The loudest sound was the scrape of sand blown against the vehicles.

Ahmed hopped down, opened the Suzuki's rear door, and pulled out a box of PowerBars. He handed several to Harry, followed by a bottle of Evian and salt pellets. They did not speak as they ate. The desert claimed all sound and stole it away.

At a hand signal from Ahmed, they resumed their positions and the drivers fired up the engines. Ahmed turned in his seat and studied Harry carefully. He said, "You understand what is happening?"

Harry replied, "We're headed into territory that doesn't exist. What we see goes on no report. We don't ever talk about it because we haven't seen it."

Ahmed said, "We travel the Jibal al 'Adhiriyat. My grandfather and his before him, they come here. My family before time. Wadi Haddad says I can trust you. But I must answer to my grand-fathers."

Emma replied, "We will come and we will do our work and we will leave. Our footprints will get filled by the wind. And the secret stays buried."

Ahmed turned to the driver. *"J'allah."*

The driver beeped his horn. The pickup jolted forward, turning off the road. Into the empty reaches.

They drove across a field of black rocks ranging in size from pullet eggs to land mines. The surface of the stones looked wet-slick, pol-ished by eons of wind and sand. The rocks reflected sunlight like a billion black mirrors, and the heat turned fiercer still. The vehicles crawled forward, dipping and rising like boats in a swelling sea. Harry had no idea how long the field of rocks continued. Long enough for him to finish drinking the blood-warm water and have it all dissipate in sweat.

The rocks ended and the vehicles sped up, racing the descending sun. Ahmed continually searched behind, showing worry for the first time, urging the driver to even greater speeds. Ochre walls rose up to surround them. The vehicles strained to climb a hill of loose sand, up out of the canyon. Harry then understood their need for haste, for up ahead loomed a sheer-sided cliff, maybe fifteen hundred feet high. They started climbing, following a goat track in some places, a fragment of trail, a broken bush. The trail narrowed until it was simply a ledge jutting from the cliff face, scarcely broad enough to support their outer tires. The driver scraped his door on the rock face. Harry heard the continuous fall of rocks off behind them, even over the engine's high-pitched strain. The sunset illuminated pre-cipitous drops over endless empty vistas. Emma shut her eyes.

Then they crested the rise, and Harry took a long breath. "You've got to see this."

"I can't look."

"Emma." He nudged her. "This is too amazing to miss."

Their ridge formed one of two sides of a bowl. The opposite cliffs were even higher than the one they had just mounted. Below stretched an oasis, the central lake perhaps a hundred feet long and fifty wide, surrounded by date palms and stunted pines. Harry smelled the biting freshness of eucalyptus and desert sorrel. Beyond the oasis, fingers of rock caught the sun's final rays and became alive, great behemoths of fire and strength, guardians against the approaching night.

Their descent was much easier, a steady slide down sand and shale. They reached the oasis floor and were welcomed by the brays of donkeys and bleating sheep. They followed the pickup around the lake's southern edge and entered a cave with a mouth only inches broader than the vehicles. Inside, however, the cave extended in every direction until the sides and roof were lost to shadows.

Ahmed climbed down and greeted several men who inspected Harry and Emma with fierce concern.

Finally Ahmed walked over and said, "My friends, they say you must die for what you have seen."

Harry made a process of testing his ribs and did not reply.

BUT WADI HADDAD WAS NOT to be found. Ahmed led him about the oasis. There must have been fifty or so people involved in Ahmed's little operation, an equal number of men and women with a host of children. Several men showed genuine anger at Harry's presence. Ahmed tried to hide it, but Harry could see that not locating Wadi Haddad troubled the smuggler. And anything big enough to turn their lone protector skittish set Harry's gut to crawling.

Ahmed tried to draw a response from a nearby woman tending a washing machine sheltered beneath a palm-thatched lean-to. She pretended that the diesel generator powering her washer made it impossible to understand him. That was when Harry spotted the reception committee.

They numbered about ten. Two outriders and a bear of a leader, all of them pointing various guns straight at old Harry.

Ahmed started to pull a pistol from his belt, but Harry gripped the man's arm. "Too late for that. Check out the cave up to your right."

Three men stood on a ledge about thirty feet above the oasis floor. One of them had Emma by the hair, a revolver jammed into the base of her skull. He was wearing Emma's sunglasses and grinning hugely. The other two were barely teens, but they held their carbines like they knew what they were doing.

Ahmed shouted in rapid-fire Arabic while advancing toward the burly man. The bear heard him out for about thirty seconds, long enough for Ahmed to get in close enough to wave his arms in the man's face. Then he reversed his pistol and hammered Ahmed once between the eyes. Ahmed staggered but refused to go down.

As the bear took aim for a second blow, Harry stepped forward and said, "I think my pal's got the picture." He gripped Ahmed by the arm and turned him toward where Emma waited. "Marching up there is the only real choice we've got."

The farther they climbed up the path leading to the cave, the louder Harry's body protested. Emma managed to shrug off her captor's grip and hurried over to take Harry's weight. Harry grunted his thanks and took as long a breath as his ribs permitted. They were ushered toward a cave whose door would not have looked out of place on a medieval dungeon. The iron frame was molded to the cave's mouth and bolted to the rock. The door itself was six inches thick and studded with nails. Harry had a final image of dark, leering faces, then the door boomed shut.

He figured a coffin would have had more light.

Then he heard a click, and the glow of an electric lantern illuminated Wadi Haddad. "You come to rescue me. How very nice."

TWENTY-FOUR

ANTONIN TARKA'S PRIVATE JET WAS the first to depart from London's City Airport the next morning. Storm had been awakened long before dawn by Tanya arriving with coffee and Storm's suitcase. Storm was given a Polish ID with a photograph that might have resembled her as long as nobody looked too closely. As Poland was now part of the EU's security zone, Tanya explained, it should be enough. If anyone spoke to her, Tanya would respond.

The jet lifted through the lingering rain and clouds into a brilliant dawn. Storm was seated across from the two men, Antonin Tarka and the Polish priest, Father Gregor. She could feel Tarka's cane resting upon her shin. Between them was a table of burled walnut embossed with a double-headed eagle. The plane was far larger than Raphael's but nowhere near as pristine. The leather of her seat was stained in places. The carpet down the central aisle needed replacing. Tanya was busy behind the galley curtains. Storm could smell fresh coffee and baking pastry.

"I'd like to call my friends and let them know what's happened," Storm said.

"I would respectfully ask that you wait until our return this evening." Antonin Tarka was dressed in identical fashion to the day before, suited and starched and impeccable. "Officially, this trip is not taking place."

Father Gregor asked, "Do you recall what we spoke of yesterday evening, Ms. Syrrell?"

"A mystery buyer with bottomless pockets started acquiring religious artifacts, mostly from Eastern Europe. This was followed by news that a second buyer started competing against him or her, this one represented by me."

"Just so. Before we heard of this first man's wild expenditures, we received word of a theft." Tarka nodded to the priest.

"What I am about to tell you, Ms. Syrrell, must be kept in the strictest confidentiality."

"If word was to escape," Tarka added, "the results would be catastrophic."

"I understand."

"The Black Madonna of Czestochowa is a painting of Mary holding the baby Jesus. According to tradition, this icon was painted by Saint Luke himself. The painting was completed while Mary told Luke of Jesus' life. Luke then incorporated these stories and teachings into his Gospel. He painted the Black Madonna upon a cypress tabletop made by Mary's husband, Joseph."

The engines whined at a comforting distance, and the sun shone brilliantly upon the side window as the two somber men seated across from her discussed events two thousand years old. They spoke with the gravity of generals around a table of war.

Father Gregor went on, "The picture remained in Jerusalem until the year 326, when it was gifted to Helen, the mother of Emperor Constantine. She brought it back to her son's new capital, where it was housed in the city's cathedral. When the eastern Roman Empire fell to the Ottomans, the picture was first taken to Belz, then brought to its current home in 1382. The painting is called the Black Madonna because of the soot residue that discolors the figures, caused by centuries of votive candles and incense."

Tanya emerged from the galley bearing a silver coffee service. She set it on the table, poured three cups, then departed. Storm studied the woman's features yet found no indication of what Tanya might think of all this.

"There have been almost two thousand years of miracles associated with the painting," Father Gregor continued. "Spontaneous healings, the repulsion of invaders—the list is endless."

Tarka said, "What you must understand, Ms. Syrrell, is that the painting's importance goes far beyond any particular miracle. The Black Madonna of Czestochowa represents Poland's ability to survive as a nation."

Storm watched Tanya return and set down three steaming-hot croissants. The pastries rested upon plates bearing the double-headed eagle. Tanya refused to meet her eye as she padded back to the galley. Storm tore off one tip from the croissant. It was as delicious as the coffee.

"Our nation's greatest flaw is its position," Father Gregor said. "We occupy a plain utterly lacking in geographical defenses. No great mountain ranges, no fierce rivers. During our two thousand years of history, we have been invaded from every side. Mongol hordes. Tatars.

Hussites. Swedes. Ottomans. Prussians. Austro-Hungarians. Nazis. And most recently, Stalin's tanks."

Antonin Tarka said, "During the Communist era, when Poland became locked behind the Iron Curtain, the Black Madonna took on special significance. The center of resistance against the Soviets was the Polish Catholic Church. When the Soviet occupiers tried to eradicate our heritage, the Church taught Polish history and language. In our darkest hour, when the powers that opposed us were overwhelming and hope was all but lost, the Black Madonna represented the eternal flame that kept us alive."

Tanya returned from the galley and announced, "We are about to begin our descent."

Storm took that as her cue. "So this painting has been stolen."

"Well, yes and no, Ms. Syrrell. If the Black Madonna had simply vanished, the whole world would hear our cry of anguish." Tarka's face had never appeared more grave. "It was replaced with a forgery so exact we have no idea when the original was taken."

THE DRIVE FROM THE KRAKÓW airport to Czestochowa was a journey through epochs. The nation's scars were evident everywhere. Communist-era apartments, drab as prison block-houses, brooded over medieval daub-and-wattle farm buildings with thatched roofs. They passed villages with impossible names—Olkusz, Slawkow, Zawiercie, Myszkow, Poczesna. They traversed a forest of silver birch, the new leaves glinting like mirrors. Then came an industrial complex tattooed with grime and poverty and hopelessness. Silent cranes hovered about a half-finished apartment complex.

Where they left the main highway, the road became lined by wild cherry trees, the knobby limbs almost lost beneath clouds of blossoms. A sudden gust of wind buffeted their car, and a snowfall of pink blossoms obliterated their vision. When the windshield cleared, they faced a green hillside crowned by a medieval structure unlike anything Storm had ever seen.

"The Monastery of Jasna Gora," Father Gregor said. "Which translates as Luminous Mountain. The central edifice is over seven hundred years old."

The parking lot was vast as an asphalt sea. There were hundreds of buses. They parked and joined a constant stream of penitents walking toward the monastery. Storm became surrounded by people of all ages. Some pushed wheelchairs, others ambulance-style stretchers. All eyes were upon the edifice that rose up ahead. The people's footsteps were as constant as rain.

They let the crowd set the pace. As they walked, Father Gregor said, "On holy days, as many as two million pilgrims visit this shrine. It is common for many seeking miracles to walk from their homes in far-flung towns. The journey from Warsaw takes nine days. Villagers still line the streets and hand out provisions to pilgrims."

They entered the monastery beneath a triumphant arch topped by a statue of winged victory armed for righteous battle. The monastery was the size of a medieval village. At its heart, a magnificent church gleamed in the sunlight.

The cathedral was vast, but even so it could not adequately hold all the supplicants. The overflow jammed open-air tents situated to either side of the main entrance and spilled down the front lawn. Loudspeakers carried the mass, which was given by different priests in a number of languages.

Father Gregor led them through the priests' entrance into a side alcove. They waited until the mass ended, then slipped through heavy velvet curtains and entered the nave. The main chamber was fully three hundred feet long and half as wide, with massive pillars supporting an arched stone ceiling. The fragrance of incense was overpowering.

"Poland's story is one of triumph in the face of impossible odds." Antonin Tarka leaned heavily upon his cane and surveyed the chamber with an expression so intense Storm thought the man might weep. "We represent a different world, one the West would do well to study. What happens to faith when all else is lost, when the human existence is reduced to rubble and tears? That is what our nation can teach." He waved the priest forward. "Show our guest what happened."

Father Gregor led her closer to the front of the church. The hall resonated with thousands of voices in prayer. Every side alcove was packed, as were niches holding prayer benches and votive candles and crucifixes. Double doors of embossed metal bars were folded back, opening the nave to the rest of the church. The icon resided upon the rear wall of the nave, over-looking the altar table. Flowers were banked about the nave in piles thick as clouds.

The portrait displayed a traditional composi-tion used by many Orthodox icons. The figures' positions formed what was known as a *Hodegetria*. One of Mary's hands held the infant Jesus. The other hand gestured toward her son, directing attention away from herself. In turn, the child extended his right hand toward the viewer in an act of blessing.

The portrait was sealed within an inner frame of beaten silver. The outer frame was covered in a sheaf of gold leaf. The result was not so much primitive as timeless. The impact was fiercely compelling, as though the image itself held the power to reach across the sea of two thousand years.

Father Gregor began, "Eleven days ago, a

brother arrived to prepare the sacristy for dawn devotionals. He was in his eighties and had been performing this duty for sixty-three years. The brother had been a novice during Polish independence between the world wars. He survived the Nazis, he survived Stalin, he survived capitalism."

Father Gregor pointed at the banks of flowers lining the floor and walls around the portrait. "Every night the flowers brought by pilgrims are gathered up and disposed of. The doors to the nave are sealed. As is the sanctuary. That particular morning, the old monk was assisted by two young acolytes, who trim the candles and lay out a fresh altar cloth and sweep the floors and so forth. The elderly brother turned off the alarm system. Only he and the senior cleric knew the code. Then he unlocked the Madonna's compartment using a key he kept with him at all times. The only other key is locked inside the senior cleric's safe. That morning, the brother opened the nave, approached the icon, and cried something that the acolytes claim sounded like 'Sacrilege.' Then he gripped his chest and fell down dead. The brother had seen the icon every day for decades, adored it, and knew every detail of the surface—every whorl in the wood grain, every slight crack in the wood, every scar on its ancient surface. We can only hope he realized that it had been replaced by a duplicate the very day the theft occurred."

"Are there security cameras?"

"They have not worked in weeks. Longer." Father Gregor's features had become tormented. "The senior cleric brought in an expert from the Vatican. The expert confirmed that the Madonna you see there is a forgery."

Storm said, "Whoever did this spent a fortune on the forgery so the theft would not be discovered. Why would somebody go to all that trouble? And who would do it?"

Father Gregor said, "A government perhaps."

Antonin Tarka limped forward to stand at Storm's other side. "There is only one government that would be so brazen. The Soviets would take great pride in such an act."

"Nowadays they are known again as Russians," Father Gregor said, correcting him.

Antonin Tarka shrugged. "Same wolf, same fangs, same threat."

Storm asked, "Why am I here?"

Antonin Tarka said, "After we learned of the theft, we frantically searched the international arts market for any hint of the Black Madonna. It was a long shot, of course. These days, most art thefts are done to order. The item never surfaces. Then we hear of a mystery Russian buyer. He pursues every early Christian artifact that comes up for sale. His interest borders on fanaticism. Money means nothing. He hides himself extremely well. Almost too well."

Father Gregor said, "My sources at the Vatican have no idea who this buyer might be. They are naturally alarmed. Any number of treasures from our early Christian heritage are being swallowed up. Who is he, and why has he chosen this moment to surface?"

Antonin Tarka said, "And could this obsessive interest of his be behind the theft of our national treasure?"

Father Gregor said, "Then suddenly, out of nowhere, Raphael Danton appears. He represents a *second* mystery buyer."

"And Danton selects you as his dealer," Antonin Tarka said. "Of course, we were delighted with the choice, given your grandfather's reputation. And your own."

Father Gregor asked, "Can you determine the name of Danton's new buyer?"

"I'll ask. But he has every right not to tell me." Storm found a certain satisfaction in having her concerns voiced by another. "Do you have any idea who Rausch represents?"

"We have been trying to determine that," Tarka replied. "So far, we have come up with nothing."

Father Gregor asked, "Perhaps your friend the Homeland Security agent can help us?"

"The American intelligence community is apparently in the dark like everybody else." Storm hesitated, then she asked, "Can I tell her why we're here?"

Both men frowned. "The more people who know, the greater the risk of this becoming an international crisis."

Tarka said, "Perhaps that is what the Russians had in mind all along."

"They are devious," Father Gregor said in agreement. "Brutally so. Our own history is testimony to that. But they also possess a certain Siberian logic. And I fail to see how they might gain from creating a public scandal."

"They steal it," Storm said, thinking out loud. "Then they offer to help you find it. And when it's recovered, they have a lever to pull you away from the West."

Both men stared at her. Tarka asked, "You have experience dealing with Russian treachery?"

"I deal in treasure," Storm replied. "There's no market more devious than mine."

A bell sounded from high overhead. Father Gregor touched her arm. "The next mass will soon begin."

"I'll meet you outside." Storm stepped away from the men and started down the central aisle. She moved against the incoming tide of penitents, a multigenerational horde that poured through the rear doors.

Every surface in the vast hall was covered. Walls, pillars, all the way up to the ceiling a hundred feet and more overhead. Canes and crutches and miniature icons and rosaries and folded prayer shawls and letters. Tens of thousands of letters, all set in cheap frames, many of them so ancient the yellowed pages no longer held any words. This was more than testimony to answered prayers. Storm felt like she walked through a cave that hearkened back to another era, one where humans struggled against forces so potent the people were left utterly powerless. Their fates were gripped by forces that cared nothing for their hopes, their dreams, their lives. They had no recourse except to pray. The church was a lone haven, the ancient icon in the sacristy a single gateway to a power that might, just might, be able to save or heal or return them to happier times. Sunlight through the eastern windows sparkled over the immense array of desperate testimonies. Storm felt as though she was surrounded by everything that defied her Western mind, her ingrained beliefs in self-determination and personal freedom.

When she emerged from the front portals, Father Gregor and Antonin Tarka waited for her just beyond the throngs pressing politely for space inside the church. For the first time, Storm felt as though she could connect to the forces that had etched the two men's features. Tanya stood some distance farther away, a stalwart woman who shared a similar conviction.

Storm walked up to them and said, "Thank you for bringing me here."

TWENTY-FIVE

T HE CAVE WAS THE SIZE of a county lockup. The air was spiced with bundles of clove and cinnamon and dried herbs hanging from head-high shelves bolted to the stone walls. The ceiling was just high enough for Harry to stand upright. Burlap sacks of beans and brown rice and dates and dried fruit were stacked against the walls. More shelves held canned goods. Wadi boiled water over a paraffin cooker and made instant coffee. They all drank from the same lone mug.

Wadi refilled the mug, added more sugar than Harry preferred, and said, "Soon as Ahmed left for Aqaba, they took me. Morning and night, guards walk me to the latrine. The rest of the time, I am here."

The cave was floored in sand fine as face powder. Illumination was supplied by a battery-powered lantern. Harry shifted his back against the wall. His entire body burned. "Who is after you, Wadi?"

"Some people. Very angry. They pay much money to have me." The Palestinian looked around the cave. "I think maybe soon enough I wish I was back here again."

"Let's pretend we've still got a reason for having this conversation," Harry said. "I'll start off, you tell me when I get it wrong. How's that?"

215

Wadi continued his silent inspection of the rock walls.

"Little honesty up front. I was hired by the Israelis to identify a source of extremely high-quality counterfeit artifacts."

Ahmed groaned, "This is the man I decide to trust."

"That was then and this is now," Harry said. "This thing has moved way beyond fake treasures. Hasn't it, Wadi?"

The man did not respond.

"So I'm brought into contact with a guy operating out of Hebron," continued Harry. "Just as the deal is going down, I get a signal from Hassan, my driver. I ram you into the wall, which probably saves your life. Then somebody lights up the night sky."

Wadi asked, "Why you are saving me? This I do not understand."

"I hate counterfeits with a passion," Harry said. "But a man who can make this level of copy is a true artist. I couldn't just let you go down."

Wadi hefted a handful of sand and let it slip through his fingers. "One moment I am wondering why you push me into the wall. Then a fireball blasts where I am standing one second before. You are between me and the bomb, so the flames hit your face and not mine. I am not knowing whether you live. Then I look down, and the only thing that is left of my guard is his ID. Right there at my feet."

"I'd take that as a sign," Harry said. "No question."

"When I hear sirens, I drop his ID on your chest. In Hebron clinic, Palestinians get first beds and best treatment." Wadi looked at Harry. "I am thinking much of this, sitting here in my prison."

Harry pressed on. "But making counterfeit artifacts, no matter how valuable, wouldn't have this level of beast tracking you."

Emma added, "Not to mention that suddenly we're getting alarm calls from all over the place. CIA, Homeland Security, some high-powered secondary buyers, Polish priests, invisible Russians, the works."

Ahmed said, "Polish priests do not find us here. This is somebody with many allies in Jordan."

"And much money," Wadi said. "I hear the guards say I am worth half a million dollars alive."

"So here's what I think happened," Harry said, looking at Wadi. "You were approached by somebody who wanted you to do some work. Something that required a counterfeiter as talented as you. But like any decent smuggler, you saw a chance for even more profit. Somehow you got an idea who was behind this whole deal. And you threatened to go public. So they decided to take you out. The bomb was meant for you, and I got caught in the backdraft. How am I doing so far?"

Emma said, "You should be working for Homeland."

"I'm happy with my own craft, thank you very much," Harry replied.

"Oh, sure," Ahmed said. "Look where it brings you now."

Harry asked, "Who's your artist, Wadi?"

When the man remained crouched over the little stove, Ahmed supplied the answer. "His daughters. They live in Damascus with their mother. They are best I have ever seen."

"Which brings us to the million-dollar question," Harry said. "Who did you manage to get so angry they've tracked you here to the back of beyond and caught us all up in the same net?"

Ahmed struggled to rise. "This does not matter if we stay trapped here."

"It matters," Harry said, watching Wadi Haddad avoid his gaze. "It matters a lot."

"First we escape," Ahmed said. "Then we see what matters."

"I checked the door," Emma said. "It's bolted shut. And I heard guards talking on the ledge."

"Door. Guards. Hunh." Ahmed stood unsteadily, cupping his badly bruised forehead with one hand and bracing himself against the cave wall with the other. He shuffled toward the rear of the cave. "I tell you before, my family control the oasis since this was Bedu kingdom." Ahmed kicked a burlap sack holding dried beans. "We must move all this."

"Is just beans," Wadi protested.

218

"No, mate. It's a back door, is what it is." Harry turned and grinned at Emma. "I'm liking this guy more and more."

When the sacks were shifted and the sand scraped away from the floor, they peeled back a rattan mat to reveal an ancient trapdoor. Harry asked, "Where does this go?"

"You see," Ahmed replied. He motioned to Wadi, who heaved on the door. Below, all was dark. But a soft puff of wind promised freedom. "I go first."

"Maybe I should take it first, help you down," Emma said.

"American agents know footholds in secret tunnels?" Ahmed unfurled his headdress and tied it around the lantern's metal base to keep it from scraping on the rocks. He slithered feet first into the tunnel and winced at the pain in his head. "You step where I step, breathe when I breathe."

"Hold it right there," Emma said. She scrambled through her purse, came up with a small packet, which she tore open. She offered Ahmed a palm holding two pills. "Secret agents always carry Advil."

Ahmed grinned in Harry's direction. "She have sister, this one?"

"Sorry, mate. One of a kind."

"That's very good. My wife, she is one jealous lady." Ahmed swallowed the Advil dry. "My head is better already. Okay. We go."

● ● ●

THE TUNNEL WAS SCARCELY LARGE enough for Harry to maneuver through. The descent gradually grew both steeper and more claustrophobic. The lantern was a dim glow up ahead. At the steepest point, the tunnel was carved with niches that formed regular foot- and handholds. Harry descended the tunnel as he would a ladder. Though his ribs complained loudly, he could not stop grinning. A hundred or so bearded bandits above them with assault rifles on auto. A hundred miles between them and the nearest road sign. For company he had a smuggler, a counterfeiter, and a woman who had come halfway around the world to save his sorry hide. And there wasn't a hope of ever getting paid for his troubles.

No question about it. This was living large.

Where the tunnel leveled off and began to widen, Ahmed cut off the lantern. Harry spotted a dim glow in the distance. The way the light flickered and cast ruddy shadows, he figured it for a campfire. Their footsteps were cushioned by sand as soft as confectioner's sugar. The firelight caught tiny diamond-flickers in the walls, suggesting mica or quartz mixed with the sandstone. Then Ahmed hissed them to a halt and moved forward alone.

Harry gingerly felt about his chest. The climb down had shifted something internal. Harry did not feel broken so much as permanently bruised.

But the adrenaline surge was enough to push his discomfort aside. At least for now.

At Ahmed's signal, they slipped forward, silent as the firelight shadows. They emerged through just another tight crevice, one of millions that dotted the hillside. Their path was a ledge that snaked in and out of sight. In the distance, a dozen or so people gathered around a fire. Then they slipped around an edge and entered a new landscape, one illuminated only by a quarter moon. Below them the palms whispered soft warnings. The oasis waters were dark as blood.

They descended another series of narrow steps, clinging to the rock face with desperate fingertips. When they finally reached ground level, Harry would have danced a jig if his body hadn't been aching so badly. Wadi had no such impediment, however, and he flung his arms upward and mouthed a silent greeting to the stars.

Which was when the guard rounded the corner.

It was hard to say who was more astonished, the bandit or the escapees.

Emma stepped forward and hammered the guy between the eyes.

The guard's eyes gave a little butterfly-flutter, but he refused to go down until she chopped him at the juncture of jaw and neck and ear.

Ahmed caught the man and Wadi the gun. Both Arabs flashed Emma grins of approval and dragged the guard into a natural alcove. They lashed his hands with Emma's kerchief, stuffed Wadi's into his mouth, and used Ahmed's belt for his legs.

Ahmed kept the Suzukis between them and the group clustered by the fire. He led them into a side alcove, which held a single vehicle, one so massive it completely filled the chamber. When Harry realized what he was looking at, he huffed a quiet laugh.

Ahmed murmured, "You know this?"

"Never driven one," Harry whispered. "But I've blown up my share."

Emma slipped up beside him. "What is it?"

"Iraqi armored troop carrier," Harry replied. "Russian make. First Gulf War vintage."

"We take it in exchange for saving driver and men." Ahmed shook his head. "Until now, I am thinking we make very bad bargain."

Quietly Wadi opened the driver's door, then he cursed softly. "No keys."

"Step aside." Harry slipped into the driver's seat, grunted as he eased himself over. And grunted again as he tugged out the wires beneath the steering column.

Ahmed grinned at Emma. "Now I am understanding why you save this man."

"Harry has a degree from the university of serious trouble," Emma replied.

"Everybody who's leaving on the Aqaba bus better climb on board." Harry cleared the sheathing off the wires with his teeth, then said, "I'll take a couple of those Advils now."

AS SOON AS HARRY FIRED the engine, the cavern was filled with the sound of angry men.

He slammed the gearshift into first and eased off the clutch. "Flight attendants, please cross-check doors." The vehicle lurched forward. "Hands and feet and personal items out of the aisles."

The first guard jerked into view, trying to wave them to a halt and bring his gun around at the same time. Harry replied by aiming the truck at the man.

A bullet whanged off the roof of the truck and another off the side window. His passengers flinched away in fear. But Harry knew from experience just how well the Russians built these suckers.

A dozen or so shouting men formed up by the cave entrance. The problem was, if enough bullets were fired at the same point in the glass, there was a risk that the windshield might eventually give. Then he had an idea and shifted his aim to the right.

Harry lined up behind the Suzuki pickup and hammered the rear bumper. "My sincere apologies."

In response, Ahmed laughed and shouted something that required no translation.

The vehicle ahead of Harry jerked and shuddered against its own parking gear, sliding over the sand until it struck the second Suzuki. The half-track's engine bellowed from the strain and kept on moving, pushing the two vehicles directly at the men who were frantically trying to take aim around the newly formed train.

Harry decided the moment deserved a song. The only thing that came to mind was, "O Lord, Won't You Buy Me a Mercedes-Benz."

Bullets whanged and punched the metal and the glass. But as far as Harry could see in the scattered firelight and the manufactured mayhem, no fractures were developing.

Ahmed showed Harry a smuggler's grin. "Janis Joplin, yes? Very good tune. But you, my friend, cannot sing."

The Suzukis crawled sideways, herding the guards like metal sheepdogs. The first vehicle struck the cave's entrance and began to accordion on top of the second. A spark must have caught the gas tank, or perhaps it was just the pressure of being compressed from behind. Whatever the reason, the pickup gave off a soft whuff and the cave mouth was a balloon of flame.

Harry kept straight on, through the wall of flame and out into a hail of gunfire. He shouted, "Which way?"

"Left! Left!"

As the second Suzuki tumbled away, Harry

shifted to a higher gear and aimed straight for the campfire. Ahmed gave another thoroughly Arabic yell as they cleared all four wheels over the fire circle, scattering people and blazing logs. Sparks showered the vehicle as Harry took aim for the night. As they climbed the long, sloping trail they had entered by, the half-track was clipped by a few parting shots. Someone wailed a furious farewell.

Harry put the headlights on bright. Emma found the controls for the side-mounted searchlight and aimed it at the nonexistent road. Harry took the descent at a gut-wrenching crawl. He did not breathe again until the road leveled off.

Then it was just the stars and the silver sand.

TWENTY-SIX

ANTONIN TARKA'S JET WAS READY and waiting when they arrived back at the Kraków airport. Storm would have liked to hang around for a few days. Kraków was the ancient capital of the Polish kingdom, and its medieval center had survived both the Nazis and the Soviets largely intact. But Tanya and the two men carried the single-minded focus of pros on the clock. Storm kept her desires to herself and boarded the jet.

Once they were airborne, Storm said, "Back to my earlier question. Why would the Russians want to steal an icon and replace it with a copy that cost a fortune to produce? There needs to be a concrete reason for them to have gone to all that trouble."

"If it was the Russians at all," Father Gregor added.

"Do they have any special connection to this icon?" Storm asked.

"They do not need one," Antonin Tarka replied. "When I was ten years old, I watched Stalin's soldiers murder my entire family. We lived in what is now the western Ukraine. I was on the run for six months, traveling only at night, stealing what food I could from farms, until I made it across the Czech border. I speak from brutal experience when I say the Russian mentality is unique. They live with a perpetual sense of being under threat from all sides. Their enemies surround them. Their inbred attitude is to strike first, to dominate, to oppress. In their twisted form of logic, they see this as their one true hope of survival."

"And the icon?"

"The Black Madonna represents the heart of a people they have oppressed for centuries. But now our nation is on the rise. We have the largest economy in Eastern Europe. We are also one of the West's strongest allies. The Black Madonna is a lever. Their hope is to draw us back into the fold."

Storm sensed that Father Gregor did not agree.

But the priest frowned at his hands upon the tabletop and said merely, "We still have no concrete evidence that the Russian buyers are somehow connected to the icon's disappearance."

"And yet I am certain it is so."

"For all our sakes," the priest said, "I hope you are right. Time is fast running out."

Tarka nodded grave acceptance and said to Storm, "Beyond the West's safe borders, beyond this generation's comfort zone, there exists a different world. A world where many people do not have the luxury of schooling. One where words come with difficulty and reading is impossible. One where they hold to a faith, even though their leaders are quite willing to torture and maim and murder to extinguish religion. The people of this other world use something they can see and touch as a means to look *beyond.* Understand this, and you may fathom what a vital role the Black Madonna has played for my country."

Storm waited while Tanya laid out plates of sandwiches, then said, "There's something else we need to discuss. The Amethyst Clock."

Father Gregor said, "It is a fable. A lie."

"Even so, the people we're up against think it is real. And they're hunting it."

Antonin Tarka said, "You have heard the story of Catherine the Great, yes? Her rule was one of Poland's darkest hours, a Russian czarina who saw our land as too rich and our army as too threatening. So she gathered her cousins, the emperor from Vienna and the Kaiser from Berlin, and over a very fine meal they carved our nation into three segments and swallowed it whole." Tarka looked at his friend. "During that harsh era, legends sprang from soil watered by the blood of patriots. Fables of impossible powers. Hope from mythical realms."

Father Gregor said, "There is a difference between faith grounded in God and fables fed by human misery."

Tarka said, "But that does not change what Ms. Syrrell has correctly pointed out. Someone has a reason to believe the clock exists and has the power to stop time."

Storm corrected him, "Someone wants to believe this so badly, they are willing to suspend disbelief."

Both men were watching her now. "What are you saying?"

"Does that sound like the Russians to you?"

DAYLIGHT HAD DIMMED TO A slate-gray smudge on the western horizon by the time they landed at City Airport in London. The day had taken its toll on Antonin Tarka. The man's features had turned cavernous, and the jet's narrow metal stairs were hard going for him. Father Gregor helped him as much as he could, and Tanya hovered one step down, there to catch him if he fell. Antonin Tarka fussily tried to shoo both of them away, but they took no notice.

Once in the taxi, Tarka said, "I would urge you to remain at the Ognisko, Ms. Syrrell. We will be better able to ensure your safety."

The prospect of returning to her drafty room in the club was utterly unappealing. But so was the threat of being abducted. "Are you sure I can't tell my friends what is happening?"

"The more people who know, the greater our risk," Antonin Tarka replied.

"Particularly this Raphael Danton," Father Gregor said. "We must ask that you tell him nothing."

"Why?"

"Danton was once a soldier of fortune in Africa, yes?"

"He had personal reasons for joining the fight."

"But he was paid for combat. A mercenary." Tarka's face was a graven image in the passing streetlights. "If he will offer his life for coin, what would he do with our secret?"

"On this matter, we must insist," Father Gregor said in agreement. "Do not trust Danton with anything."

TWENTY-SEVEN

HARRY DITCHED THE TROOP CARRIER in a highway truck stop outside Aqaba. Ahmed bought caps, sweatshirts, long drawstring pants, sunglasses, and a disposable phone from the shop. Emma did not wait for his explanation that the Western woman needed to disappear. She smudged her face with road dust, tucked her hair into the cap, slipped on the shades, and pulled the bulky sweatshirt over her head.

They bribed a trucker to carry them through Aqaba and farther south. The road to Haql and the Saudi border paralleled the silent gulf. They descended from the truck just as the eastern sky showed the first faint hint of dawn.

Their destination was a cluster of fishing dhows. Nets dried on makeshift lean-tos. The rocky beach stunk of fish. Ahmed led them to a wooden vessel perhaps twenty-five feet in length. As they flipped the dhow, two scruffy teens scrambled from one of the lean-tos, holding vintage Enfields at the ready. When they saw who it was, they waved a sleepy greeting and retreated. A smuggler departing with the night's final shadows was clearly nothing new.

As Ahmed and Wadi prepared the dhow for departure, Emma used the cell phone to coordinate with the U.S. embassy in Amman. Harry listened to Emma obtain bargaining power over Wadi Haddad and arrange their extraction from the Gulf. Every time she glanced his way, he smiled encouragement and did his best to hide his growing discomfort. It felt to him like something important inside his chest had decided now was a good time to call it quits.

The two Arabs pulled the vessel out through blood-warm water. Emma went back to shore for a pair of oars while Ahmed stepped the mast and lashed it into place with hemp rope. Emma and Wadi began rowing while Harry played like ballast. A light breeze pushed away the morning mist and revealed an Egyptian borderland of desert sands and ochre cliffs, while the Saudi coast diminished to a yellow smear on the eastern horizon.

A cluster of other boats eventually joined them. Fishermen cast quiet greetings with their nets. The last sight Harry had before falling asleep was of Ahmed raising the dhow's single parchment-colored sail.

He awoke to find Emma's hair flickering across his face. She had fitted herself onto the same bench, head to head with him. Wadi sat on the stern platform beside Ahmed, the two Arabs searching the horizon and talking softly. Emma's hair brushed Harry's face with feather strokes. Despite the gathering heat, his body was racked with chills. He eased himself up to a sitting position, cupped a hand, and dipped it over the side. Harry scrubbed his face, then slipped to the stern. Ahmed offered him a bottled water and an energy bar and observed, "You don't look so good."

"I'm okay." Harry turned to Wadi. "We need to finish our discussion. We're out here in the middle of nowhere, and my offer is the only one you're going to get."

Wadi squinted into the sunlight and said nothing.

Emma slipped onto the gunwale beside Harry. "Are you all right?"

"Fine."

"You don't look fine. You look . . ." She touched his face. "You're burning up."

"Let's finish with this, then I'll go back and collapse." Harry turned back to Wadi and said, "Something big is going down. Big enough to get the interest of some powerful people in Washington. These people are ready to make you a onetime offer. Give us what we need, and we'll do the same for you."

"You know me so well, you can tell me what I need?"

Emma took a long drink from Harry's bottle, then said, "Mr. Haddad, the U.S. government is willing to grant you and your family permanent residency."

Wadi said to the shimmering waters, "An agent we do much business with. He comes and says, 'Make me something.' He offers very much cash."

"What was the item you copied?"

"Very old painting. Religious. Woman and baby. Painted on wood. Both people wearing crowns. How you say?"

"Icon," Harry said.

"Yes. Very hard work." He extended his fingers like radiating light. "Many carvings on inner silver frame. But primitive. Very old."

"A lot of time and effort," Harry said.

"Too much work, too many days. The agent, he comes too many times. Always with the pressure. My daughters, they work all day, all night. Three months and two weeks they work. One gets very sick. The other sleep for three nights and days when it is done."

"You know who the agent was representing," said Harry. It was not a question. "You made it your business to discover. You figured there might be profit in it for you to know."

"Big mistake," Wadi muttered.

Emma asked, "What was the man's name, Wadi?"

"Vladimir Abramov."

"Say that again." When he did, she asked, "You're certain it was him?"

"What, you think they chase me for a wrong name?"

A slow puttering noise drew them around.

Harry, Emma, Ahmed, and Wadi watched the approach of an inflatable landing craft. The vessel was operated at low speed by a trio of dark-suited navy divers. They halted about twenty feet off. A woman called softly, "Agent Webb?"

"That would be me."

The boat drew closer still. "You mind if I take a look at your creds?"

"Not at all."

As the officer examined the badge and the picture ID, Wadi said, "I cannot swim."

"No worries, sir. Not getting your feet wet is part of our job." When she handed back Emma's badge, she caught sight of Harry. "Sir, are you all right?"

"Fine."

"I'm only asking on account of how you look pretty far gone, sir. And there's nothing in my book about allowing one of my passengers to expire."

"I'll make it." Harry let Emma and Wadi cross first, then he said to Ahmed, "Where do we send your money?"

"We have not discussed the price."

"That's right," Harry said. "We haven't."

The smuggler grinned and offered a slip of paper. "I was right to trust you."

Harry shoved the paper into his pocket. "Will you be okay?"

"Oh, very yes. Is good time for housecleaning."
He studied Harry. "The lady is right. You are
looking bad."

"Between you and me, I feel even worse."
Harry slipped over the edge and eased onto the
inflatable's reinforced side. He turned back and
called across the waters, "Anytime, anywhere."

Ahmed lifted a hand in farewell as the woman
officer said, "Okay, Bert, take us home."

TWENTY-EIGHT

THEIR INFLATABLE CRAFT RENDEZVOUSED
with a naval destroyer on Gulf duty. A
chopper was prepped and winding up before
they reached the main deck. They were still
settling in as the machine lifted and swooped
out over the azure waters. Harry pretty much
shivered his way through the transfers.

They landed at the U.S. military base outside
Jeddah, where they were placed in polite isola-
tion with MPs for hosts. Harry barely managed to
reach his bunk before collapsing. An hour or a
day later—Harry had no idea—Emma arrived
with a doctor in tow. The young woman had a
thoroughly efficient military air about her.
"Agent Webb informs me you're a little worse for
wear, Mr. Bennett."

"I'm feeling much better, now that I've had
some rest."

"Glad to hear it." She inspected his face. "What exactly happened to you?"

"Bomb. Probably an IED."

"Where was that?"

"Hebron. West Bank."

"Who treated you there?"

"I was in a Palestinian clinic for a couple of days." Harry swung his feet to the floor and leaned his back against the sidewall. Keeping his voice steady and his face calm took about all he had to give. "They were great."

"Did they scan you for internal injuries?"

"No equipment," Harry replied. "And no need. I'm fine."

"Are you."

"Absolutely tip-top."

Emma's phone chimed. She checked the readout and said, "I have to take this."

When she stepped into the hall, Harry asked the doctor, "Think maybe you could help me lie back down?"

"That was all show for the lady?"

"Absolutely." Even though the doctor took most of his weight, Harry groaned all the way down. He confessed, "I hurt right down to my toenails."

"Where is it worst?"

He pointed at the space below his rib cage. "Here."

"Can you take a deep breath?"

"Not anymore."

She checked his vitals, listened to him wheeze, then probed his midsection. Harry huffed against the pain.

The doctor straightened. "Have you experienced any further trauma since the explosion?"

Laughing should not have hurt him so much. "You could say that."

"My guess is you had a minor tear to the abdominal wall from the initial blast. This has been aggravated by your recent activities, resulting in internal bleeding."

"Please don't tell Emma."

"Mr. Bennett, I'm not sure you understand how grave your situation could be here. Peritonitis is as serious as it gets. You can die from this. And soon."

"We have a friend who is in worse danger than I am. If Emma knows how bad things are with me, she'll stay. There's nothing she can do for me. But our friend's life hangs in the balance."

Emma chose that moment to open the door. "How's our patient?"

Harry kept his eyes on the doctor. "Please."

The doctor was in her midfifties, with graying hair cropped tight and stern features only slightly softened by age. She said, "Mr. Bennett, you are one very lucky man."

Harry sighed his relief. "Tell me."

The doctor checked her watch. "Your travel

orders are being cut as we speak. In just over an hour our regular transport departs for Ramstein Air Base in Germany. I'll phone ahead and make the arrangements for Mr. Bennett here to be checked over at the Landstuhl base hospital."

Emma exclaimed, "What's the matter?"

"Nothing much," Harry said. "The doctor just wants to play it safe. Right, doc?"

"We need to make certain there's no seepage into the chest or abdominal cavity. That's common enough with IEDs. They'll check you out, maybe insert a catheter to drain the fluid." The doctor swabbed Harry's arm. "This first part of your cocktail is an antibiotic. I'm also going to give you an injection to ease any congestion in your lungs, plus something for the fever and the pain."

Emma said, "But he's all right?"

"Never better," Harry said.

When the doctor was finished, she closed her bag and said, "A pleasure doing business with a gentleman, Mr. Bennett. Have a pleasant flight."

WHEN THE DOOR SHUT BEHIND the departing doctor, Emma said, "That was Tip who just called. Washington is doing a workup on this Vladimir Abramov. Tip expects to find he was one of Putin's KGB buddies. Apparently these guys are the new Russian princes. The line between politics and industry has been erased.

Which leads us to the next problem. Are you sure you're up for this?"

Harry drifted on a now-familiar current, the pain receding with each shallow breath. "Sure thing."

"Tip says the CIA is in a panic. Apparently they had Storm under electronic surveillance. She was attacked yesterday. Reports are confusing. They claim she was abducted, but I just checked my messages, and Storm claims she's fine."

The military medicine was nowhere near as explosive as the ice injections the Palestinians had given him. But the results were pretty much the same. Harry felt the world begin to recede with the pain. He said, "You have to go help her."

"What about you?"

"I'm fine."

"You're anything but fine."

"They can take care of me. Storm needs you."

"And you don't?"

Harry watched Emma's hand drift up to caress his forehead. It required a world of effort to reach up and clench her hand with his own. "We're together even when we're apart."

She gave him that same open yet fearful look. Harry held on to that as he drifted away, searching the cocooned darkness for something that might make it easy for them to do whatever came next.

TWENTY-NINE

THE FLIGHT FROM JEDDAH TO the Ramstein Air Base in Germany took five hours. They were met planeside by a military green sedan, there to take Harry straight to the base hospital. Emma was politely but firmly shepherded through a swift farewell, then she was sped down the autobahn to Frankfurt's main airport. She barely had time for a German food-court meal before boarding the next flight to London. Once on the flight, however, she gave herself over to the big quandary she had been running from ever since Harry had been found. She could dress it up any way she wanted. Put it down to a dismal family life, the Washington grind, whatever she liked. But by the time the plane was descending into the London mist, Emma had returned for the dozenth time to the undeniable truth. She loved Harry desperately. If they did not grow as a couple, they would die. And she could not let that happen. But she was terrified of what came next.

Emma's internal argument carried her through customs and out the airport's main doors. She wished she could do what she had done a billion times before: flee from what she could not handle and bury herself in work. Only this time there was a new voice, soft as the English afternoon breeze, whispering that she wanted nothing more than to become Harry Bennett's lifelong love.

Which was when they struck.

The snatch-and-grab defined slick. No training exercise she had been involved in even came close. She was walking toward the taxi stand, just another weary woman focused on internal dilemmas. Two men walked up with easy smiles and open jackets and leather ID wallets in one hand. One said, "Agent Webb, we were sent to meet you."

"That really wasn't nec—"

One hand took her elbow to draw her toward the car that swept to the curb, lifting her arm just enough for the man's other hand to jab a knife at the nerve juncture below her ribs. The man said pleasantly, "Come with us or die. That is your only choice."

The other man bundled into the rear seat, dragging her inside. She braced for a strike, but the man in the front seat planted the barrel of a silenced pistol on her knee.

The lead man slipped in beside her and reinserted the knife into her ribs. "Do not force me to press harder, Agent Webb. It is ever so difficult to clean blood from seat leather. Believe me. I know."

The man's eyes were dark and fathomless. As clear a promise of agony as she had ever known. She froze.

"Excellent decision." The car pulled smoothly away. She glanced back, or tried to, but the knife pressed more deeply still. "We will make one circuit of the airport. We will speak. We will then deposit you back where we met. And we will vanish."

The man to her right was silent, unblinking. He was very compact, very still. He held her arm with a grip that Emma recognized from her time in training. His strength and his abilities were such that he did not need to prove anything. She knew this sort of man quite well.

The man holding the knife was more senior. Emma placed him as midfifties trim, with the polite detachment of a man who could maim and torture with soothing ease. His accent was crisply mid-Atlantic, the product of intense training. She asked, "Are you Russian?"

"We are nothing, Agent Webb. How could we be anything else, since this conversation is not taking place?"

"What do you want?"

"Sometimes mere words are so useless. I could have arranged a meeting and informed you politely that your Homeland Security and your CIA are chasing ghosts. And what would it prove? Nothing."

They reached the final roundabout marking the airport's perimeter. The Mercedes S-Class swept through the traffic and returned to the airport.

Emma took an easier breath. "You think this abduction proves anything?"

"But of course, Agent Webb. Think about what has just happened. We have demonstrated to you just how easy it would be for us to make you vanish." He said to the driver, "A little more slowly, please."

Emma said, "My superiors will issue a formal protest."

"Oh, I doubt that very much. Tip MacFarland is a true professional. He has suspected from the beginning that there was nothing behind the mire of double-dealing and myths."

"I'm still not clear on why we're having this conversation." She tried to break free of the man's grip on her right arm, but he merely slipped his hold down a half inch and probed the pressure point at her elbow. The pain was astonishing.

"No, Agent Webb, don't reach, don't shift; we won't be together much longer. Let us finish on a polite note." When she stilled, he nodded to the man opposite, who loosened his grip. The senior man went on, "Think on this, Agent Webb. We have just demonstrated how easy it would be for us to rip you from your life and make you disappear. We are professionals. Just like you."

"This proves what, exactly?"

"That is the first stupid thing you have said."

243

The car pulled into the middle segment designated for private cars to leave departing passengers. The man to her right slipped out and used his grip on her elbow to draw her with him. The senior man leaned over so that he could look up at her through the open door. The airport lighting turned his hair transparent. He offered her another polite smile. "Do be sure and give Agent MacFarland my warm regards. One professional to another."

THIRTY

STORM ARRIVED BACK AT THE Ognisko after midnight. She used the downstairs hallway phone to call Emma and Raphael and left terse messages, saying simply that she was fine and would be in touch. She showered in a bathroom from another age, then spent a while staring out the ancient sash window. Her upstairs room overlooked a busy street. Modern hotels rose in the distance. After a while she lay down. It felt like she was asleep before her head hit the pillow.

When she emerged late the next morning, Tanya was waiting in the front hall. "The dining room has shut for breakfast, but I can make you something. Would you like coffee?"

"Absolutely."

"Raphael Danton has phoned three times. I refused to disturb you. He was not pleased."

"I can imagine."

"I promised I would have you call him as soon as you woke up." She reached into her pocket and came out with a cell phone. "This is a pay-as-you-go phone. There is a hundred pounds' worth of credit on it."

"Thanks." Storm waited until Tanya disappeared into the kitchen to place the call.

The first words Danton spoke were, "Please tell me you are all right."

Hearing the voice of a man she had thoroughly detested until their last encounter should not have left her weak at the knees. "You won't believe what's been going on."

"Is it true what I heard about an abduction?"

"Sort of. I got saved at the last minute."

"Who did this?"

Storm hesitated. "I'm not supposed to say."

Danton asked, "Is it my fault?"

"It's definitely tied to whatever is going on."

He sighed. "I'm on my way to the Budapest airport. I should be in London by two. Where are you staying?"

"A club called the Ognisko." Storm glanced around. Tanya had vanished. Other than a bartender stacking glasses, the club appeared empty. "It's not all that great."

"I'll book you a room at Claridge's. It has the finest security system in London. I'll meet you there."

Tanya appeared bearing coffee and a plate of bread and butter and cold cuts. As she ate, Storm managed to get Harry on the phone the Arab woman had given him. His voice sounded reed-thin, but the man remained as cheerfully defiant as ever, insisting that he was fine, the doctors were nuts, he was getting out and joining them the next day. She then heard a nurse come in and beat the man with a verbal stick. Storm cut the connection and swiped her face. Her fingers came up dark with mascara.

She then called Curtis Armitage-Goode and said, "I'm sorry I stood you up."

"Great heavens, is this really you?"

"None other. Weary but intact."

"I heard you had been kidnapped. When you didn't arrive and I couldn't raise you by phone, I drove over to the auction. The police were positively swarming. Was that horrid Jacob Rausch behind your abduction?"

"I have no idea. What did you hear?"

"Only that he bought a round for the house after he heard you were abducted. That man is a weasel."

"Is the item we discussed still for sale?"

"Most certainly. But tell me what happened."

"Questions have to wait. Are you certain the owner is still motivated to sell?"

"Positively salivating."

"When can we wrap this up?"

"Soon as you arrive at my place."

"You have it in your possession?"

"My dear girl, I acquired it." Curtis was enjoying himself immensely. "Could hardly have done otherwise, could I? Not when that weasel Rausch started sniffing around."

"You are a dear, sweet man and I owe you."

"You do, actually, and rather a lot. When Rausch realized I was not going to resell the item to him, he had some particularly nasty things to say about my forebears."

Storm did not need a map and guide dog to track him. The item was hers so long as she matched Rausch's offer. "Can I have an item I purchased at the Cirencester auction be delivered to your shop?"

"Most certainly. Here, let me give you the name of my bonded shippers."

As Storm arranged the transfer of the paten to Curtis's shop, Tanya emerged from the kitchen. When she set down the phone, Tanya said, "I have been called away."

"Thank you again for saving my life back there in Cirencester."

"It was my job." Tanya handed her an embossed calling card with nothing except a telephone number. "Antonin Tarka says, call this day or night. Give your name, say what you need."

"Who is he?"

"A patriot. Antonin Tarka fought with Lech

247

Walesa against the Communists. Then he served in Walesa's government."

"You like him."

"I like working for a patriot. It makes for a nice change."

"What about you?"

"Some questions you cannot ask." Her gaze turned opaque. "Officially I am nothing. A tourist visiting London. You wish to see the Victoria and Albert Museum? I hear it is very nice."

"You believe all the stories about the Black Madonna icon?"

"The history, the legends, nobody knows. But I tell you something I do believe. I come from one of the towns we passed, Zawiercie. My father, he is an electrician. We have a little land. We raised some pigs. We did okay. I was the first of my family to go to university. My mother, she went to pray for me at Czestochowa. Every year she went. Sometimes with her local church in bus. Other times, she walked. Sixteen hours it took her. She walked and she prayed the rosary."

"I think I understand."

"The politicians and the educated people and the new rich, when they hear the Black Madonna is stolen, what will they do? They cry scandal, they point fingers, they shout and wave their arms. But the other Poland, the country still trapped in Soviet muck, they will suffer." Tanya pointed at the card in Storm's hand. "You hear something, you call the patriot. And remember. We only have a few more days. Then the politicians will learn what has happened, and my country will bleed."

CURTIS ARMITAGE-GOODE'S SHOP WAS ON the opposite side of Hyde Park, in the Mayfair district of London. The taxi drove to where Storm could see the minty green of Berkeley Square. The door gave a cheery ping as she entered.

"Great heavens, if it isn't my adventurous client." Curtis Armitage-Goode was as foppishly dressed as ever. Blue blazer, gray slacks of summertime flannel, college tie, and a silk handkerchief draped ever so casually from his jacket pocket. "Here, let me take that case. How are you, my dear?"

"Grateful I wasn't kidnapped."

"Your travails do suggest there are fates worse than bankruptcy. Tea?"

The Mount Street shop had two well-appointed rooms at street level and twice that space underground. When the Cirencester auctioneer's transport arrived, Curtis personally carried her acquisition downstairs, took the other article from his office safe, and arranged both on viewing stands. Storm knew the dealer wanted to give her the sort of polished presentation he would offer any respected client. So she spent the time on a bittersweet tour of his shop. Most of

Curtis Armitage-Goode's clients would hunker down and weather this economic hurricane. Curtis would survive intact. It was hard not to feel a little jealous.

Curtis walked over to where she admired a Rubens portrait and asked, "Will you tell me what happened?"

When Storm finished her quick rundown, he said, "You do run with a dangerous crowd. It leaves me positively giddy. Here I am, the most exciting part of my day is opening a tin of caviar for one of my overfed buyers. While you're out there defending yourself against international gangsters."

"You're making fun of me."

"Well, only a little." He waved her toward the pair of stands in the center of the room. "Shall we?"

The fact that they were in a glorified cellar was masked somewhat by high ceilings, two chandeliers, and a trio of fourteenth-century French tapestries covering the walls. The velvet display stands were placed beneath the room's central spotlights. Storm focused first upon the item Curtis had acquired for her, a single piece of rock crystal shaped like a grotto. The crystal cave contained a gold statue of Mary, mother of Jesus. Such carvings became a component of the early iconic tradition, when only a tiny minority of the population could read and write. Tradition had it that after Vespasian's invasion of Galilee in AD 67, the Holy Family relocated to a cave on the island of Patmos, where the apostle John wrote the book of Revelation.

Curtis rolled over a professional restorer's magnifying glass. The instrument was the size of a makeup mirror and rimmed in adjustable lights. "Perhaps this would help."

Storm settled onto a stool. The crystal grotto was framed with twelve images carved in gold, depicting the apostles, and topped by a gold crown embossed with gemstones. The crown, known as a diadem, contained a special carving at its uppermost point. Time had worn the emblem down to a mere shadow, but there was enough remaining for Storm to declare, "Leo the Second."

"My thoughts exactly."

In the fifth century, emperors began weaving the Chi-Rho symbol together with the imperial seal. Many such images held reputations for miracles.

Curtis noticed Storm's frown and asked, "Is something the matter?" When she did not respond, he said, "This is without question an exceptional piece. I know half a dozen museums that would match your offer and make this the pride of their Byzantium wing."

"My research has uncovered no link between any of the items I've acquired for my client," Storm replied. "Not their provenances, the list of previous owners and experts who had formally inspected the pieces. No overlaps. Nothing." What was more, the two treasures before her held no connection to Russia. Storm had searched back to the point where their histories had disappeared into medieval mists and come up empty. Yet she remained trapped inside a battle between two mystery buyers, with unnamed attackers and government spooks hovering in the background. "I don't get it."

"Well, if you don't mind me saying, perhaps you'd be better off not inspecting this particular gift horse too closely. After all, your company is surviving these perilous times because of this new buyer."

But the dealer's words only added to her frustration. "We're missing the point."

"Which is?"

Storm bent back over the magnifying glass. "I have no idea."

THIRTY-ONE

STORM SPOTTED EMMA AS SOON as the bellman tipped his hat and opened Claridge's brass Art Deco door. Emma was seated across the main foyer inside a formal gallery. Her table backed up to massive floral display. The pedestal was four feet across and supported a mountain of ivory-colored roses and lilies. Emma stared at nothing, her features tight with sunburned exhaustion.

A man's voice shouted, "Storm!"

Claridge's was not the sort of place where people normally yelled. Or ran, which Raphael Danton did, down the central staircase and across the marble-tiled foyer.

He met her beneath the main chandelier and swept her into an embrace. Storm caught sight of her own astonished reflection in a gilded mirror as he murmured, "I was so worried."

Storm normally hated anything that tore life out of her control. She also loathed being the center of attention, unless she chose to put herself there. Yet here she was, clenched by a man handsome enough to slow foot traffic in the next area code. Every eye in the hotel was on them. And all she could think was, He's so tall.

Over Raphael's shoulder, Storm watched a young woman follow him down the formal staircase. She was some exotic mixture of Asian and Western bloodlines and as precisely made up as a geisha. If Storm spent a full year in front of the mirror with an army of pros to do the makeover, she would never approach this girl's elegance.

This stylish young woman gawked in open-mouthed astonishment at Raphael.

Raphael broke off his embrace, touched Storm's face, started to speak, then noticed his watch. "We have to hurry."

"Excuse me?"

"We're expected at the Athenaeum in less than an hour." He glanced around. "Where is your luggage?"

"I left it with the man outside. Why?"

"You must change."

She looked down at herself. The gray suit carried the rumpled stains of a hard day. "This is the nicest thing I've got with me. And you need to—"

"No, no, this won't do at all. Sir Julius is extremely formal." Raphael spotted the hovering Asian woman.

And snapped his fingers.

The woman actually jumped. "Sir?"

Raphael said to Storm, "This is Muriel Lang. She is one of my personal—"

"Raphael."

"Storm, it is vital—"

"Don't snap your fingers."

It was hard to tell who was more shocked, the man or his aide.

Storm went on, "If you made a list of all the things that would send me straight through the roof, snapping your fingers at somebody would be at the tippy-top."

He colored. Started to speak. Then clenched down hard on whatever it was he was about to say. The effort left him sounding a bit strangled. "Tippy-top?"

"Be glad I'm not armed."

"Yes. Very well." He turned to the woman. "Take Ms. Syrrell to Bond Street. Chanel, perhaps. You know what is required. And give my compliments to the manager at Cartier; ask him for the loan of—"

"Raphael."

"Storm, please, it is vital—"

"We're not going anywhere." Storm pointed to where Emma stood by her table. "We have to speak with my friend."

"My dear, it simply is not—"

"Now, Raphael." She already had him by the arm. "Your people in Athens will understand."

"The Athenaeum," he said, correcting her. "It's a club."

"Swell. But we need to sit down and figure out what is going on."

Muriel said, "Sir, if I might suggest, I could shop for the lady myself."

Raphael allowed Storm to pull him toward the gallery. "Something elegant yet understated."

"I understand. Madame, might I ask your shoe size?"

"Nine and a half."

Raphael said, "Take the car. Bring back several selections. Don't forget Cartier. Hurry."

Emma frowned at Raphael's hold on Storm's hand as they approached. Storm rounded the table and hugged her friend. "Are you okay?"

"I'm alive. So is Harry. The rest is detail." Emma nodded a tight greeting to Raphael and said, "I need to ask you some questions."

"We are late for a most urgent—" He caught sight of Storm's warning glance and sighed. "Perhaps we should sit down."

Emma said, "I need to know who your client is."

Raphael studied her carefully but showed none of the outrage Storm would have expected. "Such information is highly confidential."

"This thing is moving too fast and has grown too big for you to play coy. Besides which, your client list is not legally protected. I know because I've checked. If it's necessary, I'll go to my British counterparts, explain the situation, and formally request that you be held in custody until it can be determined if any of your clients are actively involved in the financing or direct promotion of terrorism. But I'd prefer to deal with this over tea, wouldn't you?"

From the adjoining chamber, a violin trio began playing Gershwin. Raphael said simply, "I would rather like a cup of coffee."

"Order it yourself."

Storm said, "Emma."

"What?"

"Raphael is not our enemy."

"You sure about that? I'm trying to figure out what role he played in my abduction."

Storm said, "What abduction?"

Emma said, "I'm waiting, Danton."

Raphael signaled a passing waiter, ordered coffees, then asked, "How far will this information go?"

"I'm in the business of keeping secrets."

"My client is Sir Julius Irving."

Storm's own surprise was mirrored on Emma's face. "He's British?"

"Sir Julius Irving is a corporate solicitor who has risen to the pinnacle of British establishment. Knight of the British Empire, member of the Queen's Privy Council. He is related to the Earl of Gloucester, but as youngest son to the youngest son. According to one source, Sir Julius inherited all of the aspirations and none of the means. His fortune is his own."

"What are his connections to the Russian government?"

"None whatsoever that I have been able to determine. Sir Julius is fabulously wealthy. What is more, it is legitimate wealth. When all this started, I checked. Thoroughly. He holds interests in a number of Britain's oldest companies, a string of castle hotels in Scotland, several distilleries."

Storm asked, "Why is he bidding against Rausch's client?"

"That is a mystery for which I do not have an answer. Six weeks ago, the PA to Sir Julius contacted me. I was carefully vetted. I had no idea why. You must understand, most of my clients belong to the newest class of the wealthy. What I offer is not merely the power to acquire but also an understanding of how to be wealthy on an international scale. This goes far beyond where to shop. It amounts to a complete cultural make-over. That is why I am successful. But people like Sir Julius rarely use my services. They have family estates, private secretaries, butlers. They are conservative in their habits and established in their routines."

Raphael's calm candor did little to defuse Emma's ire. "None of this explains what happened to Storm. Or Harry. Or me. Or why we're attracting the attention of multiple intel divisions."

"I quite agree."

Storm asked Emma again, "You were abducted?"

"This afternoon." Emma related the events in terse bullets.

When she was finished, Danton said, "This was intended as a message. Russian intelligence has demonstrated to you in the clearest terms possible that if they had been behind Storm's kidnapping, she would not be alive."

"My boss in Washington said the same thing." Emma studied him, then went on. "I have been instructed to share some intel with you. In

258

strictest confidence. We have identified Rausch's client as one Vladimir Abramov."

Danton showed genuine surprise. "That is utterly impossible."

Emma said, "What are you talking about?"

"Vladimir Abramov is bankrupt."

"He is the buyer, Danton. We know that for certain."

"And I am telling you the man does not have ten cents to his name."

Emma said decisively, "So you know something Homeland Security doesn't?"

"About the new Russian billionaires, perhaps. And about Vladimir Abramov, apparently so."

"Homeland has done a careful rundown on the guy. He owns the majority share of Russia's largest aluminum producer."

"But over the past ten days the value of his holdings has effectively evaporated. In exchange for making Vladimir's debts vanish, the Russian government is quietly in the process of eating his assets whole." Danton held up his hand. "Please, Agent Webb. On this I am absolutely certain. One of my Russian clients is on the verge of collapse because of Abramov's unpaid debts. He is in Moscow as we speak, begging for crumbs."

Storm said, "So we have a British lord with no ties to the Russians, bidding against a Russian with no money. Does that make sense to you?"

"Not in the least." Danton rose to his feet.

"Which is why I am taking you to meet Sir Julius yourself. But we must hurry. The man positively despises being kept waiting."

THE SUITE RAPHAEL DANTON HAD booked for Storm was as intimate as an Art Deco teacup. The mirror frames were hand-embossed with the image of a slender woman in a flowing gown. The bed's headboard was inlaid with the design of two ballroom dancers ready to waltz her into sleep. The glass shower and the closet doors held etchings of similar figures. More were printed on the silk divan in the parlor. Storm wanted to stretch out and enjoy the place for a month. But Raphael's elegant young assistant laid out dresses on Storm's bed and pressed her with silent urgency.

Muriel stood with her hands clasped in front of her, not looking directly at Storm but keeping her in her field of vision at all times. Storm joined her beside the bed, surveyed the four dresses, and declared, "Wow."

"I think they are rather nice, given the short notice."

"They're fab. Which one would you choose?"

"Perhaps the green one here."

Muriel expertly helped Storm slip into the froth of emerald silk. The dress was fashioned as a twenties ball gown minus the train and ended just above her knees. The dress was gathered at two points, the left shoulder and the left hip, so that the hem flowed in an asymmetrical fashion. Storm stared at the strange apparition in the mirror and asked, "Is this Chanel?"

Muriel tore the wrapping off a pair of patterned stockings. "Balenciaga."

"You had time to hit two shops?"

"Seven. The shoes are from Ferragamo. Purse from Louis Vuitton. Jewelry from Cartier. And the gray shift is from Max Mara. But I see now it is too flashy. With your striking looks, it would be, well . . ."

"Overkill?"

"Quite."

Storm accepted heels of pale-green lizard skin, slipped them on, and rose to her feet. "Unless, of course, Raphael goes for overkill."

"Ms. Syrrell, I have served as Mr. Danton's personal aide for three years and two months. Until today, I would have thought it impossible for Mr. Danton to be diverted away from an urgent meeting with Sir Julius." Muriel joined her by the mirror. "If anyone on the planet needs less overkill than you do, I have yet to meet her."

"Will you do my makeup?"

"Certainly, madame."

"My name is Storm."

"Sit on the vanity stool, please."

"How much time do we have?"

"You and Mr. Danton are already late. Sir Julius

will be livid. He positively abhors being kept waiting, even by the queen." Muriel brushed at Storm's hair with strong professional strokes. "You will make your entrance and both gentlemen will instantly suffer from complete amnesia."

THIRTY-TWO

EMMA LEFT THE HOTEL, CROSSED the street, walked down a pedestrian passage, and slipped into a Starbucks. She doubted the coffee here would be as good as Claridge's. Certainly the paper cup did not measure up to their china. But the hotel was so much like her mother's idea of heaven that Emma had felt surrounded by years of bitter dispute.

She took a seat at the rearmost table and dialed Harry's number. "How are you?"

"Not bad, considering." Harry breathed with a slight wheeze but sounded alert. "The docs are holding off on some chest thing until the antibiotics kick in. They spent a couple of hours picking Hebron bricks and mortar out of my face. They say it should heal clean now."

"Are you up to hearing what's happened at this end?"

"You kidding? I'm laying here staring at a wall, wishing I was there to keep you two out of trouble."

Emma gave him a quick rundown of the airport abduction and finished with, "Those were the six most terrifying minutes of my entire life."

"And I wasn't there to protect you." Harry huffed a tight cough. "Man, if I wasn't already sick, that would just about do me in."

"I hate to tell you, sport, but even at your best you couldn't have done much against that crew." Emma related the events at the hotel. "I have been lied to by pros, Harry. And much as I don't like saying it, I think Raphael Danton is telling us the truth."

She was half expecting him to argue, which in a twisted sort of way would have suited her just fine. Put a little distance between them, given her ammo for pushing him away. Instead, Harry said, "Claridge's is one amazing place, isn't it?"

"Harry, did you hear anything I just said?"

"Every word. And a lot that wasn't spoken at all."

"What is that supposed to mean?"

"I've spent a lot of time here flat on my back thinking about us. I know something is eating away at you inside. All I want to tell you is, I think I'm fighting the same old ghosts. There's a lot I'll probably never get right in this life. But I've been staring at the truth, Emma, and I know I can't afford to be wrong about us. I trust you, lady. With my life. Whatever you want to give me, it's enough. That's all I've got to say."

She was still sitting there, holding the silent phone to her ear, long after Harry hung up.

HARRY HANDED THE PHONE TO the hovering nurse. He breathed as deep as the rising constriction allowed. "Thanks."

The nurse was a hard-bitten veteran of many battlefield hospitals. Even so, the light in her gaze made up for her gravelly voice. "I've met a lot of charmers in my time. You'd be amazed at how nice a fellow can be, flat on his back and staring at that final door."

Harry watched her slip the tourniquet up his arm and cinch it tight. "I can imagine."

"Lot of guys, they play macho until the moment the anesthetic shuts them down. Like they've got to prove they're still in control." She inserted the needle into his arm. "I thought that's what you were up to, waiting for this lady to phone before we wheeled you upstairs."

Harry realized she was apologizing. "I just needed a chance to set the record straight," he said.

"You were doing more than that, sport. You were being honest. That's a rare gift. I hope the lady appreciates that."

Harry watched her phone the operating room and say they were on their way. When she hung up, he pointed at the metal bedstand and said, "There's a letter in there addressed to the lady. If something happens, would you mail it to her?"

"You're a tough old bird. You'll do fine. But yes, in the unlikely event, I'll be happy to help out." She then called to the male orderly holding up the wall outside his door.

As they wheeled his bed out of the room and down the hall, Harry said, "The lady deserves more than I could ever give her."

"I wouldn't sell myself short, if I was you."

Harry felt his eyelids drifting south. "Wish I knew what to tell her."

She waited until they had him snug inside the elevator to pat his arm. "Trust your heart. From what I just heard, it's working wonders so far."

THIRTY-THREE

STORM'S SUITE IN CLARIDGE'S WAS on the British first floor, one level above the lobby. The lobby's ceiling was two stories high. Storm walked along an open-sided balcony to arrive at the staircase. She watched Raphael pace the lobby below her, arguing into his cell phone. He had changed into a suit dark as a tuxedo, a starched white shirt, and a black silk tie. His cuff links caught the chandelier's light as he waved his free arm in the air. His gaze drifted upward just as Storm started down the steps. The staircase was Georgian and shaped in a gradual curve. Raphael murmured a final word, stowed away his phone, and stood planted with treelike stillness by the bottom stair.

If Storm had ever known a finer compliment than this man's unblinking gaze, she could not recall it. Storm walked up to him and released a half-dozen thoughts all in one breath. "You look fabulous. I never knew black could look so good on a man. I want to pack Muriel up and take her home with me. I'm sorry I kept you waiting." She took a breath. "That didn't come out in very good order, did it?"

Raphael blinked once. "I have no idea."

They were bowed out the front door and into a waiting Rolls the color of old smoke. The driver took Storm's coat, a silk Balenciaga that shifted tone through the simple act of being folded and settled on the front seat beside Raphael's briefcase.

Raphael turned so that he could face her full-on. "The Athenaeum, Roger."

"Certainly, sir."

"And, Roger?"

"Yes, Mr. Danton."

"There is no need to hurry."

The driver shot Storm a tight smile in the rearview mirror. "As you say, sir."

Storm said, "In that case, could we stop by Mount Street and let me pick up one of Sir Julius's treasures?"

"Why not?" Raphael lifted a glistening bottle from the silver ice bucket. "Champagne?"

"Better not. I'm already flying."

He liked that enough to form dimples. "Do you mind if I have a glass?"

"Of course not."

"Thank you. I'm celebrating, you see."

"What's the occasion?"

"I'm not exactly certain." He popped the cork. "Does it matter?"

Storm caught another flash of humor from the driver's gaze. "Not a bit."

THE ATHENAEUM ANCHORED ONE CORNER of Pall Mall, the nexus of British political power. The structure was part Georgian palace, part Grecian temple. The entrance was reached by stairs broad enough to support a mounted honor guard. A liveried servant stood at attention beneath the Corinthian columns. He managed to bow a greeting and block the door in one smooth motion. Raphael Danton announced, "Sir Julius is expecting us."

"Certainly, sir. Your name, if you please?"

"Raphael Danton."

They were ushered through brass doors twenty feet high. A pair of guards flanked a reception desk that Storm would have been happy to place in her shop's front window. The doorman announced, "Mr. Danton and guest for Sir Julius."

"If you would be so kind as to sign the register,

sir? Might I have a look in your bag, madame?" When Storm opened the drawstring and showed him the sacramental plate, the man's eyes widened. He turned to his aide, a young man with a soldier's brush cut and white gloves. "Show our guests to the main library."

The interior stairs were thirty feet wide and flanked by more columns. Midway up, a Grecian statue saluted visitors from a recessed alcove. The entire establishment was meant to intimidate. But that evening Storm was immune. She liked the way Raphael looked up close. Which was surprising. Given what she knew of his background, she would have expected to find traces of hard living and too many close calls. "Who are you really? I'm only asking because the last time I was in London I met this other guy."

"Oh, him." Raphael shrugged. "He died in Africa."

"And that makes you who, exactly?"

He showed dimples once more. "I have no idea."

THE LIBRARY ROOM WAS FORTY feet long and almost as high. A circular staircase rose to a brass-railed balcony that ran around the walls. Every shelf was crammed with books. Storm would have stopped and gawked if not for the man seated at the oval table at the room's center.

Sir Julius Irving possessed a patrician's beak

and a Roman scowl. He lifted his attention from the magnifying glass he had been using to study an ancient text and glared. "Really, Danton. This is *utterly* unacceptable."

Storm had years of experience with the kind of man who blasted his ire across formal chambers. Her grandfather had been a master at the craft. Storm disengaged from Raphael and crossed the library alone. "Sir Julius, my name is Storm Syrrell. And I am the reason why we are late tonight."

"Storm—"

"No, Raphael. I will not let you take the blame. Sir Julius, may I?" Storm knew the best way to handle such a menace was speed. She unfolded the plate's display and set it atop what appeared to be a tome of eighteenth-century maps. She drew the paten from the sack, set it into the display, and stepped back with, "I wanted to personally deliver your most recent acquisition."

The room's principal illumination came from a massive brass chandelier directly overhead. Torchlight might have had a stronger effect, but the present atmosphere would do in a pinch. Especially when Sir Julius said, "Most impressive."

"Thank you, sir."

"But you should have accomplished your duties and arrived at the appointed hour."

"I'm sorry. But that simply was not possible."

Sir Julius wore his pinstriped suit like robes of imperial power. He surveyed her coldly for a moment, then reaimed his ire across the room. "In that case, Danton, you should have instructed your staff person to retrieve this item on her own while you arrived here on time."

Storm replied, "I asked him to accompany me, Sir Julius."

"That simply will not do. I despise tardiness, young lady, as Danton well knows."

"Just the same, Sir Julius, I was attacked two days ago while acquiring this item."

He lifted the magnifying glass and inspected the paten's rim. "Attacked how?"

Raphael replied, "There was an attempted abduction."

Storm watched the gentleman lean in closer to the plate and decided he already knew about the abduction. He asked, "And where is my second treasure?"

"In the safe of the dealer who helped me track it down."

He set down the glass and declared, "The rim is not original to the paten."

"It was a common practice for icons and other holy articles to which miracles had been attributed to be given further decorations," Storm replied. "Many considered it an act of veneration. My estimate is that the border was added around the tenth century."

He examined her with the same calculating chill he had applied to the plate, then pushed his chair back from the table. Only when he rose to his feet did Storm realize the man was almost seven feet tall. "Allow me to show you out."

THIRTY-FOUR

MORE THAN FIFTY OF OUR club's members have won the Nobel Prize, at least one in every category. Makes for a rather nice fillip for future generations, wouldn't you agree?"

Sir Julius walked with a marked stoop, which granted him a false sense of vulnerability. This was magnified by his diffident manner of speech. But one look into his ice-blade gaze left Storm certain Sir Julius would send a man to the gallows or a nation to war without pause or a backward glance.

Their progress was tracked by the same footman who had led them upstairs. Only now he carried the velvet sack in his white-gloved grip. Sir Julius halted before the staircase and said, "It was here that Charles Dickens finally made up his rather violent quarrel with Thackeray. They had not spoken for more than twelve years, but Thackeray was dying, and Dickens did not want to have his former closest friend carry their argument to his grave. I've always found that rather touching."

Storm sensed this running commentary was his way of keeping her from asking any questions. She broke in with, "Do you have any idea who is behind the attacks against me?"

He peered at her with the same displeasure he might have shown a wayward serf. "Your question, young lady, is unreservedly incorrect. What you should be doing is reporting on who dares bid against me."

"We have a name."

"Then be so good as to tell me."

"Vladimir Abramov."

Sir Julius possessed the ability to frown with his entire being. "Has he not recently suffered a setback?"

"The man is bankrupt," Raphael said. "Completely."

"Then what you are telling me makes no sense whatsoever."

Storm nodded. "I agree."

"This is not acceptable. If you wish to remain in my employ, I expect you to deliver not merely the merchandise but the opposition." His farewell was a brushing gesture of those long arthritic fingers, shooing them away. "You may be in touch when you have something of value to offer."

They were shepherded downstairs and ushered with polite firmness out the front doors. They exited the building to discover a light rain had settled upon the city.

Raphael peered through the gloom. "I don't see our car."

The footman stopped in the process of shutting the club's front door and said, "They're quite strict about stopping here, sir. I saw him make a circuit not long back."

As Raphael took out his phone, Storm walked to the top stair and watched the passing traffic. He joined her and said, "My driver is not answering."

"I don't mind waiting."

"You did very well inside." He studied her. "To be honest, I'm surprised you don't seem more angry."

Storm sniffed. "My grandfather on a bad day would have fried Sir Julius hard as he liked his eggs."

"The first time he shooed me off I was livid for a week."

"He's paying the bills, Raphael. Big ones. He can treat us any way he wants, and he's enough of a snob to enjoy it. That's his problem."

"Now you're stealing my best lines."

"If you keep making dimples at me I can't concentrate."

"Sorry. How's that?"

She wanted to kiss him. Just hurl herself into his arms and kiss him so hard it bruised both their lips. But at that moment a car sliced through the wet night and halted by the curb.

Raphael said, "Let's talk on the way to dinner."

Storm sighed over lost opportunities. "We're going to dinner?"

"I made us reservations at Cipriani." He halted at the first stair. "Is that all right?"

"Yes, Raphael. It's fine."

"You look disturbed. I should have asked. Is that it?"

"No . . . well, yes, okay. A girl likes to know if she's going on a date. But that's . . ." Suddenly Storm was glad the footman had slipped back inside, leaving them alone with the night. "I wanted to kiss you."

"You're blushing."

"Never mind."

"I've never seen you blush." He closed the distance between them. "Or look more beautiful."

WHEN RAPHAEL FINALLY RELEASED HER, Storm carried the feel of his arms into the night. As they left the alcove and began to descend the steps, the rain felt marvelous on her face, a veil soft as his scent.

Raphael asked, "Why isn't Bernard out of the car?"

Storm pretended she needed his arm to manage the slick stone stairs. "Who?"

"Our driver. He should be up here with your coat and my umbrella."

"He might get wet."

"He might . . . that was a joke."

"A bad one."

"No, no, it was actually quite . . ."

"What's the matter?"

"Something is wrong." He stopped and raised his voice. "Bernard!"

"He hasn't seen us. Let's just get—"

"He hasn't seen us because he isn't looking." Raphael spun her about. "Move back up the stairs."

The feel of his lips lingered like the tendrils of deep sleep. Her mind simply refused to accept the change. "But that's—"

He pushed her, rougher now. "Go!"

Raphael's features were taut with feral alarm. He bundled her up, lifting her off her feet like she was weightless, and ran for the club entrance.

Over his shoulder, Storm saw a man rise from the car. Instantly she recognized the attacker from Cirencester. "That's him!"

It was not the clearest alarm she had ever spoken. But it was still enough to spur Raphael to greater speed. The attacker settled his arm upon the Rolls's roof and aimed a pistol at them. The bangs were as sharp as the light, hard flashes of sound and flame.

Raphael jerked and coughed and literally tossed her behind the first pillars.

He collapsed half inside the alcove's protection. Granite chips splintered from the column above Storm's head. She scrambled across the landing before her feet actually found purchase on the wet granite. Someone shouted from the doorway behind her. Storm heard a scream closer at hand. And realized she had made the noise.

The car door slammed and the vehicle sped away. Raphael clutched at his shoulder with one hand and reached toward her with the other.

Storm slipped down beside him, gripping him as hard as she dared. Her hands and her body felt drenched by a slick lava. Raphael arched up, as though the top stair's corner cut into his back.

"I'm a doctor. Are you hurt?" The voice came from above her.

Storm knew she should respond. But it would have meant turning a fragment of her attention away from Raphael.

"Step away, miss. Give me room."

She did not move so much as allow herself to be slid back. She made no protest until her grip on Raphael's hand was threatened. She must have complained, because the hands allowed her to remain where she was. But she heard nothing. There was no room for anything except Raphael's face.

He blinked slowly, his lashes long nets that captured the misting rain. His eyes tracked her, even as the doctor and two footmen shifted him slightly so as to inspect his back. He tried to speak. She saw him shape her name. Then his gaze drifted up and away.

And he saw no more.

THIRTY-FIVE

THEY HAD TO RESTART RAPHAEL'S heart twice on the ride to the hospital. Storm refused to let go of his hand even while the doctor and the ambulance aide worked on him. The ambulance was one of the newer versions that in an emergency could serve as a pre-op unit. Storm knew this because the doctor told her. He was the same man who had knelt beside her on the Athenaeum's front steps, a member of the club who happened to be inside when the shots sounded. He was an older man and quite stout. He had difficulty bending over his belly to work on Raphael. But work on him he did, and with a dogged tenacity that Storm found reassuring.

The second time he applied the paddles, the doctor got down tight in Raphael's face and shouted so loud his voice broke, telling Raphael to hang on. The ambulance aide worked alongside the doctor. His face was bone pale in the flashing lights. Storm gripped the stretcher's steel railing with her free hand and knelt on the vehicle's metal flooring. She was tossed about every time the top-heavy vehicle took a corner. Up ahead a police car wailed, ramming through the city traffic and the rain. Storm knew she shouted at Raphael as well, begging him not to leave her. But she still could not hear her own voice. She could hear everything else perfectly well. But the only way she knew she was shouting was that her throat hurt worse than her knees.

When they pulled up in front of the hospital, two orderlies threw open the doors and hauled her bodily from the back. "Are you hurt, miss?"

"Leave her," the doctor barked. "This is the one you want."

One orderly helped the doctor and the ambulance aide pull out Raphael's stretcher and extend the wheels. But the other man remained by Storm's side. He spoke with a Caribbean accent. "The blood here, miss. Is any of it yours?"

Storm looked down at herself. The silk dress clung to her body. The front was black from neckline to hem.

The strength in her legs simply departed.

The orderly was both experienced and strong. He caught her easily and settled her onto the ambulance's broad rear step. "You steady up, now. Your man in there needs you to be strong for him, you hear?"

Storm watched the stretcher roll through the emergency room doors. "I'm okay."

"You're more than that, lady. You been strong all this night. You rest easy there; you can't go with him now anyway." He reached into the ambulance and came out with a blanket that he settled around her shoulders. "You're not hurt?"

"No." The rain coalesced at the edges of her eyes. "He shielded me."

"So now you do the same for him, hear?" The orderly pointed to where two police officers hovered. "There's some hard people looking to ask you some hard questions."

THE POLICEMAN'S ATTITUDE TOOK A turn for the worse when he established that Storm was linked to an earlier shooting and possible abduction. Storm could not have cared less. "Are you aware that the police have been trying to contact you, miss?"

"Can we please go inside? Raphael is—"

"When we're done." He was big boned and muscular but so fleshy as to erase all angles. "Wouldn't it seem obvious that someone involved in a shooting should make themselves known to the authorities?"

"I was out of the country." Storm heard the rain speak to her then, a sibilant whisper that anything she said would only trap her further. She turned toward the hospital's urgent-care entrance.

The policeman's firm grip anchored her to the night. "Not so fast."

A voice shrilled, "Hold it right there!"

As soon as Storm heard Emma's voice, she released her own tight hold on control. She was already sobbing so hard she could not draw breath when Emma shoved herself between Storm and the policeman and said, "Steady."

"They shot—"

"I know. Muriel called. She heard about it from somebody called Julian or Julius."

The policeman demanded, "And you are?"

"Emma Webb. U.S. Homeland Security."

The woman officer said, "We definitely need to move this lot to the Yard."

"You go anywhere you like," Emma snapped. "I am taking this woman inside."

"We'll move when and where I say and not—"

"You are so far out of your pay scale we're not even breathing the same atmosphere. Now back off."

The policewoman said, "I'm calling for assistance."

"You will do no such thing!" Leather heels marched smartly across the tarmac, and a tall shadow inserted himself into Storm's fractured gaze. "My dear young lady. What an utterly dreadful turn of events. And on the front stairs of my club."

The policeman demanded, "And which part of this circus act do you play?"

"How *dare* you take such a tone with me. I'll have you know I'm a member of the Queen's Privy Council!"

"The lady is soaking wet," Emma said. "And she's covered in the man's blood and trembling so hard I'm worried she might be going into shock."

"You don't mean to tell me they've kept you out here in the—"

"Sir, we have every reason to believe this woman is involved in crimes against the state," piped the blond officer.

"Oh, piffle. She *defines* the very concept of victim," said Sir Julius. "And at the hands of our own constabulary. Which is why I intend to make your careers vanish in a puff of smoke. Now out of my way!"

SIR JULIUS TOOK CHARGE. EMMA played the silent friend, a comforting strength who filled the seat beside Storm and held her hand. Eventually the ward sister brought towels and a set of surgical blues. The nurse dismissed the police's objections with a sniff and led Storm back to a private shower.

When Storm returned, the policewoman was talking on her phone and the male officer looked cowed. Sir Julius turned from the doctor speaking with him and said, "This doctor refuses to tell me anything whatsoever of value."

The doctor explained, "We won't know anything for another few hours."

Sir Julius flicked the doctor away, much as he had dismissed Storm earlier. "Look here, Ms. Syrrell. I am late for a function where I am the guest of honor. Do be so good as to let me know of any development. No matter what the hour." Sir Julius turned to the hovering police. "I assume we understand one another now. Yes? Splendid."

As the tall man strode down the hospital corridor, Muriel Lang hurried toward them. She carried a suitcase and a practical air, despite her red eyes and broken voice. "How is Raphael?"

"Still in surgery."

"I apologize for not being here sooner. But Raphael left explicit instructions on what steps to take in just such an emergency. I was not about to let him down." She handed over the valise to Storm. "I stopped by the hotel for your things."

"Thanks."

"When I leave here I'll move you out of Claridge's and into the guest room of Raphael's Chelsea loft."

"Fine." Storm saw Emma frown over the news. Storm did not care. She wasn't going anywhere.

Three hours later, the doctors moved Raphael into a room in the hospital's newer wing. The hallway formed a horseshoe around the central nurses' station. The patients' rooms all had walls of glass facing the station. The beds were stationed so that the patients faced the nurses. Gauze curtains could be swept across to offer incomplete privacy. Only one visitor at a time was permitted inside. There was no sign saying this wing housed the hospital's new crisis center. None was required.

Raphael was wired and tubed. He breathed because a machine beside Storm's chair pumped up his lungs and beeped in time with his heart. His chest was bruised in a multitude of places that did not make sense. His skin had a waxy translucence. His eyelashes looked impossibly long. The man was handsome even when unconscious.

The doctor who had saved Raphael's life during the ambulance ride was named Jeremy Brenneman and was the former president of the Royal College of Surgeons. "Your gentleman friend is with us because I had declined the offer of a vintage armagnac and was standing in the foyer when the shots rang out." He watched the way she stroked the hair on Raphael's forearm and changed course. "Your fellow was struck by two bullets. His ribs deflected the first. The other unfortunately punctured a lung. Either because of blood loss or trauma or our need to restart his heart, he has slipped into a coma. This is the sort of blanket term we doctors like to use when we have no earthly idea what precisely is going on."

Muriel drifted over from the nurses' station. To avoid breaking the one-visitor rule, she hovered just outside the sliding glass door.

"My guess is, he might breathe on his own if we let him. But I am keeping him on the ventilator in order to offer a bit of assistance. Keep him regular, as it were."

"Will he . . ."

"I have no earthly idea. Nor does anyone else. In my forty years of practice I have seen patients suffer the most horrendous of shocks and fall into such comas as part of the recuperative process. Why this happens, nobody knows. His bodily signs are strong. But he is not fully with us. There may be something we missed in the repair business, but I doubt it." To give his hands something to do, he fitted the stethoscope to his ears and gave Raphael's chest a careful listen. He stowed the instrument back in his pocket and declared, "Heart is strong as an ox."

Storm knew he was talking for her benefit and struggled to shape the words, "Thank you, doctor."

"Observe this, if you would." Brenneman probed a deep cavity by Raphael's right shoulder. "If I were to hazard a guess, I'd say this was caused either by shrapnel or a ruddy great spear."

"Raphael fought in Africa."

"Did he now. I suppose that's where he picked up the burn marks across his thigh?"

Storm wiped her eyes and shook her head. "I don't know."

"What I mean to say is, this fellow has been through some very rough scrapes. And he's survived. I see no reason why he shouldn't do so again."

"How long before we know?"

"I cannot say." He walked around the bed and

slipped between her and the patient. "Now I'll tell you what I do know, if you'll be so kind as to pay close attention. That's better. What we have learned from talking with patients who return from such forays is this. They are still with us. How precisely, we have no idea. But many are able to repeat almost verbatim everything that was said while they were incapacitated. They say they were utterly aware, simply unable to reply."

"You want me to talk with him."

"I want you to do more than that, young lady. I want you to *engage* him. Because we have also learned that such discussions seem to draw them back from wherever they might currently reside."

"I can do that."

"I should hope so. But first you must maintain your strength. I'm going to ask the sister to bring you a tray. I want you to eat everything on it. Including the napkin and utensils. If you don't, I will come back and be most cross with you. And if you ask any of the wretched students who have suffered my wrath, this is something to avoid at all costs." Brenneman moved for the door. "I'm also going to prescribe something I want you to take. No, young lady, don't even think of objecting. You've been through your own shock. You will take the tablet and you will have a good night's rest. I'll have them make up the divan there so you can remain at his side. But sleep you will, or you and I will have words."

The ward nurse brought Storm a tray and insisted she leave Raphael's room to eat. The main waiting room was a collage of cheery pastels. Sky-blue floor melted into butterscotch walls with creamy drapes covering nighttime windows. The children's play area was done in lavender and rose. One door led off to a conference area, the other to a small chapel. All the rooms had interior windows so that the nurses could sit at their station and observe everything.

Eating proved to be a terrible trial. Storm tasted nothing. All she could smell was the hospital. Twice she almost lost it, the gorge rising as she struggled over another bite. Emma basically stalked her, standing so close her shadow loomed over the little table rolled in front of Storm's chair.

Muriel was stationed in the doorway, from where she could look back and see the entrance to Raphael's room. "The sister is going to give her a tablet to make her rest."

Emma shot the woman a tight look. "Can you give us a minute?"

If Muriel was offended, she gave no sign. "Of course. I'll just go have a few minutes with Raphael."

Emma waited until she left the room, then asked, "You trust her?"

"Raphael did and so do I."

Emma mouthed a silent okay. "What about Sir Beanstalk?"

Storm tried for another bite of the overboiled potatoes, then set down her fork in defeat. "He helped me with the police."

"Which would make sense, if he didn't want the cops looking too closely at something."

"Do you distrust everybody?"

"Almost." Emma waited while the nurse brought in a pill and stood over Storm while she took it. When they were alone once more, Emma went on. "You're going back to the man's apartment?"

"His name is Raphael, and I'm not going anywhere. They're making me up a bed in his room. What about you?"

"Muriel's booked me into a hotel around the corner. The lady is efficient, I'll give her that." Emma stared through the glass wall, past the nurses' station, to the open glass door leading to Raphael's room. "I need to report back, let Tip know what's happened."

"And Harry."

Emma nodded, then lowered her voice. "I left Harry on a sour note."

It felt good to have something else to worry about. "You two argued?"

"It would probably have been easier if we did. But no. Harry was a perfect gentleman. I was the one in a borderline panic." Emma kneaded the soft leather of her shoulder bag. "I'm a United States federal agent. I'm highly skilled in unarmed combat. I hold an expert rating in small arms. A couple of days back I took out two armed men with my bare hands. Now I've been totally undone by the finest man I've ever known."

Storm replied, "I'm going to sit here and pretend that makes sense."

"You're not helping. At all."

"Harry loves you. You love him. I don't see the problem."

"You don't know what baggage I'm carrying."

"Oh, and Harry is mister perfect?" Storm was suddenly engulfed by a wave of fatigue. "Wow."

"What's the matter?"

"The pill she gave me feels like a velvet hammer." Storm gripped the chair arms and forced herself to her feet. "I'm going to bed."

She walked past the nurses' station and arrived at the entrance to Raphael's room. She found Muriel seated in a chair. One hand clutched the sheet, the other held Raphael's limp fingers. Muriel's face was buried in the bedcovers. She wept softly.

Storm returned to the waiting room, determined to make a little more noise on her next arrival. She found Emma still seated there, staring at nothing. Storm declared, "Muriel is on our side."

THIRTY-SIX

THE PILL KEPT STORM DOWN for almost eight hours. Several times she relived the attack, great booming flashes that shredded a soft rain and softer kiss. Each time she almost surfaced, drawing close enough to wakefulness to hear the hospital sounds and smell the sharp odors. Then the drug's languid claws dragged her back down again.

She finally rose from the narrow divan just after seven. The ward nurse smiled a professional good morning as she checked Raphael's status. Storm tried to shape the words, but her brain was still clogged by the pill. The nurse understood her anyway and said, "Your young gentleman had a restful night. At this stage, you should take that as good news."

Storm carried the words, along with the things Muriel had brought, into the shower room. She returned not restored but at least awake. She sat for a time beside Raphael's bed. He seemed a bit paler than the day before, the bruises protruding from his shoulder bandage much more savage in color.

She knew the ward nurse would probably bring her breakfast, but she had not left the hospital floor since her arrival the previous evening. Even a visit to the cafeteria was a welcome break.

As she crossed the lobby and passed the hospital gift shop, a rumpled bear approached her. That was how he appeared to Storm in her coffeeless state, a frizzy-haired man over six feet tall, wearing a dark, wrinkled suit. "Tell me you're Syrrell."

"Excuse me?"

"Storm Syrrell. That is you, right?"

She edged closer to the entrance of the hospital gift shop, scouting for someone who would hear her scream. "And you are?"

"Your new best mate." He moved in close enough for her to catch his stale odor. "The bloke who can bring you the Amethyst Clock."

She backed up. "Where did you hear about that?"

"A little bird." He leered. "A cockatoo, to be exact. Drapes a silk hankie from his pocket. Likes to think he's better than the rest of us."

It could only be Curtis Armitage-Goode. "The Amethyst Clock doesn't exist."

"You know that. I know that. So does the cockatoo. But he's asking about it anyway. Which means you've latched on to a client with too much of the ready and no brains to speak of. Tell me I'm right."

Emma stepped through the hospital's front doors, spotted her, and rushed over. "Is this man bothering you?"

The bear took on an affronted air. "The lady

and I happen to be having a conversation of the private variety."

"She stays," Storm said. A faint chime sounded in her brain. One strong enough to pierce the pill's fading haze. "Go on."

The guy glared at Emma but continued. "I can have a clock like that made up. We'll split the take."

Emma started to speak, but Storm shook her head, both to squelch the outburst and to focus the jumble in her brain. "Go on."

"I got my hands on a Chilean amethyst. Single geode. Eleven and a half inches tall. Shaped like an egg. Primo grade."

His kind was known as a predatory dealer. They lurked around the edges of her profession. They dealt in false certificates of authenticity and goods with no past. Storm had spent years avoiding just such a conversation. But just then, she feared if the man walked away she would lose this thread of an idea.

"I know a bloke, he's got his hands on a sixteenth-century chronograph. The workings fit inside the geode like they was made for each other. I know on account of how I scoped it out yesterday, soon as I heard from your cockatoo. I got me a mate, he can do wonders with gold. Carve us a stand that'll sit up and beg for your buyer to take it home."

But the idea would not take shape. Storm

stepped away from the stale cigarettes on the guy's breath. "No, thanks."

"This is fate, I'm telling you. Banging on your front gate, begging for you to open up, make us both rich."

But Storm was already moving away. "Good-bye."

STORM CUT UP TWO PEACHES, mixed them into yogurt, and forced herself to eat it. Emma sat across from her at the hospital cafeteria table and complained over her willingness to listen to the predator, until she realized Storm was paying no attention to her.

Storm took her last cup of coffee upstairs. She settled Emma into the waiting room, then returned to Raphael's bedside. The idea sparked by the predator stayed with her, nebulous and just out of reach. She settled into the chair by Raphael's bed. She should talk to him like he was awake, the doctor had said. Not just talk; engage him. Use her voice to draw him back.

"I need to walk through everything that's happened. It's the only way I can think to make sense of it all." Storm felt funny sitting there, talking to a guy whose only response was the dual beeps of his heart monitor and lung pump. Then the nurse at the central station looked up, smiled at Storm, and went back to her paperwork. Like it was not only normal but proper.

Storm shifted her chair so the partly open drapes blocked her view of the central station. She looked straight into Raphael's face, which was disconcerting at first, but then it no longer mattered, because she became increasingly drawn into the one-sided conversation.

Storm found an odd semblance growing among the various events. Like a puzzle built of fragmented lives and hidden motives and a love demolished before it could take form. She had not seen this before. She had been too caught up, first in finding a way to save her company, then in Harry's supposed death, then in the sudden chance to experience international life in the first-class fast lane. Twenty minutes into her lopsided conversation, Emma delivered a cup of tea, then leaned in the doorway and listened. At first Storm felt uncomfortable chatting with an audience, but Emma started nodding in time to her points.

A few minutes later, Muriel slipped in and fitted herself into the corner. Tanya followed soon after. Emma greeted them both with hard frowns. Neither gave any sign she noticed.

When Storm took a break, Emma asked point-blank, "Do you trust these ladies?"

"Yes." She nodded a greeting to Tanya. "It's good to see you again."

"I bring the respect and sympathies of our friends," Tanya replied. "We only heard this morning."

"I should have called. But—"

"They say to tell you that I may remain here with you until we resolve the issue or it goes public. That is, if you find this acceptable."

"I could think of nothing finer."

Emma sighed. "Storm . . ."

"What, Emma?"

Emma stared at the linoleum by her shoes. Shook her head. Said nothing.

Storm looked from one woman to the next, then she said, "Maybe I should take it from the top. Start over. See if you can help me connect the dots."

"I would like that," Muriel said. "Very much."

Emma sighed but did not speak. Storm got a firmer grip on Raphael's hand and began anew. She found a greater sense of clarity in the retelling. No sudden bursts of illumination, but a clearer fix upon the bonds between the various elements.

Fifteen minutes into her second round, the ward nurse slipped past Emma and said, "There is a perfectly good reason for our one-visitor policy."

"This is important," Storm replied.

"Very," Muriel said.

"Vital," Tanya agreed.

The nurse took Raphael's pulse. She checked the monitors. "Be that as it may, you should take your discussions into the waiting room."

"We can't," Storm replied.

"Whyever not?"

"Because," Muriel replied. "Raphael needs to hear this."

"Does he now." The nurse studied them in turn. "Well, in that case, I suppose you'd best bring in some extra chairs. Only do please unblock the doorway so we can keep watch on the patient."

With the other women in place, Storm resumed her story. When she finished describing the attack in Cirencester she paused, wondering if she would be violating Tanya's confidence if she continued. She looked the question at the Polish woman. In reply, Tanya spoke directly to Emma. "You are U.S. intel, correct?"

"Homeland Security."

"Can you accept this information and not pass it on to anyone else?"

Emma bristled. "You're singling me out?"

"I know all about lines of authority and official reports," Tanya replied. "You and I, we speak the same language in different tongues. So yes, I am asking."

Muriel asked Tanya, "Why are you trusting us at all?"

"Excuse me," Emma said. "*She* is trusting *us?*"

Tanya pointed at Storm. "This woman has taken us far and paid the price. But we are still at a loss for answers and running out of time. I begged my superiors to let me return here because I think—no, I hope—she may have the answer. How, I do not know. Or why. But this is what I am hoping." Tanya kept her gaze on Emma. "Keep the lid on what you are about to hear for two days. That is all I am asking for."

Emma looked from one woman to the other, then said, "I'll wait for your word before reporting in."

"Everyone here must understand, this is highly confidential." Tanya searched the three other faces and must have found what she sought, because she nodded at Storm. "You may tell them."

Storm outlined what had happened at the Polish club, then recounted the trip to Poland and the missing Madonna.

She summarized their meeting with Sir Julius need to say anything about the attack. The results were lying in the bed between them.

Emma broke the silence with, "I don't get it."

"I agree," Muriel said.

"With all due respect," Emma said to Tanya, "there's no way your missing icon would have the U.S. intelligence community so interested. I mean, let's be realistic. You could have the crown of thorns go missing and the CIA would just yawn."

"Emma is right," Storm said. "We're all looking in the wrong direction."

Emma asked Tanya, "Why two days?"

"People in my government have begun to whisper. Rumors are circulating. In two days, we go public with news of the theft. And then, everything changes."

THIRTY-SEVEN

MURIEL LEFT TO CHECK ON Raphael's business. Emma could not reach Harry, but she spoke with the military hospital nurse and hung up somewhat reassured. Tanya stationed herself in the waiting room and made several calls of her own. Storm felt swamped by waves of fatigue, which she took as a good sign. If she was going to track the attackers, she needed to rest well and return to full alert. Identify the enemy, hunt them down, and end this thing. Which meant giving in to her need for rest. Storm stretched out on the divan beside Raphael's bed. She closed her eyes and was gone.

The dream arrived in a very subtle fashion. Storm dreamed that she opened her eyes to discover Raphael watching her. All she could think to say was, "Are you awake?"

"I should be asking you that." He pointed to the chair beside his bed. "Come sit beside me."

She did so and took his hand in both of hers. A current passed through her fingers, strong as breath and so vivid she felt her body begin to tremble. "Am I in love?"

"You want me to look into your heart and tell you?"

"Of course."

"It doesn't work like that."

"Why not? I want to love you and I want you to love me back."

"Storm."

"Where are your dimples? You're smiling but your face isn't creasing."

"Listen to me, Storm."

"I love how you say my name."

"You need to finish the discussion you have started with your friends. You need to identify the answer."

"I know. I will."

"Do it now."

But she didn't want to talk about attackers and threats and trauma. She wanted to sit there and stare into that lovely face and be in love. "Can I kiss you?"

"Pay attention. This is important."

"It sure is."

"You know the answer. It's right there waiting for you."

"All right."

He took a long breath and then softly sang the words, "And now I must go."

"No. You can't."

He removed his hand from hers. Storm didn't want to let him go, but she was powerless to stop him. He sat up and slipped his legs from the bed's other side. "Good-bye, Storm."

"I won't let you leave." Only now she was the one trapped and he was moving. She tried to rise from the chair and follow him as he started from the room. She intended to scream the words, yet they came out a fragile whisper of woe. "Wait for me."

As Raphael passed the nurses' station, he turned and smiled at her once more. Then he was gone.

AS STORM CAME SLOWLY AWAKE, an idea drifted into her consciousness. She was fairly certain it was the same one that had come to her while she listened to the predatory dealer pitch his fake clock. Only now it carried a whisper of clarity.

Then she opened her eyes and the idea vanished. A nurse leaned over Raphael. Storm flashed back to the dream's final image and started to lunge for the bed.

Then she realized the nurse was smiling.

"What is it?"

"I thought I saw him move," the nurse replied. "There was a blip on the monitor, a slight change in his rhythms. I came in for a peek, and I thought he shifted. I've been waiting to see if he'll do it again."

Storm watched the nurse fit the stethoscope to her ears and give his chest a listen. When the sister straightened, she asked, "Anything?"

"Not yet. I will admit, I've had worse duties than watching this lad sleep." The nurse made a notation in Raphael's file, then said, "A police inspector is in talking with your friends. He wanted to wake you but I wouldn't let him. He was most insistent."

"I'm glad you refused." Storm slipped into the bedside chair and took hold of Raphael's hand. The idea that had come to her upon awakening was gone now. She sat there a minute, trying to draw it back. Then she said, "I dreamed we were talking."

"Perhaps you were. You hear of some quite remarkable events in this unit." The nurse gave her another moment, then quietly said, "You should go see to the inspector."

Storm rose from her chair, looked down at Raphael, and whispered, "Was it you?"

The heart monitor beeped. The lung compressor sighed.

The nurse waited until Storm rounded the bed to ask, "Your young man told you something nice, did he?"

THE MAN QUESTIONING HER FRIENDS wore a tan suit with creases so deep that they looked ironed on. He was trim and compact, with the lean features of an aging runner. He watched her enter the room and said, "Storm Syrrell?"

"That's right."

"Inspector Mehan." He offered her a card. "Scotland Yard."

Emma said, "He is investigating the murders."

Mehan rose to his feet. "I'd like to speak with Ms. Syrrell alone, please."

Muriel said, "As her attorney, I cannot permit that."

That brought them all around. Storm asked, "You're a lawyer?"

"The proper term," Muriel replied, "is solicitor."

The inspector demanded, "Why should Ms. Syrrell require representation?"

"Why do you wish to speak with her alone?"

Storm held up her hand. "What do you mean by 'murders'? Raphael is not dead."

"Raphael's driver was found stuffed in the trunk of the Rolls," Emma said. "Along with the shooter. Both professional hits."

Mehan looked pained. "Might I inquire how you obtained information related to confidential police inquiries?"

"Sir Julius stopped by." Emma said to Storm, "He says you may call him at any time, for any reason."

The detective liked this even less. "Precisely what connection does Sir Julius Irving have to this matter?"

Storm replied, "He is Raphael's client. We were leaving a conference with him when Raphael was shot. He feels responsible for the attack."

"Was Sir Julius the target?"

"No," Emma replied. "Storm was."

"You seem remarkably clear on the matter, Miss Webb. Especially for someone who was halfway across London when the attack occurred."

"This was not the first attack," Emma said. "What you should be asking is, who would be so well connected as to know in advance that the meeting with Sir Julius was taking place?"

Storm asked, "You're saying the man who shot Raphael was left with the driver?"

Emma said, "My guess is, the shooter was executed by his bosses for bungling the job. He brought everything into the open with two very public attacks. Both failed. His death was payback for a bad job."

Tanya said, "This is my thinking also."

The inspector asked Emma, "Might I inquire as to Homeland Security's interest in this matter?"

Emma said carefully, "Storm is my closest friend. She was threatened. She called. I came."

"So you are here strictly in an unofficial capacity."

"I assumed so. Only my superiors are taking a very keen interest in this incident. Why, I do not know."

Mehan turned his attention to Tanya. "And you, miss?"

"Also a friend."

He continued to examine Tanya as he asked, "Is Raphael Danton tied to any intelligence service?"

"No," Muriel said.

"Or any government operating in a clandestine manner within our borders?"

"Absolutely not," Muriel replied.

Mehan met one hard gaze after another. He said carefully, "None of you at present are under investigation. I am merely here seeking your help." He pulled out a notebook as rumpled as his suit. "Ms. Syrrell, be so good as to walk me through what happened at the Athenaeum, please."

When Storm finished, Mehan asked, "Might I have a copy of Mr. Danton's client list?"

Muriel laughed out loud.

"A judge may see fit to rule otherwise, Miss Lang."

"Then I shall see you in court," Muriel said. "We have tried to be helpful, and now you respond with a threat."

"On the contrary," replied Mehan. He rose to his feet and stuffed his notebook in his pocket. "You have only appeared helpful. We have agents of foreign governments operating clandestinely within our borders, hovering around events involving two murders and one attempted kidnapping. I would say you've offered me very little in the way of anything concrete."

"You know what we know," Emma said.

"Oh, I doubt that in the extreme, Agent Webb." He stalked toward the door. "Sir Julius can only protect you for so long."

303

. . .

THE TWO WOMEN DEPARTED SOON after the detective left, Tanya to meet with her superiors and Muriel to take care of urgent matters at the office. Storm expected Emma to come back at her with further reasons not to trust them. But Emma must have sensed her readiness to argue the point, for she merely pulled out her phone and said, "I need to check in with Tip."

Storm sat and listened to one side of the discussion. Finally Emma shut her phone and said, "Tip agrees that my abduction and release at Heathrow was Russian intel's way of showing they're not involved. Tip expected the CIA snoops would vanish like old smoke as soon as he reported the news of my abduction and release. Instead, he says they're swarming around him like angry ants."

Storm sat and struggled to fit that into her mental puzzle. Emma appeared content to wait. The silence was broken by an announcement over the hospital speakers. A nurse passed by the glass portal, glanced inside, and kept moving. Her shoes squeaked on the hall's linoleum floor. The elevator doors pinged open, then shut. Finally Storm turned and looked at her friend. "What if we're missing the Russians' real message?"

"I don't follow. They demonstrated that if they'd been the ones behind the Hebron bombing and the attacks in Jordan, Harry would be history."

"I'm not so sure."

Emma just pressed harder. "Ditto for your attempted abduction in Cirencester. Maybe even the missing icon. They meant for us to understand they had nothing to do with these events. They're clean."

"But remember what Father Gregor told you back in Washington. His contacts in the West Bank insisted the Russians were involved in the Hebron attack."

"You're saying the Russians hijacked me just to lie?"

"Not exactly. What if everything we're facing is all tied to one guy? What if this guy is so powerful the Russian government was forced to help him out?"

Emma did not respond.

"What if some people inside the Russian government don't like being manipulated into this international situation? What if they orchestrated your abduction to pass this message on?"

Emma nodded slowly. "They were specifically ordered not to say anything. Which they didn't. Instead, they delivered a message that was just smoke."

"But the real message is, 'Somebody is pulling our strings, and we don't like it.'"

"The reports we're getting suggest the new Russian oligarchs hold that kind of power. They back Putin, Putin backs them."

"Antonin Tarka said pretty much the same thing."

"But we already know that Abramov guy, the one you bid against, is bankrupt. So he can't be manipulating anybody."

"Forget him. Abramov was just a ruse."

"Which leads you back to square one, right?"

Storm said, "Think back to what happened in Spain. I made a deal with Rausch. They took two of the auctioned treasures, we took two, and we saved each other a ton of money. To me, it was a logical move. But Raphael's client was furious. He wanted me gone. Which means Raphael's client wasn't after the goods. He was after . . ."

"He was after everything."

"No, Emma. When I was at the Cirencester auction, Raphael told me the client's instructions were to *crush the opponent.* Publicly humiliate him."

"To what end?"

"That's what we need to figure out. That is the key to everything."

Emma said, "So what happens now?"

"Food," Storm said. "I'm starved."

THE HOSPITAL CAFETERIA WAS LOCATED in a wing that predated modern medicine. The lighting was so stark it embalmed the living. A boiler hissed sullenly behind the serving counter.

Storm took a soup and a salad and some fruit, then walked to the room's opposite side. Narrow windows revealed a cloudless sky. Storm set down her tray and stared at the windswept day. Across from her was another brownstone hospital wing. The wall clock above the window aimed at meaningless numbers. Such things as time belonged to an entirely different realm.

Between bites, Storm told Emma about the dream. Emma listened in silence, then said, "Maybe it really was him."

"I want it to be real. So much. But what about when he said he had to go?"

"Maybe he said you had to go, not him."

"He said what he said. And to back it up, he got up and left."

"Get a load of us, arguing over what a guy in a coma told you. While you were asleep."

Storm set down her spoon. "I'm in love with a man I may never speak with again."

"For what it's worth, I understand you a lot better than I would ever want."

The confession was ragged enough to draw Storm back. "Why don't you just call Harry and say you'll marry him?"

Emma pushed her tray away. "The corridors of Washington are littered with marriages that were doomed long before the rings were bought."

"Harry is different, and so are you." Storm wished she could clear her head enough to offer something solid, but all she could think of was, "What do you want? I mean, really?"

"Really?" Emma's features twisted in a semblance of agony. "I want to smother the man with my love."

"Harry will not desert you, Emma."

"Who says I'm worried about . . ." She pointed across the chamber. "Here comes trouble."

Inspector Mehan was entering the cafeteria flanked by two uniformed officers. Mehan spotted them, signaled to the officers, and walked over. "Ms. Syrrell, Agent Webb, I'm ordered to take you both into custody."

Storm asked, "On what charges?"

"No charges, miss. None required. You have all been deemed undesirable aliens in our fair land. Your visas are hereby revoked." He searched the cafeteria, then turned to one of the officers and said, "Go check upstairs for the Polish lady."

By now all the cafeteria was watching as Emma snapped, "My agency will be lodging an official protest."

"They can do whatever they please, Agent Webb. In the meantime, your deportation orders take immediate effect." He swept them up. "Move or be moved. That is your only choice at present."

THIRTY-EIGHT

T HERE WERE NO SIRENS. NO guns. No shoving or physical abuse. They were hustled into a police van with polite efficiency and swept away. As Storm watched the hospital disappear through the wire mesh covering the rear window, she learned an important lesson about herself. She had noticed it before. Yet she had never identified it as a personal trait. Or perhaps she had, but was forced to relearn it with each new trial.

The world was never clearer than when she faced impossible pressures. Her thoughts were never so precise as now, her emotions never farther removed. She was aware of her heart's lament, the silent keen of anguish over leaving Raphael. Yet it did not overwhelm her. In fact, her ability to separate the immediate circumstances from her emotions was so complete she could observe her torment with the same distance she used to study Inspector Mehan.

The detective was seated on the hard bench across from her. He had said nothing since refusing her entreaty to see Raphael one last time. He revealed a professional detachment, swaying in easy cadence to the van's bumpy progress. There was nothing to suggest he was anything other than completely satisfied with the events.

Yet Storm was certain the man was enraged.

The police officers had fetched her purse from Raphael's room. Storm pulled out the cell phone Tanya had supplied. "Is it all right if I make a couple of calls?"

Mehan did not even glance over. "My orders say nothing about sequestering you from outside contact, miss."

She phoned Muriel and received the answering service. Storm related what had happened and asked Muriel to call back immediately. She then dialed Sir Julius's number. The phone was answered by a woman whose frosty edge matched that of her boss. "Sir Julius is unavailable."

"Could you please tell him that we are being deported?"

The woman's sniff was loud enough to be heard over the rattling van. "I doubt most sincerely, madame, that such matters will be of any interest whatsoever to his lordship."

Storm shut her phone and cradled it to her chest. She compressed her hands, as though trying to squeeze what she sensed but could not identify from the instrument.

Emma was seated beside Storm. She made a call, spoke behind a cupped hand, slapped it shut, fumed, then said, "I can't raise Tip."

Storm resisted the urge to tell Emma that she was focused on the wrong direction. The swirl of thoughts and images and ideas had not crystallized. Storm simply nodded.

Tanya was seated between Storm and the rear doors. Her expression was pinched. Pale. Worried. She made two quick phone calls, then stowed her phone and stared out the rear windows with unblinking blindness.

Storm's phone rang. Muriel said, "I received your message."

"Where are you?"

"Back in the hospital waiting room."

"Can you stay there? I don't want Raphael left alone."

"Of course. I will lodge an official protest—"

"Never mind that. We're going to be deported. We need to face that fact and move on. Can you find somebody who can do a check for bugs?"

"You mean listening devices? Of course."

"Have them scan the waiting room. And Raphael's room. As quickly as possible."

"I will get on this immediately."

"Until they arrive, you need to remain planted where you are. Don't leave there for an instant. Give the nurses precise instructions that nobody other than you is allowed into Raphael's room. And arrange for some security to camp out in the waiting area."

When Storm cut the connection, Inspector Mehan was watching her carefully. But it was Emma who asked, "You think our boy's in danger?"

"Maybe." Storm met the inspector's unblinking gaze and said, "You left the hospital waiting room and were gone, what, two hours?"

Something flickered deep in the policeman's gaze. Storm hoped it was approval. All he said was, "A bit longer."

"Then you returned with orders to deport us. Something happened in that period, and it wasn't your idea. Something you don't like."

Mehan replied, "I will do as I am ordered, miss. And so shall you."

Storm pressed. "Three principal suspects in a murder investigation being evicted from Britain. This can't be a good idea."

"You were never suspects."

Emma demanded, "What kind of answer is that?"

The inspector's gaze did not waver. "The only kind I am permitted to offer."

Storm asked, "What happens when we arrive at Heathrow?"

"We will of course follow standard procedure. You will proceed to a room rather like the one you just left at the hospital, only the furniture in this one will be rather more seedy and the door will only open from the outside. There I shall read you the riot act. After which you will be required to wait until your flight is announced."

Emma asked, "Where are you sending us?"

"That is not the question," Storm replied. "Is it?"

The faint glimmer returned to the inspector's gray gaze. He did not respond.

"The question is, where do we need to go next? Your orders were to get us off British soil. We can choose our own destination."

Tanya turned from her inspection out the rear window. "You have an idea?"

"Maybe. But first we need to settle something." She turned to face Emma straight on. "I need you to accept that we can fully trust Muriel. And Tanya. Without reservation."

Emma glanced over Storm's shoulder, then back again. "On what grounds am I supposed to accept such a totally unfounded premise?"

"Let's assume Muriel is not to be trusted. She's a spy for Rausch. How do you see all that working out?"

"How should I know? Maybe she wants to take over the business. She looks like a smart girl. She's tired of working for the jerk. So she accepts an offer from Rausch's buyer."

"But why, Emma? She helps shoot her own boss? Wouldn't she be the first to come under suspicion?"

Mehan said, "She most certainly was."

Emma glanced over, then back. She did not reply.

"Why not just go off and set up her own shop?" Storm said. "You said it yourself. Raphael can be a major pain. How many of his employees and clients are there because of Muriel and the team she probably holds together?"

"It was just a suggestion," Emma replied. "She could be working for one big score."

"But what would be the motive behind Rausch's client making such an offer to her?" Storm continued. "This mystery guy has spent a ton keeping his identity secret. All of a sudden he'd trust Raphael's number two so much that he will rely on her to help him shoot her boss?"

"Ms. Syrrell," Mehan said, "has a point."

Emma gave a tight nod. "All right. I'll go with you on this. Unless I have strong evidence to the contrary." She shifted her gaze to the woman seated on Storm's other side. "Which I sincerely hope I never do. For all our sakes."

"Great." Storm turned to Tanya. "Call Antonin. Tell him we're looking for a Russian so powerful he can order armies to war."

Tanya shrugged. "Russia has maybe a hundred such oligarchs. More. We need something to narrow the search."

The same idea that had whispered to her when she woke from Raphael's dream returned now. "All the items I've bid on are tied to miracles," Storm said. "Each of them is bound to events so huge the stories have endured for over a thousand years. Centuries of miraculous healings. Visions, holy men, powers and events beyond mortal men. Even the power to stop time."

Mehan said, "You're suggesting our culprit is some religious wacko who's moved in close to Russia's new throne."

"No." Only now was the concept fully formed, clarified by the confines of a police van drawing her ever farther from Raphael. "I think we're after someone who has lost all earthly hope. He needs a miracle."

Tanya nodded slowly. "I like this. Very much."

"Tell Antonin to search for a Russian oligarch with a problem so serious he's given up all connection to logic. Maybe somebody who's cheated death before, and he's looking to do it again. He wants his own personal stairway to heaven. Buy his way out of his latest problem."

Tanya swiveled around to face the rear window and hit the speed-dial button.

Storm opened her own phone. She could feel Mehan's gaze raking over her. When Muriel answered, Storm asked, "Anything?"

"Two gentlemen in suits just stopped by. They took one look in Raphael's room, spotted me, and left."

"Do you have access to the upper echelons of the British power structure?"

"Most certainly."

"We need to know who Sir Julius Irving really is."

Mehan leaned forward.

Storm went on, "Raphael was emphatic that Sir

Julius held no connection to Russia. But he *is* the second buyer. Which means he has a hidden motive for fighting with Rausch's client over these items. We need to find out who is backing his play and why."

"I will have my team get on this immediately."

"One other thing. Can you find us a plane?"

"I can do better than that," Muriel replied. "I can find you an ally. Where are you now?"

She passed the question on to Mehan, who replied, "Just coming onto the A4. Thirty minutes from Heathrow in this traffic."

Muriel said, "Unless they carry heads of state, private planes are rarely granted landing privileges at Heathrow. Can you get to City Airport?"

When she asked Mehan, he said to the driver, "Turn us around and head for City."

The driver objected. "That airport has no facilities for detaining deportees, sir."

"Just do it."

THIRTY-NINE

TANYA'S PHONE RANG JUST AS the police van reentered London's stop-and-go traffic. She spoke briefly, then handed the phone to Storm. "The patriot has succeeded."

When Storm answered, Antonin Tarka said, "We have a name. Kiril Temerko. Does that mean anything?"

Storm lowered the phone and repeated the name to Emma, who frowned. But Tanya leaned back against the van's metal side and smiled at the ceiling. She said, "Is perfect."

Storm raised the phone and heard Antonin Tarka say, "Kiril Temerko is an intimate crony of Russia's president. You have heard of Mikhail Khodorkovsky, perhaps?"

Storm recalled the name. "The disgraced oil tycoon."

"Khodorkovsky backed Putin's opponent in his last race for president. Khodorkovsky thought having a billion dollars in the bank was enough to protect him. He was wrong. History is filled with such stories, where princes mistakenly think they are as powerful as kings. When his company, Yukos, was broken up, Kiril Temerko was permitted to purchase the assets for pennies."

"So Temerko now owns Russia's oil."

"Quite a considerable portion. Kiril Temerko also controls two-thirds of Russia's natural gas fields. And more than half of western Europe's gas comes from Russia."

More puzzle fragments swam together. "Is Temerko sick?"

"His daughter. An only child. She has cancer of the bone marrow. Her chances are nonexistent."

Storm waited as the van took an overly tight corner, then she asked, "Now give me the bad news."

"You are quite correct. The next item is certainly not good." Even so, the old man's voice rang with optimism. "Kiril Temerko owns eleven houses. They are everywhere. His official residence is a private island in the Moskva River from which the Kremlin is visible. He owns another island, near Papua New Guinea. A penthouse in New York. A town house in Versailles. The list, as far as we are concerned, is endless. He employs a small army. He travels only by private jet and helicopter."

"Maybe so. But if this Temerko has spent a ton on items tied to miracles, my guess is that he has a priest-confessor on call day and night. Can you reach Father Gregor?"

"He is seated across my desk from me. Ms. Syrrell, I wish to share something with you. My definition of a professional is someone who can think coolly in the heat of battle." Antonin Tarka gave that a beat, then said, "One of us will be in touch as soon as we have something to report."

THE SUN FROLICKED THROUGH THE city, flashing off windows and buildings and cars. The sidewalks were crowded. Many people walked with faces turned to the cloudless sky. Storm watched them through the van's wire-mesh rear window and wished she held the power to rejoin them. To cut away this distance between herself and any hope of a normal life. To bring Raphael

318

back to consciousness and give herself the chance to love a man who could actually respond.

Emma must have caught a hint of her remorse, for she slid an arm around Storm's shoulders. Drew her close. Did not speak. They remained like that, knit tight as shared sorrow, until Storm's phone rang.

Muriel reported, "Raphael's jet has landed at City Airport. The pilot is Eric Siegler, Raphael's former partner. Also, our security team just found listening devices in the hospital waiting room and attached to Raphael's bed. Highly sophisticated. Not commercially available."

"You need to stay safe," Storm said. "Is the security in place at the hospital?"

"I am surrounded by hulking men."

"Stay by your phone." Storm cut the connection and repeated to everyone in the van what Muriel had said.

City Airport was located within shouting distance of London's financial district. The economic crisis might have depleted the ranks, but private jets still outnumbered the commercial aircraft by a factor of ten to one. Raphael's jet was visible from the parking lot, a tiny sparkling gem between two Boeings with crossed swords and Arabic lettering down their sides.

The van stopped in front of the wire mesh gate. Mehan said, "I need to inform my superiors where you're headed."

"We don't know yet."

Mehan stared at her. "You're asking me to let you sit on the tarmac and wait for word?"

Storm met his gaze. "Exactly."

FORTY

THE MAN WHO STEPPED DOWN from Raphael's jet looked warped. Like a perfectly normal human being had been attacked by a force as strong as the sun. The left side of his face was nothing but scar tissue. Same for his neck and left arm where it emerged from his short-sleeved shirt.

Only Emma was unaffected. She walked over, offered her hand, and said, "Emma Webb. Homeland Security."

"Eric Siegler."

Emma introduced the others, then said, "Raphael was your buddy?"

"Is." He looked at Storm. "Raphael is my friend."

Storm liked that so much she rushed over and took his hand in both of hers, seeking a link strong enough to keep her own hope alive. "Thank you."

"You look just like Raphael described," he said.

Up close the man's scars were even worse. The bone above his left eye threatened to poke through the scar tissue. His left ear was a mockery. Storm asked, "He told you about me?"

"Three times," Eric replied. "Where are we going?"

Mehan said, "An excellent question, that."

"As soon as we find out," Storm replied, "I'll let you know."

THEY WAITED IN RAPHAEL'S JET for three hours and twenty-seven minutes. Storm knew because of the two clocks set above the cockpit windshield. The clocks were separated by a compass. All three dials were rimmed in silver and burl. Storm watched the clocks tick together, counting down lost minutes in both London and New York.

Through the bulbous windshield Storm watched Inspector Mehan pace back and forth in front of the jet. A police car was parked between the jet and the airport gates. The deportation van was gone. A uniformed officer was in the police car's rear seat. The officer's head was settled on the headrest. He appeared to be asleep. Mehan draped his overcoat and his yellow-beige jacket on the jet's stairs. A dark stain of perspiration had formed between his shoulder blades.

Waiting.

Emma hovered by the cockpit's entrance but did not speak. Storm felt a mounting pressure, an ache like she was being repeatedly struck just below her rib cage, the blows timed to each tick of the dual second hands.

Storm's phone finally rang, and Father Gregor announced, "I have news."

As Tanya crowded into the cockpit portal beside Emma, Storm said, "Just a moment. I want us all to hear." She keyed on the speaker and set the phone beside the engine controls. "Go ahead."

"The Vatican has made enormous strides in building bridges to the Orthodox community. We have a thousand years of wounds to overcome. But we are progressing. A new ally agreed to check for us to see if Kiril Temerko has a personal priest. I apologize for the delay in responding. But with the man's residences spread all over the globe, this has taken quite some time."

Tanya called softly to the inspector, who vaulted up the jetway and crammed himself in behind her. Father Gregor went on, "A high-ranking Orthodox bishop was flown from Saint Petersburg to Switzerland recently to perform their version of last rites for his daughter."

Eric Siegler demanded, "Switzerland? You're certain?"

Tanya said, "Antonin's list includes a villa in the Engadine Valley."

Father Gregor said, "The bishop described landing between a village and a lake."

Eric nodded. "He landed at the Saint Moritz airport."

Storm asked, "You know the region?"

Eric's smile was a twisted affair. The muscles

on the burned side of his face did not move at all. "Raphael and I commanded troops on the Italian border."

Father Gregor went on, "The priest described a palace set on a hill in the middle of the valley. The palace was surrounded by a high fence. In the far distance he could see a towering wall of ice."

"A glacier tongue. Which means it was probably east of the city." Eric pulled out a clipboard holding an international flight plan and began writing. "Saint Moritz has an excellent airport. I have used it many times."

Emma lifted her buzzing phone. "It's Tip."

Emma slipped to the rear of the plane. Mehan accompanied Eric to the control tower where the pilot filed his international flight plan. Storm watched planes land and take off. Raphael seemed to grow more distant with each tick of the clocks. She had never hated waiting so much as now.

When Emma returned to the cockpit, her expression was grim. "Tip has ordered me back to Washington."

"You can't go." When Emma did not respond, Storm raised her voice. "I need you here, Emma."

Emma sighed her way into the empty pilot's seat. "If I stay, it's the end of my career."

"Think about the timing," Storm pleaded. "The inspector interviewed us in the waiting room.

323

He left. You and I talked. Two hours later, we're deported. Now Tip is locking you up tight. Why?"

Emma tapped her phone against the engine controls and did not reply.

"Whoever bugged Raphael's hospital room and overheard our conversations decided we were getting too close," Storm said. "They're covering something up. Something bigger than just the identity of Rausch's client."

Emma had still not responded when Eric returned to the jet. Eric took one look at her face and asked, "What's happened?"

Emma stared at the sunlit runway and did not reply.

Storm was about to plead once more when her phone buzzed. Muriel reported, "I've had considerable difficulty finding anyone who was willing to speak about Sir Julius. I finally obtained the information after calling a source who owes Raphael his reputation. He insisted we speak over a secure line. You understand?"

"The man is scared."

"Terrified. According to this one source, Sir Julius is the British intelligence agency's representative on the Queen's Privy Council."

Storm thanked her and rang off. When she repeated the news, Emma recalled, "The listening devices in the hospital were special government issue."

Tanya asked, "Do you suggest British intel is involved in the murders at the Athenaeum?"

Storm shook her head. "That's not the question we need to be asking."

Emma said, "We need to understand why British intelligence would be so keen to acquire these religious artifacts."

"They don't care about the items," Storm said. "They want a lever to use against Temerko."

"All right." Emma rose from the pilot's seat. "I'll give you two days and not one second more."

FORTY-ONE

ALL STORM SAW OF SAINT Moritz was a concrete landing strip and a lake surrounded by early summer green. To the north a road curved around a hillock and merged with a cluster of roofs. A windsock shivered in a snow-laden breeze. Directly ahead of them, two police cars blocked the airport exit.

Eric taxied over to where a dark-gloved policeman waved them to a halt. Eric powered down the plane, lowered the stairs, and said, "Everybody stay close."

The wind was brisk and spiced by the surrounding ice-capped peaks. As Storm's feet touched ground, her phone rang. "This is Storm."

The woman's frosty tone had not altered one

iota since their last conversation. "Hold, please, for Sir Julius Irving."

A series of clicks, then, "My dear Ms. Syrrell, how and where are you?"

"Your secretary did not seem to think that was of any interest whatsoever."

"Ah, yes. A most unfortunate misunderstanding, that. I failed to leave word with her of the situation. I was rather shaken by events."

As far as apologies went, it barely shook the needle. "I understand."

"Most kind. Now then. I am calling to ask if you could bid on my behalf."

"You're interested in acquiring another piece?"

"My dear young lady, you didn't think that simply because your employer met with this accident—"

"It wasn't an accident."

"No. Quite. I misspoke. But simply because Mr. Danton is temporarily laid up does not mean we can cease in our quest."

"I thought . . ."

"Yes?"

"Nothing."

"I only learned of this particular article an hour ago. The auction begins tomorrow morning at Basel's international convention hall and runs for three days. I have already inquired as to security. You will be most well taken care of. Now then. Where are you?"

"Saint Moritz."

"How timely."

Storm stared at the mountains that walled her in. "As I have not dealt with you directly before, I will require the funds in advance."

"Inform my assistant what is required. The transfer will be made within the hour. Ms. Syrrell, I want this item. Whatever the price."

As Storm recited her bank details to the frosty secretary, she watched Eric turn his back on the police and walk toward them. When she hung up, he announced, "We are being refused permission to disembark."

"Did they tell you why?"

"One of their officers served with me and Raphael. He says the orders came from security headquarters in Bern. He knows nothing else. I must give them our next destination."

"Can you take us to Basel?"

"That should not be a problem. They do not order us from Switzerland, just from Saint Moritz."

When Eric returned to speak with the police, Emma asked, "Does this mean your thinking is off course?"

Storm watched the sunlight crystallize into plans as solid as the surrounding peaks. "No. Nothing's changed."

"You're saying Sir Julius ordering you to Basel is a good thing?"

"It's better than that," Storm replied. "It's perfect."

● ● ●

STORM SPENT THE FLIGHT OUTLINING her plans. Eric connected her with Muriel over the plane's radio system, so she only needed to go through the ideas once. When she finished, Emma said, "I'm glad I agreed to stay."

Tanya said, "This is a good plan. It has great promise."

Emma said, "I wish my directives from HQ were this clear."

"I quite agree," Muriel said. "I will ring off now. Everything you requested will be ready upon your arrival."

They descended through nighttime clouds and landed in heavy rain. When they exited airport security, they were met by a tall, angular man in a severe gray suit. "Storm Syrrell?"

"Yes."

"I am Klaus. I was sent by Muriel." When he gestured toward the entrance, he revealed an earpiece and clear cord running into his jacket. "I have cars."

Four more men waited by a pair of dark Range Rovers with tinted windows. They wore earpieces and rain-spotted overcoats. Two more men sat behind the wheels. They were all huge. Muriel had done her work well.

Emma said, "Money can't buy you love, but it sure does a bang-up job with security."

When they piled inside, Storm asked Klaus,

328

"Do you have the items Muriel asked you to acquire?"

"Five cryptophones, yes?"

"Tanya is not coming with us," Storm said, "so we need to find a quiet place and take care of this now."

Klaus spoke to the driver. They pulled away from the terminal and halted by the airport exit. Klaus reached into the luggage hold and passed out white plastic bags. Tanya opened hers and said, "I know this equipment."

Klaus said, "It is the latest model and uses ten-digit algorithms. It has no black box, which means it would be easily broken by experts."

Storm said, "I'm hoping the experts won't have a reason to suspect anything."

"Then these phones should be satisfactory. They work like regular phones. Turn on here, dial here." Klaus handed out note cards with five hand-printed telephone numbers.

When they had made note of the names belonging to each phone, Storm said, "Circle back to the airport."

When they pulled up in front of the terminal, Storm got out of the SUV with Tanya. The Polish agent studied her a long moment, then said, "What your friend said on the plane was correct. You would be excellent at my job."

"Sorry," Storm replied. "I don't have the nerves."

As they pulled away, Emma said, "You sure could have fooled me."

FORTY-TWO

THE BASEL MUNICIPAL AIRPORT WAS in a trination enclave surrounded by the Rhein River. The hotel was in the same international free-trade zone as the small airport and the convention center, where the auction was slated to begin the next morning. Their two SUVs pulled up to the hotel entrance and Emma watched the security team move into action. Storm rose from the first vehicle, her hair wrapped in a dark scarf and her face lost behind large sunglasses. The security surrounded Storm and marched her inside. The team had obviously alerted the hotel, because a dark-suited manager was on hand to escort them directly to the elevators.

After Emma checked them in, she stopped by the hotel shops, then went upstairs. She and Storm ate a room-service meal and strategized until exhaustion set in.

The next morning, Emma arrived downstairs fifteen minutes early. She wore a new dress of café au lait silk with a matching jacket. She ordered an espresso from a passing waitress and seated herself in an alcove that granted a semblance of privacy. When the coffee arrived, she switched her phone back on. She scrolled through a sheath of increasingly irate messages from Tip and decided nothing would be gained by making that call. Her time on the firing line would come soon enough.

Instead she phoned Harry and found some comfort in how improved the man sounded. If only the same could have been said for her own conflicted heart. Then Emma spotted the men entering the hotel's doors. She said her farewells, stowed her emotions with her phone, and rose to greet the approaching trio.

They were led by a gray-haired man with a hunter's thousand-yard stare. "Agent Webb?"

"That is correct."

"Randolf Barnes. May I see some ID?"

"I was about to ask you the same thing."

He traded his leather portfolio for hers. "We were sent by Sir Julius—"

"Your services are not required."

He hesitated in the act of handing back her badge. "Pardon me?"

"We decided," Emma said, "to handle Storm's security ourselves."

"But . . ." He glanced at his partners. "Sir Julius specifically ordered—"

"Sir Julius Irving is not responsible for Storm's safety," Emma replied. "I am."

"This is most irregular."

"So is our friend getting shot on the steps of his club." The elevator doors pinged and four agents exited, surrounding a woman masked by dark sunglasses and a scarf. Emma said, "I have to go."

The four security men were so tall as to dwarf the woman at their center. As they marched in tandem across the lobby, Emma gave the woman a careful inspection. The actress Muriel had hired to play Storm would do fine, so long as no one came too close. As they approached the exit, two SUVs pulled up and the drivers jumped out, a tightly choreographed dance of tension and risk.

"Ms. Syrrell, a moment please." The British security agent started forward. "Sir Julius wishes to have a word—"

Emma inserted herself between the British agent and Storm's stand-in. "Sir Julius has Storm's number. He can call her any time he likes."

"THIS IS UTTERLY OUTRAGEOUS!"

For once, Sir Julius and his ire left Storm unfazed. "I'm sorry. But Emma Webb felt it was best to handle the security issue herself."

"I went to a great deal of trouble to arrange the highest-quality service. What possible good could arise from that woman countermanding my orders?"

"First of all, she is not 'that woman.' She is my friend. Secondly, this is not some casual change of direction. I have been the victim of two attacks."

"Which is why I arranged—"

"Emma Webb is a professional agent. She

wanted to take personal charge of my safety. I know her and I trust her."

Sir Julius gave her a British version of sullen. "I thought your friend had been ordered back to Washington."

"Who told you that?"

"I can hardly be expected to recall every small detail."

"This is a vital bit of highly confidential information."

"Ms. Syrrell, I did not phone you to be interrogated. Now I really must insist—"

"Emma Webb is remaining in place until she is certain that I am safe. She is handling security."

"Your attitude is most unreasonable."

"I'm sorry you feel that way. Do you want me to handle the bidding?"

He made no effort to hide his discontent. "For the moment."

Storm shut her phone and sat staring through the side window of the taxi. The house was almost lost behind a line of willows.

Eric asked quietly, "Are you certain you want to do this?"

Storm responded by reaching for the taxi's door.

"Wait just a minute." Eric Siegler rose from the taxi, scouted in all directions, then said, "All right."

"Are you coming?"

He stared up at the house. "This is as close as I ever need to get to those people."

Storm walked up the tree-shaded walk. The house dated from the nineteenth century, with a gabled roof and miniature turrets at each end. Broad stairs shaped like an open fan rose to a door as forbidding as a Swiss safe, tall and bound by iron bands and studded with nails. She rang the bell.

The young maid wore a uniform from the Victorian era, a black smock and crinoline apron and starched cap and lace-up shoes. *"Ja, bitte?"*

"My name is Storm Syrrell. I am here with news about Raphael Danton."

The maid's features constricted. "You will please to wait here." She shut the door in Storm's face.

The door was opened a second time by a woman who resembled Raphael to an astonishing degree. "Yes?"

"My name is Storm Syrrell. I have news of your son."

"Very well." She crossed her arms beneath the single strand of pearls. "I'm listening."

"Perhaps it would be best if I came inside."

A masculine voice from within said, "Oh, let the woman in, Gilda."

The house felt as cold as a cave. Granite floors, peaked stone ceiling, barred windows, even the paintings were severe. Storm was led into a cheerless parlor. The stone floor was covered by a beige Berber carpet. The furniture was leather and as severe as the man standing by the unlit fire. "You bring word of Raphael. Say it."

"He's been shot."

The woman sank onto the sofa. She turned and stared at the man, who said, "The last time, we learned of Raphael's injuries from some reporter. He also said Raphael had been arrested for being a mercenary." The man bit off each word like he was measuring a compound in the lab. "And plotting a coup."

"That time he was struck by a spear," the woman softly added. "The reporter wanted a comment."

"Spear, gun, knife, bomb, Raphael has chosen his life and must accept the consequences." The man wore a brown tweed jacket over a forest-green vest and matching tie. Trimmed sideburns extended down to where they almost met at his chin. He did not stand by the mantel so much as pose. "I suppose you're here to tell me his injuries are more serious this time."

"I'm afraid so."

"It was inevitable. Simply a matter of time." He glanced at his wife. "He was born with an over-abundance of recklessness. He has sought this end his entire life."

The woman wiped at her face but did not speak.

"Thank you for seeing me." Storm headed for the door.

When they were back outside, the woman asked through the open door, "Where is he?"

"Guy's Hospital. That's in London."

The woman started to speak, but the man called, "Gilda!"

The woman lowered her gaze and shut the door.

FORTY-THREE

WHEN THE VEHICLE PULLED UP in front of the auction hall, Storm's stand-in watched from the second SUV as Emma entered the building. Emma obtained passes from the front desk and entered the crowded chamber. Illuminated cases flanked the entry and marched down the side walls. Waiters drifted about bearing trays of mimosas.

Emma slipped through the dealers and high-end buyers, up to the cluster of power by the auctioneer's dais. She saw the flash of recognition within Aaron Rausch's dark eyes. "Remember me?"

"My dear Ms. Webb. However could I forget?" The old gentleman offered the suggestion of a courtly bow. "How very good to see you again."

"I have a message from Storm."

"Allow me to show you an item I find of particular interest." He gestured toward the sidewall. "Is she here?"

"In a manner of speaking."

"Is she safe?"

"That's what I want to speak with you about." She felt eyes track them across the room. "Can we talk somewhere more private?"

"If we leave the premises, people will notice." He tapped the display case's glass top. "I assume this is what we'll be fighting over."

Emma saw a gold, jewel-encrusted box shaped like a cathedral, right down to tiny gold pillars lining what she assumed was the front. "What is it?"

"A reliquary, eleventh century or earlier. It is reputed to hold a finger of Saint Peter himself." Even his smile was courtly. "Most likely a chicken bone. That was the animal of choice in those days. Quite a number of miracles are linked to this item."

As Emma relayed Storm's message, Rausch drew a small magnifying glass from his pocket and leaned closer to the glass. When she was done, Rausch remained bent over the reliquary. "So you have inserted a double for Ms. Syrrell, and you want my assistance in, shall we say, establishing her provenance."

"Storm needs to be elsewhere. We need to mask her movements from any potential watchers."

"Provenance is a vital word in my profession, Agent Webb. You are asking me to risk my good name for, if you will excuse me, something of questionable value."

Emma had come expecting this. She leaned in close and murmured, "Vladimir Abramov is not your client."

Aaron Rausch straightened slowly. His fingers trembled slightly as he slipped the magnifying glass into his vest pocket. "I'm sorry. What did you say?"

"But you already knew this, didn't you." She was close enough to see the perspiration bead his forehead. "Shall I name the man pulling your company's strings?"

"That will not be necessary." He hesitated, then asked, "Is our firm in danger?"

"Not if we are successful in pulling this off."

"You may tell Ms. Syrrell that I stand ready to assist you."

"Storm asked me to tell you that she is in your debt. I'll add my own vote to that."

"I sincerely hope I shall have an opportunity to call upon you. And that you shall both be around to respond." This time his bow was deeper. "Good day, Ms. Webb."

EMMA EXITED THE HALL AND signaled the security team. They alighted and fitted them-selves around Storm's stand-in. As Emma handed each team member a pass. The actress was slightly taller and a little heavier than Storm. But with the sunglasses and the dark head scarf and the agents blocking anyone from coming too close, she might pull it off. Maybe.

They entered the main hall with Emma in the lead. Dealers scanned the assembled objects and clustered and spoke softly into phones with their hands cupped around the mouthpieces. The entire room froze as Aaron Rausch shouted, "You said nothing about that woman showing up here!"

Emma ignored Rausch's outburst. She turned to Storm's stand-in and pointed to the room's opposite side. "Item one hundred and forty-six."

The old gentleman rushed forward. "This is positively the worst abuse of dealer privilege I have *ever* seen!"

A bespectacled gray-suited man set his auctioneer's hammer on the podium and hurried over. "Is there a problem?"

"A problem, did you say? A *problem?*" Aaron Rausch collided with the outstretched arm of the nearest guard and windmilled backward. "Take your hands *off* me!"

Emma said, "Keep your distance and there will be no trouble."

"You speak to *me* about *trouble?*"

The auctioneer inserted himself between Emma and Rausch. "What is the meaning of this?"

"Ms. Syrrell simply wishes to bid on one particular item."

Rausch yelled, "This woman has no more right to be here than my pet cat!"

The auctioneer pointed at her guards. "And these people?"

"At a recent auction in England," Emma replied, "Ms. Syrrell was the victim of an attempted abduction."

"Ah." The auctioneer's gaze took on a tightly avaricious gleam. "I recall hearing something about that incident."

"Then you also heard how Mr. Rausch's son threatened Ms. Syrrell after she won their battle over a particular piece."

"Slander! I'll sue you for every cent you own!"

The auctioneer asked, "Does Ms. Syrrell represent a bona fide buyer?"

Rausch yelled, "She's nothing but a cheap trickster and a charlatan!"

"She absolutely has a buyer." Emma offered the auctioneer Sir Julius's card. "You can call this number to confirm."

"In that case, I shall expect all participants at this event to maintain proper decorum." The auctioneer adjusted his chin so as to look down upon Aaron Rausch. "Do I make myself perfectly clear?"

Emma moved to where the woman posing as Storm leaned over the case. "The item does not actually come up for auction until the day after tomorrow. Do you wish to remain any longer?"

In response, the woman straightened and headed for the exit. The guards surrounded her more tightly than ever. As they passed through the main doors, Aaron Rausch shouted, "Outrageous!"

From her position by the exit, Emma cast the old man a look of pure gratitude. "I couldn't agree more."

FORTY-FOUR

EMMA AND TANYA REJOINED ERIC and Storm at the airport. After they took off and climbed to cruising altitude, Tanya stepped forward and confirmed that all the arrangements were being made according to Storm's plan. Storm knew she should be asking questions and making preparations. But afternoon sunlight glinted off peaks rising like ice-clad islands from a frothy sea, and all Storm could think was, This is Raphael's home.

She asked Eric, "Will you tell me about Raphael?"

"What do you want to know?"

"Everything."

Eric occupied the left seat, which meant she could watch emotions flicker across the mobile side of his face. "Raphael blamed himself for Valerie's death."

"Valerie was his wife?"

"Yes. She was pregnant. She wanted to return to Switzerland for the delivery. Raphael agreed but refused to travel with her. We had a contract, a big-game hunter flying in from Bavaria. Valerie refused to leave without him. Three nights after we left on safari, the rebels attacked."

"Poor Raphael."

"Raphael buried his laughter with Valerie. His smile. His heart. After it was over, Raphael and I fought against those who took everything from him. When I was injured, I went home to Switzerland. Raphael moved to London. He got rich. He met you." He glanced over. "Now you know everything."

Storm stared out at the endless horizons and thought about all that lay ahead. "Do you believe in miracles?"

"Absolutely not." Eric turned so that she could see both sides of his face. "Until I heard Raphael speak about you."

THE WEATHER CLEARED AS THEY entered Italian airspace. Eric chattered with the Milan controllers and aimed south. The storm clouds had filtered away, revealing minty green plains. In the distance Milan's earthbound cloud glowed an ugly shade of yellowish gray. Eric held to his course for about fifteen minutes. Then he spoke with the control tower again, announced a change in course, and banked the plane north.

Eric said, "Italy's air traffic controllers are notorious for avoiding paperwork. My flight plan says Rome. They might report our altered course. Someday."

Eric began descending as they reentered the Italian Alps. The surrounding peaks looked razor sharp and far too close. Eric pushed the nose down. From this perspective, the mountains appeared to cage the valley, hemming in tightly on all sides. A single road formed a tiny dark snake far below. As the village grew in front of them, Storm said, "It looks so quiet."

"The Livigno Valley missed the twentieth century entirely. Both world wars, the fascists, Mussolini—for the people here it was all nothing but rumors. There are only two roads in and out. The one into Switzerland crosses the Narrow Pass. The road into Italy crosses the Foscagno Pass. Both are above seven thousand feet. Avalanches close the valley off several times each winter. There is no industry. The mountains are too steep for ski resorts. Also there was the matter of Livigno's unsavory reputation. Livigno has been a smugglers' haven for centuries." The undamaged side of his face smiled at her. "Which makes the place perfect for us."

But her idea of walking into Switzerland, with Eric to guide them past the police, no longer seemed such a great one. She swallowed, trying to force down the dread. "I guess."

"I told you. Raphael and I commanded troops along Italy's border with the Engadine for two years. I have hiked all over these mountains. They are my friends." He banked the jet through a steep turn. "It's a good plan."

The airport was a single north-south landing strip. Eric did a flyover. The airport came and went in the blink of an eye. Storm asked, "Can you land on that?"

Eric banked a second time, leveled off, and dropped like a stone. "Theoretically."

The plane met the runway extremely hard. Eric stood on the brakes and powered the engines into reverse thrust. The entire plane shuddered and the tires smoked. They halted so close to the end all Storm could see was snow-flecked grass and two astonished sheep.

From the back, Emma said, "Something tells me I'm glad I missed that one."

AS THEY DESCENDED FROM THE plane, Father Gregor greeted each with solemn intensity. He turned to Storm last and said, "My nation thanks you, Ms. Syrrell. Even those who will never have reason to know your name."

The steep-sided mountains framed the priest in stone and ice. "Now that I'm here, all I can think of are ways for this to go wrong."

"Which is why you do not go alone."

"Maybe we should wait and—"

"There is no time. The pressure on us to release the news is growing with each passing hour.

Antonin and I both agree. It is a splendid plan."
He waved them toward a Fiat people mover.
"Come. Your team awaits."

Emma asked, "What team would that be?"

Father Gregor smiled. "Come and see."

THEY DROVE THROUGH THE VILLAGE of
Livigno and continued north. The narrow road
ran along a ridge that dropped to Gallo Lake. The
lake was four miles wide and so long both ends
were lost to the afternoon shadows. Every time
Storm lifted her gaze from the lake's steel
waters, the mountains loomed high and tight.
Watching.

Storm squinted out the front windshield. "They
look so high."

"They are," Eric said.

"And steep."

"Extremely."

Emma said, "You're quite the salesman."

"You don't have to come," he replied.

"Yes, I do."

"I was speaking for both of you."

Emma glanced at Storm. "So was I."

Their destination was a twelfth-century
monastery. The cloister and its surrounding
pasture overlooked both the road and the lake.
The meadow extended north into its own miniature valley, over which the mountains brooded.
In the distance, sheep grazed between the

patches of snow. The view was exquisitely peaceful. So long as Storm kept herself from looking up.

They arrived just as dinner was being served. The medieval hall was jammed. One long table held the monks, while another held nineteen civilians. All but Antonin looked both young and extremely fit.

Antonin Tarka limped over, leaning heavily upon his cane. He waved to the people lining the second table and said, "My associates insisted upon sending you some help."

"But—"

"Whether you like it or not, Ms. Syrrell. My associates have insisted on this escort."

Emma protested. "They're worrying over a fake."

"You must be Agent Webb." Antonin Tarka inspected her carefully. "The answer, Ms. Webb, is that they are worrying over my nation's heritage."

Storm asked, "Who are they?"

"They are no one. They are not here. They do not exist. As for the fake Madonna, these people have brought it with them, and I can assure you that it is perfectly safe." Antonin Tarka waved them to seats at the table's center. "Your places await."

As they took their seats along the refectory table, Father Gregor stepped to an ancient

346

wooden podium set by two tall stained-glass windows. The instant he began speaking, the hall became silent, tense. Storm took a long moment to inspect the group. They were about two-thirds male. The women were hard as the men. Young, taut, intent.

The priest led them in prayer, then took the seat on Storm's other side and observed, "I have seen starched linen altar cloths with more color than your face."

Storm waited as a server placed a bowl of stew in front of her. "I don't like heights."

Antonin Tarka said, "Then don't go."

Storm forced herself to take a bite. Swallowed. Tasted nothing. "I have to."

"Why?"

Storm took another bite. She did not speak.

"Ms. Syrrell intends to take a pilgrimage," Father Gregor said. "For herself. And for Raphael Danton. Is that not right?"

Storm pushed her plate away.

"I hope you will excuse Tanya for keeping us abreast of the young man's progress." Father Gregor slid the plate back in front of her. "You must be strong. And you must be rested. Start with this meal. Then we will pray. And then you will sleep."

"I can't."

"My dear child," the priest replied, "I was not making a suggestion."

FORTY-FIVE

STORM WAS AWAKE LONG BEFORE the monastery bell sounded for matins. The ringing was gentle, almost apologetic. Storm heard footsteps in the corridor outside her door and rose from her bed.

When she had sat and talked with Father Gregor the previous evening, the chapel had been empty and lit by two flickering lamps. As she entered the chapel that early dawn, tall candles burned on stands to either side of the nave. The monks filled one side of the chapel. The group Storm was coming to think of as her team filled the other side. Antonin Tarka gestured for Storm to join him in the first pew.

Father Gregor led the morning service, assisted by two monks, wearing robes of red and white and gold. In place of his normal quiet dignity was an almost regal bearing. The candles, the incense, the deep-voiced chants, and the night-darkened windows all came together in a comforting embrace. Her fear did not vanish. Grim dangers still lay ahead. But here in this one brief moment, there was peace. Storm closed her eyes and breathed deeply, trying hard to believe that this momentary gift would see her through the coming trial.

They left the monastery at sunrise. Father

Gregor remained in his formal robes. The monks gathered behind the priest and chanted in plainsong as the group passed through the doors. The monastery had an odd little gate facing the private valley and the mountains beyond. The waist-high wall surrounding the building rose into an arch, with a font set in the right-hand wall. A Latin inscription was carved into the stones overhead. For over six hundred years, the monastery had served as a way station for pilgrims traveling from the northern reaches to Rome. The carved words had almost been washed away by the seasons and weather. Father Gregor had translated them for Storm the previous night. They came from Acts and read, "You will be my witnesses to the ends of the earth."

As the monks sang, Father Gregor sprinkled them with holy water and blessed them in Latin. Three of their Polish team carried the crate bearing the counterfeit Black Madonna. Each of the Poles dipped his or her fingers into the font and made the sign of the cross before passing through the arch. Up ahead rose the hills.

Their path lay alongside a tumbling river. They crossed the meadow, passing through herds of quietly bleating sheep, and entered a forest of alpine fir. The rise, when it began, was subtle, as though the mountains intended to lull them into complacency. Gradually the slope steepened, and the river shouted a warning as they climbed.

They rested when they reached the tree line. The padded straps of Storm's pack bit into her shoulders. She leaned against a rock and stared at the blue-black sky. Too soon they were called back to the trail. They climbed. Each time the path steepened, the snow-swollen river became a waterfall. The backwash struck the climbers like liquid bullets.

They climbed until Storm's lungs burned as fiercely as her legs. They entered a realm of rock and snow and ice. Everything green lay below them now. Here there was only winter.

She wore a pair of felt gloves with leather stitched around the fingers. The gloves were soft and flexible, yet the leather gave her purchase on the rocks even when wet. Storm did not mind the steep segments of the climb. It drew the boulders in close to her face, blocking the temptation to look back at the paralyzing distance below.

They arrived at a ledge perhaps fifty paces wide and twice as long. A waterfall plunged into a pool at the far end. The rest of the narrow plateau was covered in loose gravel and fresh snow. Immediately the outcropping became littered with exhausted bodies. Eric and Tanya set up paraffin stoves and began brewing tea. Emma filled a mug and brought it over to where Storm was seated on a rock. Emma pointed to the crate holding the Madonna. It had been carried the entire ascent by three people at a time, one in front holding guide ropes, two behind taking most of the weight.

Now that they had stopped, one Pole after another walked over to the crate. They stared down at it for a time, then touched the wood, crossed themselves, and walked away. Emma asked, "What are they doing?"

"It was a habit among medieval pilgrims. They started on the road carrying a prayer." Storm drained the mug and set it in the snow beside her rock. "Most pilgrims traveled in groups because the roads weren't safe. Someone in the group carried an icon, a cross, a prayer book, something that had been blessed by a priest and was meant to remind the pilgrims of their purpose. Every now and then, they repeated their prayer. Then they touched the object, sending the prayer off to God. This was how a lot of icons became known as sources of miracles."

Emma crouched on the rock next to Storm. "But the icon is a fake."

"Tradition has it that any true likeness carries the same power as the original icon."

"How do you know all this?"

"Father Gregor told me last night. He said if I was going on a pilgrimage, I should understand the rules of the road."

Emma watched as one military-hardened Pole after another walked forward, touched the crate, crossed himself, and walked away. "What kind of prayer?"

"Usually something acknowledging the hopelessness of their situation and affirming their faith that they are in God's hands."

"So, like a lost cause."

"Think about it. You're leaving comfort and safety behind. You're walking for days. You do this as an act of sacrifice. It all adds to the intensity of a prayer."

Emma rose slowly, testing each muscle in turn. "More tea?"

"My turn."

"I got it." Emma started toward Tanya, then veered over to where the crate leaned against the cliff. She stared at the crate for several seconds, then she reached forward and touched it. She rested her hand there for a long moment.

THEY ROPED UP FOR THE final ascent. The river that had guided them disappeared under a tongue of glacier ice, but the rocky pass remained clearly evident, framed by niches and hollows. Here and there they came upon images carved into the rocks. A cross, a Latin inscription, a crude font now holding ice and snow, a stone fish. Those climbing ahead of Storm often reached out and touched the images, then their lips. And they climbed.

Smuggler's Pass was a saddle formed between

two towering peaks. Eric identified them to Storm as he fitted on the mini-skis that would serve her as snowshoes. Monte Chaschauna to the southwest, Monte Saliente to the northeast. Both over ten thousand feet. The peaks were known as *arete*, where two glaciers had crawled up opposite sides of a mountain and formed a jagged, narrow ridge like the blade of a serrated knife.

Emma let Eric help her into a second pair of walking skis, then confessed, "I'm too tired to make it down."

"Press your heel down hard. Good." Eric rose and pointed across the expanse to where the ice saddle melded with a sky more black than blue. "We hold to the southern wall. The surface there is more stable. The distance is less than five kilometers. We overnight in a mountaineer's hut."

"Five kilometers," Emma said.

"A bit less. And most of that is flat."

"I can do that."

The stark surroundings granted Eric's half smile a semblance of normality. "I know you can."

Storm walked across the snowpack to where Tanya and two others fitted themselves into the crate's guide ropes. The skis were a welcome change, as they kept her from needing to actually lift her feet from the surface. She said, "I want to carry it."

Emma stepped up beside her. "Me too."

Tanya spoke to the two men, who helped each of them loop the crate's ropes around their neck and one shoulder. The lines were connected to hooks screwed into the crate's corners. The lines were meant for balance and as last lines of safety. One of the young men motioned for Storm to take off her pack.

"I can carry it," she replied.

Tanya said, "Let them help."

The Pole was quite handsome in an intensely blond and hard-edged manner. He accepted Storm's pack and said something softly, which Tanya translated as "We bear one another's burdens."

The crate was bulky but not heavy. As they entered the ice flow, Eric pushed a long, collapsible pole into the snow, testing the way ahead. The group followed in a slow line. The rope linking them was kept slack so as not to jerk anyone off balance. Storm and Emma and Tanya were at the line's midpoint. Progress was slow enough for her to glance around. In the late-afternoon light it seemed as though they were connected by time's own hand, linked to events and powers far beyond her ability to see.

A soft wind added a breath of urgency to the descending sun. Storm sensed that Eric was con-cerned, but he did not alter his pace.

Then the saddle ended, and the world simply dropped away.

Eric must have known they were all on the verge of collapse. He unsnapped himself from the line and remained in place, pointing ahead and murmuring the same mantra to each person who passed: "Food and water are less than a thousand meters ahead."

The drop and the lengthening shadows robbed the valley of all color. The distant scene was merely a patchwork of shadows and grays. Storm was so exhausted she could look at the drop and not care. She felt nothing.

Her lungs continued to pump desperately for air, but her throat was numb. Her hands and shoulders ached from carrying the crate.

The alpine hut was so small she would have missed it entirely, taking it for just another rock outcropping that protruded from just another snowbank. But a Swiss flag was painted on its side. The hut did not look much bigger than a walk-in closet.

Emma muttered, "Are we supposed to sleep standing up?"

At that point, Storm did not care. All she had room for was the sight of one person after another stepping around the outer ledge and entering through the door. Off the path. Into a haven of safety.

FORTY-SIX

THE HUT FRONTED ON A cave, and the cave
had been sectioned into bunk rooms and
chemical toilets and a wide main room. The
bunks and the benches were all carved from the
stone and covered by lightweight pads. Eric
slipped into the front room and lit the stone stove,
which basically meant hitting the switch. There
was no other control. The stove was run by solar-
powered batteries and had one temperature, just
hot enough to boil water at this altitude.

They dined on freeze-dried stew served in
melted snow. They drank cup after cup of tepid
tea. No one spoke. Eric assigned bunks. Everyone
slept in his clothes.

Emma was the first to wake the next morning.
She took the hut's four pans outside, filled them
with snow, and set two on the burner. By the
time they came to a boil, the chamber was
warming. A first slit of sunlight glimmered
through the hut's shutters. Emma made herself a
cup of instant coffee, sweetened it liberally from
the plastic sugar jar, and heard Storm ask, "What
does a lady have to do to earn one of those?"

Emma made a second cup and said, "Why don't
we take it outside?"

They took their boots from the line by the
door and carried the tin mugs out to the bench

facing the rising sun. The air was both still and dry enough to ease the morning chill. Storm finished her mug and asked, "More?"

"Not just yet."

Storm rose and went inside. Emma settled back, in no hurry to go anywhere. She heard people moving around and hoped they would stay indoors. The sun warmed as it rose, a brilliant orb in a blue-black sky.

Storm returned carrying Tanya's satellite phone. She dialed a number, waited, then said, "Good morning, Muriel. How is Raphael?"

When Storm took a ragged breath, Emma reached over and took hold of her free hand. Storm asked, "Can I speak with him?"

Emma kept hold of her free hand as Storm said, "Good morning, Raphael. Eric is here, leading our team over Smuggler's Pass. We're carrying the duplicate Madonna into Switzerland. Before we left Italy, Father Gregor called this my pilgrimage. Now I know he was right. I'm doing this for you and for me and for us. I'm doing it for our love." Her voice broke then. She tried twice to go on, then cut the connection. She handed the phone to Emma.

Storm's breathing gradually eased. She swallowed hard. "I can't tell you how much I wish I had your problem. At least you two have a chance to work things out."

Emma said, "Do you believe in miracles?"

The cabin door opened. Tanya emerged, saw the two of them seated there, took the phone and their mugs, and retreated back indoors. Emma said, "I'm only asking on account of how I don't see any other way out of this mess I'm in with Harry."

Tanya returned bearing a single plate and one mug. "You'll have to share. There aren't enough plates to go around."

They ate the freeze-dried stew and shared the mug in silence. Emma rose and took the plate and cup back inside. When she returned, the mug was steaming again. She seated herself, sipped, handed it to Storm, and said, "The past few days have revealed a fracture line in my life. The problem is not the other people who have failed at this marriage business. And it's not my parents. It's not my profession. And it's not Harry. It's me. Here and now. I'm terrified that I'm not able to do this, make it work, keep us together." She planted her fists together. "I've got this tug-of-war inside me. One side desperately wants to be with Harry and nowhere else. The other side wants to hide away forever, using whatever excuse is nearest to keep me alone. Loving that man from six thousand miles away was ideal."

"You can keep doing that."

"No, we can't. Either we grow or we die."

Tanya emerged from the hut once more and announced, "We leave in five minutes."

Storm rose slowly to her feet. "The only reason I have the strength to go on is the hope that miracles can touch even someone like me."

ERIC WALKED ALONGSIDE STORM FOR a time, speaking of his highland world in almost reverential tones. There were many passes through the mountains. San Bernardino and San Gotthard were perhaps the best known. But in medieval times they were often preyed upon by bandit gangs. In such cases, pilgrims journeying to the Holy City sought lesser-known routes. Smuggler's Pass had been a vital conduit for over four hundred years. The reason became clear in the morning light.

The glacier saddle descended in a series of treacherous drops. The recent snow was creased with lines tight as a woman's frown. Eric pointed out how the drifts were shifting with the rising temperatures. This, he said, was an avalanche in the making.

But the path of their descent was utterly removed from this risk. To the west, the snowfield was rimmed by massive stones. They descended on these boulders like mice crawling down a giant's staircase.

The sunlight was strong enough to melt where it touched. The water re-formed as ice in the shadows. Each of the granite blocks was between ten and fifteen feet high. Where the stones met the cliff, centuries of pilgrims and smugglers had carved a lattice of hand- and footholds. Now and then they came upon more carved messages. In many places the steps were worn down to dangerous slants. Storm found the going especially hard at first, because she could not find enough air to take a decent breath. Her lungs sucked and pumped, but the air refused to gather.

Eric pushed them hard. Every time they halted he watched the peaks overhead. As the day progressed, the wind picked up again from the south. The peaks started snagging clouds, drawing colossal shadows over their world. Their handholds became mired in shades of granite and mist.

They lost the ability to speak. They walked and rested and walked again. Eventually they left the stones and the tongue of ice behind and entered a chaotic, slanting field of boulders. In some places a path became visible. In others, they picked their way around rocks the size of houses.

Each time they stopped, Storm used what precious breath she had to speak with Eric and Tanya. Their plans were simple enough. But her head felt parched from a raw mix of exhaustion and too little air. She made Tanya repeat each step before translating it to the people who crowded about them, listening, nodding, asking quiet questions for which Storm had to find yet more answers. One of the group used the satellite phone, then returned to their group and gave

Storm a thumbs-up. Storm found it reassuring to see that others agreed with her direction.

The rocks diminished in size, and their descent became progressively easier, which was good, because Storm's legs were on fire. Eric promised them a longer rest soon. Storm longed for stable earth that did not constantly slope downward. Where she did not have to keep constant watch for ice mixed with mud and rocks. Where she was not forced to lean back and balance her weight on her heels. Where breathing came easy. Where her pack did not constantly grow heavier. And her boots. And her shoulders. A world where she could just stop and rest until the next millennium.

The pine forest rose around them in stealthy stages. One tree fought through the rocks to form a Zen-like sculpture. Then two. Then a cluster high as her head. Then suddenly the rock was gone. The world became hushed by a blanket of needles, and the trees' fragrance overpowered her senses.

As they followed a muddy trail, the clouds descended and blanketed the forest, bathing their world in a fine mist. Now and then the stillness was broken by the *whump* of snow falling off branches. Occasionally sunlight broke through the mist. Birds chirped and sang of a world where men were not aliens. Storm's lungs stopped aching. Now the air felt thick as soup.

They halted. Storm released her pack's chest

strap, and then her legs simply gave way. She would have found it funny had she not been so tired. She managed to turn over so that she faced up and could see the branches carving delicate script from the white-gray mist. Once again the sun managed to break through, the light so blinding that Storm wanted to shield her eyes. But she could not raise her arm. As the world became shrouded again, she felt another body drop beside her own, but she could not find the energy to turn her head. Then Emma said, "Wake me in a thousand years."

Tanya slipped down to Storm's other side and said, "If my training had been this hard, I would be raising pigs like my father wanted."

Storm might have laughed. Or maybe it was just a sound inside her head.

FORTY-SEVEN

EMMA WOKE TO THE JARRING chime of Storm's cell phone. She rolled over and groaned in cadence with her body's complaints. The act of crawling to Storm's backpack required several more groans. She flipped open the phone and said, "What?"

Muriel Lang asked, "Storm?"

"It's Emma." She glanced at the motionless form beside her. "Storm is out for the count."

"I just heard from Storm's double at the auction

in Basel. The item comes up for auction in two hours. Perhaps less."

Emma confirmed, shut the phone, and eased to her feet in careful stages. Gradually her tendons and ligaments and muscles reknit themselves into something that resembled a body. The mist had vanished while she slept. The air held an odd mix of snow chill and sunlit warmth. The pine needles glowed softly where they caught the light. Other than Storm and herself, the glade was empty. Eric and the Poles had vanished. All according to Storm's plan.

She drained her water canister and ate her last PowerBar. She resisted the urge to sit back down. The temptation to let the forest roots bind her to the earth was too great.

Besides which, there was something that needed doing.

Emma opened the cell phone, then held it to her chest, testing her resolve. She stared at the sunlight lancing through the boughs overhead, wondering if she really had anything of value to say. The only response came from the wind and the surrounding trees, whispering softly that she must hurry.

When Harry answered the phone, Emma launched straight in with, "You're the first man I've ever known who's made me feel like it's okay to be me."

"You're better than okay, Emma. You're the best there is."

Harry's voice still carried that same breathless quality, but he sounded fully alert now. Fully there. "How are you feeling?"

"Better." He puffed a breath, then added, "It's actually been a good thing, being forced to lie here and let others take care of me. Not easy, but good. I needed to learn what it meant to be weak. Does that make any sense to you?"

"Yes, in a scary way."

"I am and always will be a treasure dog. But I also know you have changed me forever. I love you, Emma. And we need to be together."

Emma swiped at her face. "There you go again. Taking the words right from my own heart."

"Marry me, Emma."

The words came as easy as releasing the breath she had been holding. For her entire lifetime. "I want that, Harry. So very much."

"Wow. Easy as that."

"Nothing about this has been easy, except saying yes to you." Emma realized Storm was sitting up and watching her. "The rest has to wait."

Harry did not insist. "Go save the world, lady. It's what you're best at."

FORTY-EIGHT

EMMA AND STORM FOLLOWED ERIC'S final directions and emerged from the forest exactly where he had planned. Emma set down her end of the crate and took a long look around. "I suppose there's a word for a man who brings us over a mountain pass and through a forest and lands us square in front of our destination."

Storm was glad for the chance to rest. Despite the crate's light weight, carrying it through the woods had required a good deal of maneuvering. Not to mention the fact that she was still seriously exhausted.

The forest was as precisely trimmed as everything else about this land. It bordered a highway, and the highway ran alongside a rushing stream. To Storm's right rose the perfectly ordered rooftops of Zuoz. Fifteen kilometers farther southwest stood the villages of Samedan and St. Moritz. The Engadine Valley floor was a windswept patchwork of silver-green fields. The surrounding mountains gleamed white in the late-afternoon light.

A steep-sided knoll rose directly across the stream from where they stood. A tree-lined drive veered off from the highway in front of them, crossed the rushing stream, and circled around the back of the knoll. The flat crest covered perhaps five acres and was rimmed by a high stone wall. A landing strip flanked the stream and the highway. A small jet and a two-man helicopter were stationed where the strip met the drive.

Emma asked, "Only one family lives here?"

"For one month each year, assuming our man spends the same amount of time in every house," Storm replied.

They crossed the highway and started down the lane. The bridge over the stream was a fanciful blend of stone arches and Art Deco lights that draped like flowers. Storm and Emma were both huffing by the time they climbed the slope and settled the crate down before the main entrance. The double gates were handwrought iron, a latticework of fairies and flowers. The manor within the walls was massive. A turret rose from each of the manor's four corners. Storm rubbed feeling back into her hands and studied the empty forecourt.

Emma said, "What kind of guy lives in a pink palace?"

Actually, the shade was more a dusky rose. And it was not just the manor. The inside of the wall, the outbuildings, even the paving stones framing the gravel drive were all tinted with the same pastel shade. Storm guessed, "He did it for his daughter."

"Then we've come to the right place." Emma pointed to a pair of cameras that whirred around and focused upon them. "We're being watched."

"Good." Storm moved to the crate. "We don't have much time."

THE CRATE HAD A PAIR of latches, and the latches were sealed with tape. They pried the latches loose and opened the crate's front and unwrapped the layers of padding. Emma said, "Whoa."

Storm lifted the icon. "Shut the case."

"This is a fake?"

Sunlight caught the icon's silver frame and did not so much shine as pierce. "Stand it on the top of the case," Storm said. "No, aim it toward the cameras."

"I hope you know what you're doing. My professional training would suggest a little more caution is in order, seeing as how this man is the Russian who had Raphael shot."

"Now show them your badge."

Storm steadied the icon as Emma flashed her badge at the camera.

"I need to be ready for the call," Storm said. "Can you hold this by yourself?"

"I'm good." Emma pocketed her badge and took a firmer grip on the icon's frame. "You were right about Tanya and Muriel, by the way. Those ladies are totally stand-up. I was doubting me. Not them."

"Forget it. That was two eternities ago." Her cryptophone rang. "This is Storm."

Muriel Lang said, "I have your double on the line."

"Are you ready with the other connection?"

"Just give me the word. I have a secure phone service in Basel on hold. If Sir Julius traces your call, he will see the Basel auction area as your location."

"Okay. Put my double through."

After a series of clicks, the woman playing Storm said, "The item is coming up next."

The woman's Swiss-German accent was strong enough to overpower the cryptophone's metallic rasp. Storm asked, "What is the opening bid?"

"Two hundred thousand."

"Dollars?"

"Euros."

"Okay. Don't bid yet. I'll be right with you." Storm opened her other phone and hit the speed dial. Muriel answered instantly. Storm said, "Do it."

Storm stepped to where she could stand directly beneath the camera on the gate. She said into the cryptophone, "Where are we now?"

Her double replied, "Bidding is at three hundred and fifty. The auctioneer is asking for four hundred."

"How many bidders?"

"Four in the hall. One on the phone."

"Hold one moment." In her other ear, she heard Sir Julius bark his version of hello. Storm said,

"The reliquary is up. Bidding is at four hundred thousand euros and rising in increments of fifty thousand. We have company. Four in the house and one on the line."

"Have you bid?"

"Not yet. But there is no reason not to enter. Everyone knows why we're here."

"How is that?"

"Aaron Rausch made a scene yesterday."

"Did he indeed. Very well. You may begin."

Storm received the bidding process in her left ear and reported it to her right. The cryptophone was clear enough, but its harsh edge helped Storm keep track of who was where. Storm felt the wind whip about her, a sudden gust strong enough to rattle the cell phone's mouthpiece. Sir Julius demanded, "What is that infernal racket?"

"Perhaps there is interference at your end."

"It sounds like wind."

"They are now at one point six, Julius. As your appointed dealer, I should point out that no reliquary is worth—"

"Keep bidding."

Storm was about to pass on the instructions when the manor's front door opened.

The six men who emerged did not look like thugs. They did not look like killers. They looked exactly like what they were. Consummate professionals. They wore matching beige jackets and brown slacks and earpieces. They

369

flanked a man talking on his cell phone. He stood a trace under six feet. He had once been huge. But no longer. Kiril Temerko's skin draped like a suit designed to hold two of him.

The woman told Storm, "All but Rausch have now dropped out. The auctioneer is asking me for one point eight."

Storm watched Kiril Temerko shuffle across the graveled forecourt. She could hear the pebbles clicking as his feet scraped the earth.

Lord Julius demanded, "What is happening?"

Storm said, "The bidding is down to you and Aaron Rausch. He is at one point seven. Rising in hundred-thousand-euro increments."

"Keep on."

Temerko halted on the other side of the iron gate. Storm heard him say, "Have them bring the chest down for another look." His accent was heavy, his English precise. "For one point nine million euros, they can all wait."

Storm did not need to wait for her double to report, "Aaron Rausch has just requested another inspection, Sir Julius."

"Tell them to hurry things along!"

"It is within his rights—"

"Oh, never mind. The pilot informs me we are about to take off. I will be landing in Basel in ninety minutes. I expect you at planeside, young lady."

"You're coming to Switzerland?"

"Did I not just say precisely that? I have urgent business with the government."

"What about the reliquary?"

"Let Rausch's man have it. This time, young lady, you had best be on time."

Storm relayed the instructions to her double, then she watched as a moment later the man on the far side of the gates gave a cadaver's parody of a smile.

Kiril Temerko had the palest eyes she had ever seen. He shut his phone and said, "I have won."

Storm dismissed her double, stowed both phones away, and replied, "Sir Julius didn't care about the reliquary. He just wanted to make sure I wasn't standing here. Talking with you."

"You think holding this fake Madonna makes you safe? I can send my men out, they will take this icon, and they will make you disappear." He glanced at Emma. "You too, lady with a badge."

"You might have been that person once," Storm replied. "But not now. Not today."

"You know nothing about me. Nothing."

"I know you love your daughter so much her illness is killing you."

"I know things too. I know you are nothing but a second-rate dealer hunting scraps from a rich man's table. I could bury you in my cellar and fly away."

One of his men smirked.

Emma said, "Pay attention to what she's about to

tell you, Kiril. Offers like this don't grow on trees."

Storm related what Father Gregor had shared with her at the monastery. "Last year Putin wanted the Ukraine to pay more for their Russian gas, even though they had a twenty-year contract. Putin asked you to shut down the pipeline. You control thirty percent of all natural gas used by France. Forty percent for Germany and Italy. Even more for the Baltic states and Poland. When you did as Putin asked, the world panicked. Shutting off the flow of natural gas threatened the world's economy. The governments you've been bidding against for these items want to make sure you never do anything like this again."

Perhaps his face was incapable of expression. Maybe the mixture of old woes and fresh grief was too much for one face to wear. "Why do you waste my time, telling me things the whole world knows?"

"You know how they trap a tiger? They dig a hole and cover it with brush and tether a goat as bait. I'm tired of being the bait, Kiril." Storm gestured at where Emma held the icon. "The CIA and the British secret service know about you, they know about your daughter. They know the Russian who arranged to copy the Black Madonna for you. Your counterfeiter, Wadi Haddad, is now in the U.S. under government protection. Sir Julius, who orchestrated the bidding against you, is on his way to Basel as we speak. I assume to inform the Swiss government of your actions and request a warrant to be issued and held until the need arises."

Emma added, "It's all come together, Kiril. The Western governments know you were behind the theft of the Black Madonna. They have something against you now. The next time your government tries to cut back on the gas, they're going to cage the beast."

"We're doing you a favor," Storm said. "If the Western governments knew we were here, they'd be livid."

"So maybe they will thank me when I make you both disappear, yes?"

"They might. They might also arrest you for stealing the Madonna. And who looks after your daughter then?"

Pale eyes bore into her a moment longer. Then he wheeled about and said, "Come."

FORTY-NINE

THE TALLEST OF THE SECURITY guards did not like letting Storm inside the compound. He tried to protest, but Kiril Temerko was already shuffling back toward the manor. The guard opened the gate only about a foot, and Storm had to ease through sideways. When she was in, he jostled her as he shut the gate, shoving her against the metal.

Emma jammed her arm through the bars, pushing him back. "Watch it!"

One of the guards moving alongside Kiril Temerko spoke to their boss. The Russian turned and saw what was happening. He spoke one word.

The guard threatening Storm stepped back. The moment Temerko turned again toward the mansion, the angry guard pulled a phone from his pocket, hit the speed dial, and began muttering. All without taking his eyes off Storm.

Storm called to Kiril, "You're forgetting something."

"Yes?" The man stopped and turned toward her.

"We should take the counterfeit icon with us."

Temerko registered a trace of surprise. "You will just give it to me?"

"You made it. It's yours." Storm watched the guard slap his phone shut and stalk over to stand beside Temerko. She did her best to ignore his glare. "In return, you're going to give me the original icon."

"Am I?"

"Of course. It's in your best interest. And your daughter's. All this bluffing you're doing is for show. But neither of us has time for that now. So why don't we just go inside and do this thing."

THE MANOR'S GROUND FLOOR HAD the rehearsed sterility of a Palm Beach palace. The colors in the Titian oil above the polished stone fireplace matched the silk Isfahan carpet. Standard thirty-foot ceiling. Brazilian mahogany rimmed the polished granite floor. Everything was coldly tasteful. The London hospital's waiting room had more heart.

The upstairs was divided by the sweeping central staircase. Storm assumed the double doors to her left led to the master suite. The guard who had accosted Storm remained at the base of the stairs, while the three remaining guards continued to accompany Temerko. He pulled out his cell phone and again spoke urgently but softly, shooting daggers up at Storm.

Kiril pushed open the right-hand doors, revealing a long, dark hallway. When Storm hesitated, he said, "You wanted so bad to see, come see."

The hallway was tall and domed and painted the same shade of rose as the manor's exterior. The walls held too many carved alcoves to count. Each alcove was lit by votive candles.

Storm no longer cared that Kiril and the guards waited impatiently up ahead. She set down the icon and gave herself over to the joy of discovery.

The first alcove held a carving of Jonah being cast from the whale. Such carvings had been popular in the second and third centuries. Early believers had considered it an image befitting those who had been expelled from the world of

Greek and Roman gods. The piece was of white onyx. Jonah, as the hero, was sculpted slightly larger than the whale that had just expelled him.

Storm stepped to the next alcove, which held a reliquary casket carved from olive wood and heavily embossed with silver and gilt. The casket's lid was peaked in three places like a royal throne, indicating it held the remains of a church leader. Probably sixth century.

Next came an emerald necklace, most likely worn by a Byzantine emperor when exercising his power as head of the church. The face of each stone was sanded flat and carved with the image of one of the apostles. Fifth century.

An early diptych, ivory covered with gold leaf. Because the woman depicted wore Roman dress, it was probably an image of the first Byzantine empress, Constantia, sister of Constantine. Fourth century.

A royal *globus cruciger*, a hand-sized ball topped with a cross, solid gold, studded with rubies and diamonds. Probably seventh century.

A diadem, or crown, made to commemorate the coronation of a new emperor. Because the crown was so tiny, it was probably made for a child. Ninth century.

There was a primeval air to the hall. But it was not a holy sensation. This was no church. The candles performed a macabre dance before treasures robbed of their sacred significance.

Kiril waited for her at the hallway's end, the three guards still surrounding him. Kiril's skin folded about his face and neck like a ghoulish cape.

"Enough," Kiril said. "Your prize is this way. Come."

FIFTY

THE CHILD'S SUITE WAS HALF Aladdin's cave and half shrine. The bedroom was larger than Storm's entire apartment. A turret formed the room's northeast corner, a curved fairyland filled with stuffed animals and dolls. Hundreds and hundreds of dolls.

The room's centerpiece was a pink four-poster bed topped by a pink canopy. On the bed's other side was the largest antique dollhouse Storm had ever seen. It completely covered an oak refectory table.

The guards took up stations at the hallway door just inside the bedroom. A woman in a nurse's uniform rose from a chair by the bed. She did not look in Kiril's direction. She stepped into an alcove and left the room via a recessed door in the tower's curved wall. The door clicked shut.

In the bed was a wraith, a ghost still encased in skin and bones. Her skull was covered in a grayish-white fuzz that left her head even more naked than if she had been completely bald.

Only her eyes held life, two brilliant dark orbs that fastened upon her father as soon as he appeared. She did not even glance at Storm. Her father sank onto the bed beside his daughter, took up her hand, stroked her face, and crooned to her.

The room's walls were plastered with icons. Dozens of them.

The Greek word *eikon* meant a likeness, image, or picture. In the eleventh century, after the defeat of iconoclasm and the split of the Roman and Eastern churches, artists began fashioning secondary frames around the icons known for having miracles associated with them. These frames were normally finished in silver and gold revetment, where every inch was meticulously embedded with patterns of holy ornamentation—crosses, diadems, faces, and so on. Every icon Storm could see bore such adornment.

The Black Madonna was on the wall directly opposite the bed. Storm felt herself drawn across the room. The force of the image was that strong. The table before the icon was blanketed by votive candles. In the flickering light, the icon's eyes watched her approach. Storm had the vivid impression that the child in the icon smiled a welcome.

She leaned the copy against the wall, slipped around the table, and gingerly took down the original. Her hands tingled as though a current passed through her body. She replaced it with the counterfeit. Then she stepped back. She knew she should flee. But the art historian in her insisted upon one proper look.

In the room's weak lighting it was difficult for Storm to identify differences between the two. Yet the original held a powerful sense of realness. The patina of smoke was deeper. The revetment, the gilded outer frame, was deeply marked in places. The scars beneath the woman's right eye, where invaders had attacked the icon six centuries ago, gleamed with a soft luminosity. Storm felt the strength of heritage and history reach across the centuries. She stared at the original icon, and her mind was filled with the image of Tanya's mother, walking sixteen hours to kneel and pray.

Her mind was then captured by an image of her own pilgrimage and how she had been held by such a grim desperation that to have released her prayer would have cost her every shred of control.

"You have what you came for," Kiril Temerko said. "Take it and go."

Storm turned back to where the Russian oligarch continued to stroke his child's cheek. "The guard we left at the bottom of the stairs, was he responsible for stealing this icon and making the duplicate?"

The man on the bed gave no sign that he had heard her.

Storm went on, "My guess is, he won't be all that happy watching me leave."

Without lifting his gaze, Kiril spoke to the other guards. One motioned to Storm, a lifting of his chin. Come.

But as Storm hefted the icon, Kiril said, "Find me the Amethyst Clock. I will pay you whatever you want."

"You don't believe that it exists any more than I do."

He did not look up from the child's face. "What is belief? I buy what I need. I buy you. I buy the clock. I pay twenty million dollars."

"I can't help you," Storm replied. "Sorry."

"Fifty million." The Russian's voice carried no hope. No life. "A hundred."

Storm watched the man stroke the child's cheek. The girl's eyes glittered in the half light as she stared at her father. Then the guard to her left touched her shoulder. Storm lifted the Madonna once more. She walked down the hallway, the treasures glittering in the candlelight as she passed. There was nothing for her here.

She blinked as she stepped onto the upper floor's landing. The doors clicked shut behind her.

Then she saw the gun.

THE TALL GUARD STOOD AT the bottom of the stairs. He was a big-boned man with a fighter's jaw and eyes of pale onyx. The two guards flanking Storm argued with him in Russian as they continued down the steps.

The icon was not especially heavy, but the frame was so broad she had to walk with her arms outstretched. The guards halted when the gun weaved over to include them. It was a very Russian sort of argument, a lot of hand waving and finger-pointing. But none of the other guards pulled their weapons, so Storm assumed the quarrel was going her way.

Storm settled the Madonna on the next step down. Her entire body ached. She could track the pains up from her feet, through her legs, the small of her back, her shoulders, her wrists, her fingers. Finally one of her guards walked down the stairs, plucked the gun from the other man's grasp, and shoved him to one side. Storm lifted the icon and continued down the stairs. A rising wind buffeted the north-facing windows. The branches of one of the ornamental trees tapped against a ground-floor window.

The hostile guard said as she passed, "Sir Julius sends you his regards."

THE WIND SMACKED HER WITH a cold, damp fist. The northern peaks clutched passing clouds and spun a blanket of gloom across the valley. From behind the gates, Emma called something, but her words were lost to the wind. Then she pointed, and Storm saw that another jet had landed on the private strip and was taxiing to where a police car waited.

The guards saw it too. One man reached out to pull her back into their angry huddle. But Storm lifted the icon higher and let it act like a sail, tugging her down the front steps.

The wind tried to rip the icon from her grasp, but she hung on grimly and was carried forward. Behind her, a guard yelled. Her feet traced a frantic beat across the graveled forecourt.

She heard the guards racing to catch up. They shouted back and forth, panicking as the police car started up the drive with its lights flashing.

Storm spotted the red knob set in the pillar beside the gates and struck it with her shoulder. Emma pried through the instant the gates parted and rushed over. "This it?"

"Yes." She slipped through the gates.

"Can we go? The natives are growing restless."

"One of the guards has been in Sir Julius's pay." Storm anchored the icon at her feet. "Things are about to get sticky."

Sir Julius emerged from the rear seat before the police car came to a full stop. The wind rustled his thinning hair and fluttered his pant legs. "How *dare* you attempt to deceive me!"

"Looks to me like we succeeded." Storm motioned to Emma. Together they lifted the icon and started down the lane toward the landing strip. Away from the police and the guards and the irate British nobleman.

"We'll see about that!" He flapped one arm against the wind and the day. "Seize that item!"

Emma released the icon to Storm and stepped between them. "It's not yours to take."

"Oh, and I suppose you're going to stop me?" His sneer was strong enough to defy the wind. "The agent who has been dismissed from her agency for refusing a direct order to stay out of affairs that are *none of her concern?*"

Emma took the verbal blow without a blink of her eye. "That's right," she said. "I am."

The peer's hand was shaking so hard he twice missed drawing a letter from his inner pocket. "I have arrived with orders for these policemen to arrest you."

Storm asked, "Are you going to arrest them as well?"

"What are you blathering . . ." Sir Julius turned.

Every tree lining the private lane sprouted an individual. There were more men than women. But the women were clearly as tough as the men.

Sir Julius demanded, "Where did they come from?"

"Poland," Storm replied.

His laugh held a manic edge. "You think this rabble can halt Her Majesty's government?"

"Absolutely," Storm said.

The police and the guards had gone silent. Their

attention was gripped by the sight of the ragtag group moving toward them.

"What do they expect to do, shoot us down?" Sir Julius raised his voice. "Do you have *any* idea of the firestorm that would be unleashed?"

"No more of a firestorm than your trying to mask the theft of a national treasure," Storm replied. "They are unarmed. They are taking the icon and they are leaving."

"What utter rot." Sir Julius turned to the police. "You there. Stop them."

The police shouted something in Swiss German and started forward, hands on their holstered guns.

The approaching group unclenched slightly, revealing a man whose face was half melted away. He responded in their own tongue and lifted a leather badge case similar to the one Emma carried.

Emma moved back to where Storm kept the icon anchored against the wind. "He's intel?"

Storm replied, "Swiss military."

"You knew this since when, exactly?"

"I heard Eric use the satellite phone in the mountain hut. He called down and received permission for us to enter his country. He explained what he was doing and why."

"And you didn't tell me." Emma swept the hair from her face. "Shame on you."

A distant rhythmic popping overhead grew louder. Storm said, "Here they come."

Sir Julius towered over the two women and the icon. "I will *destroy* you."

"I'm sure you will try." Storm waited while a helicopter settled onto the landing strip beside the jet. "And now, if you'll excuse me, I have an item to deliver to its rightful owner."

She and Emma began walking toward the landing strip. Tanya stepped from the group and helped Emma and Storm anchor the icon against the raging wind. The rest of the group of Poles fell in around them. One of the men began singing. Several others joined in. Storm hummed along, though she did not know either the tune or the language. But it scarcely mattered, just as her prayers did not need to name a man or even her own need, for fear of shattering her hold on the day. She heard Emma begin to hum what sounded like an entirely different tune. Somehow their melodies blended well.

By the time they arrived at the point where the lane joined with the landing strip, Father Gregor and Antonin Tarka had alighted from the copter and moved toward them, their voices joining in the song. All of them were singing. Everyone.

FIFTY-ONE

A T THE SAINT MORITZ POLICE station they were met by a man in a gray uniform with a colorless expression. Eric snapped off a salute and said to the women, "I must go with him."

"Will you be okay?" Emma asked.

Eric waited until the man had stepped away to reply, "There are some within my government who do not approve of Sir Julius's actions. They dislike using Temerko and his ailing daughter as pawns. I am safe. What about you?"

"Hard to say."

"You play the game, you pay the price, yes?" He must have understood the fear behind Emma's tight features, for he added, "Your efforts have averted an international crisis. Sir Julius is of course livid over your blocking his plan to blackmail Temerko. But there must be cooler heads in both his government and your own. They will recognize what you have done as a service to international relations."

"Let's hope my boss agrees with you," Emma said.

"I am certain of it." Eric turned to Storm. "Raphael would be very proud of you."

"Will be," Emma said, correcting him. "Will be very proud."

Storm hugged the man. "Assuming we all survive this, I just want you to know, whatever you need, wherever you need it."

"I feel the same." He saluted them. "An honor to serve with you both."

The Swiss authorities took the two women to the Zurich airport. They were ushered through customs and taken to a room the size of an office cubicle. A stout woman in her late twenties stood by the steel door. She wore a dark blue uniform and a suspicious air. Storm found it easy to ignore her.

Storm sat on one side of a plastic table bolted to the wall. Emma sat across from her. High overhead, an air conditioner rattled quietly. Shadows creased Emma's features, strong enough to defy the room's fluorescent lighting. She stared at her hands, which cupped her phone.

Storm said, "Not checking your messages won't make the bad stuff go away."

"You think I don't know that?"

Storm reached across the table for Emma's phone. Emma started to draw away, then sighed. That single breath released all her muscles. The hands and arms and shoulders and neck all went limp.

Storm turned on the phone. Dialed Emma's voice mail. Listened.

Emma asked the tabletop, "How many messages?"

"Seventeen from Tip, four from Harry."

"Leave our lad for the moment." Emma's voice sounded strangled. "Let's face what Tip has to say."

Storm listened to the first few messages, then cut the connection and sighed.

Emma swallowed hard. "Bad, huh?"

"How do I reach Tip?"

"Number two on the speed dial."

The phone in America rang once, then Tip MacFarland barked, "You missed the D-Day landing, so you decided to set up your very own Normandy, is that it?"

"This is Storm Syrrell."

"Why aren't I speaking to Emma?"

"Because." Storm hesitated, then decided the man deserved the truth. "She's terrified."

Emma turned and stared at the sidewall.

"The lady should be."

"That's very helpful, Tip." Emma looked so small and frightened, Storm could not entirely keep the fury from her voice. "She's done nothing wrong, and you know it."

"She defied a direct order from the director's office."

"Because of the CIA's maneuvers. Their aim was to let a Russian oligarch keep possession of a Polish national treasure. Which the Russian had stolen. But the Langley brigade and their pals in England didn't care about that, or the uproar that threatened to engulf central Europe. All they

wanted was a way to pull the Kremlin's strings."
When Tip remained silent, she pressed, "Did
they happen to mention how Emma helped
restore the icon to its rightful place, an act that
earned her the thanks of the Polish nation and
the Catholic Church?"

Tip spoke slowly. "You're telling me you have
documented evidence you could take public."

"I don't make threats, Tip. Unlike some
people."

The growl softened a notch. "Let me speak to
her."

Emma did not reveal a thing as she accepted
the phone and said, "Webb here." She listened
awhile, gave a soft yes, another, and then hung
up. Emma stared at the phone in her hands and
said, "I may have to lie low for a while. Drop a
ways down the pay scale. Find a cave and pull a
rock in behind me. Tip mentioned Tasmania."

THEY TOOK THE BULLET TRAIN to Weisbaden.
Storm had intended to travel straight back to
London. But two things changed her mind. Harry
revealed that he had undergone what sounded
like fairly major surgery. Then there was the
small item of marriage. As in, Emma and Harry.
They both wanted Storm to witness the occasion.
Harry had arranged for the ceremony to take place
in the hospital chapel. Storm agreed to make a
quick detour, then hurry to Raphael's bedside.

Storm's reunion with the wayward lad was made more poignant both by his weakened state and by Emma's untrammeled joy. Emma sat in the chair by his bed, held his hands, and glowed. Storm stood where she could watch them both and yearned.

They overnighted in a hotel by the main gates of the air base. Storm did not sleep well. The next morning Emma appeared wearing the same dress and jacket she had last donned in Basel. The outfit was wrinkled and road-weary, but it did not matter. Emma's face shone with a luminescence that left Storm wanting to weep—with joy for them, with worry over her own state, with relief and exhaustion.

While Emma went upstairs to check on Harry, Storm bought flowers from the hospital gift shop and followed the signs to the chapel. The chapel lighting was muted, the colors soothing, the seven pews empty. A single votive candle burned upon the altar. Storm set two bouquets to either side of the stone cross and wished it was in her power to accent the day further. Fireworks, perhaps, a hundred of their closest friends and an angelic choir and a twenty-one-gun salute. Because that was what her friend deserved.

Storm took a seat in the front pew and checked her watch. The time meant nothing. She opened her phone, speed-dialed Muriel, and spoke the question yet again. "How is he?"

"Raphael has had a bad night."

The air was suddenly filled with glass shards, each breath a scarring experience. "What happened?"

"I have no idea." Muriel tried for a professional air but achieved only a monotone flat as pounded iron. "I can't see any change. But I met with the doctors. They say his vitals are not holding up as well as they had hoped. Whatever that means."

Storm forced herself to swallow down the wail. She found herself speaking with the same dull flatness as Muriel. "Can I speak with Raphael?"

"Of course. Here he is."

Storm heard the rustling sound as the phone was settled against his ear. She felt a surge at heart level and knew the current between them was so strong it could defy even the dead air. "Hello, my darling. The pilgrimage is over. The one I did for us. I think it's maybe the finest—"

She stopped. Everything welled up inside her, pressing against her heart until the walls burst. She said what she had not allowed herself even to think. Until now. "I want a home with you, Raphael. I want a yard with a bougainvillea hedge and palms that rattle in the night winds. I want a porch and a swing. I want us to watch the water sparkle at sunset. I want children, Raphael. I thought I would never say those words. But I do.

I want to give you your heart's desire. I want to know the joy of loving you for years and years . . ."

There might have been a sigh, a quiet rush of sound. Almost like she could hear a man whisper her name.

Storm managed her farewells to Muriel, then sat cradling the phone. Raphael's absence was an empty ache, almost large enough to swallow her whole. Even so, her words to him echoed through the empty chamber. Words Storm had always assumed would never be true, as far as she was concerned. Somehow, her present had become at least partly severed from her past, enough so that she could reach beyond her upbringing and declare herself ready to love. Before this day, this very hour, she would have called such things impossible. Storm wiped her face and wondered if this was what it was like to come face-to-face with miracles.

Then Harry's nurse pushed open the chapel doors. She smiled at Storm, as though finding only rightness in a woman's tears. The nurse said, "We're ready to begin."

ACKNOWLEDGMENTS

The writing and research of *The Black Madonna* was a reminder about the power of history to transform lives. During the chaotic interval between the defeat of the Nazis and domination by the Soviet Union, my wife's parents escaped from Poland. They eventually settled in America. The family members who remained in Poland were soon trapped behind the Iron Curtain. Over the years, they have shared with me their stories and their love of their homeland. They have gone out of their way to make me feel not just included but embraced. I am deeply honored to be a part of this wonderful family and continually impressed by the heritage they have helped me to understand. Special thanks to Teodozja Tarka, Olgierd Tarka, Tadeusz Kaliszczak, Jadwiga Kaliszczak, Jan and Halina Zorawski, and Teresa Aleksandrowicz.

Debbie Bernstein is a former federal prosecutor based in Manhattan who focused on crime within the international arts and treasures markets. Today she is vice president of Sotheby's and is responsible for their compliance divisions. Basically, Debbie's remit is to keep the auction house both accountable and secure. It has been a privilege to learn from her.

Senator Bill Nelson and his wife, Grace, have

kindly welcomed me into their homes both in Florida and Washington, DC. Their extensive international network of contacts helped immeasurably in providing leads and interviews for this story. My wife and I value their friendship and their leadership. Thanks also to Tim Perrier, leader of Grace's Florida team, who continues to inspire us with his passion for politics as a force for the good.

This book involved considerable site research in England, Poland, Switzerland, the West Bank, and Italy. I am indeed grateful to all those who opened their lives and homes to me during these travels. A special thanks to Rabbi Baruch of Ashdot, Israel, whose help was instrumental in forming several scenes.

I was first introduced to glacier hiking over a dozen years ago. I still dream about that first crossing of the ice. I am grateful to all the guides and journeyers who taught me about their world above the tree line.

This period may go down as the toughest in Palm Beach's history. Many fine people have been badly scarred by the Madoff scandal, and a number of charities performing vital roles have been reduced to ashes. Our thoughts and prayers go out to these people, along with my thanks for the welcome they gave us, despite their current woes.

My heartfelt thanks goes to the superb teams at

Howard Books and Touchstone, and I am proud to be affiliated with Simon & Schuster. I am especially grateful for the ongoing assistance and wisdom of my editor, Dave Lambert. Thanks also to Tom Williams for his valuable story insights.

As with all my works, my greatest guide and truest friend has been my wife, Isabella. Her eyes have seen what my own have missed. Her ability to translate not merely the words but the sentiments behind them, as well as the history that shapes them both, has made this book possible. On the wall of our home in England hangs a framed print of the Black Madonna of Czestochowa, the same one she has known since childhood. She has placed the cover design for this novel next to it, and tells me that this book has made something very special even more so.

ABOUT THE AUTHOR

Award-winning novelist Davis Bunn has sold more than six million books in sixteen languages. His titles have appeared on numerous bestseller lists and have been featured by Doubleday Book Club, Literary Guild, Mystery Guild, Guideposts, and Crossings Book Club. He is known for the diversity of his writing talent, from gentle gift books to high-powered thrillers.

Davis has received numerous accolades, including three Christy Awards for excellence in fiction. He currently serves as writer in residence at Regent's Park College, Oxford University. Davis divides his time between England and Florida, and lectures internationally on the craft of writing.

Visit with the author at www.DavisBunn.com.

READING GROUP GUIDE

1. Key scenes in *The Black Madonna* are set in the glamorous world of auction houses. Have you ever attended an auction of any kind? What was the atmosphere? Were you inclined to bid on any items?

2. How are various forms of *power* exercised in this book? By whom and with what impact?

3. Which character in *The Black Madonna* do you most identify with and why?

4. The title of *The Black Madonna* refers to a sacred relic deemed to hold miraculous powers. Do you believe such supernatural qualities are possible, or merely superstitions? Have you had any personal experiences that could be considered miraculous?

5. At a number of points in the story, Storm Syrrell has her physical limits tested; for example, when climbing a mountain over cold and rough terrain. Have you ever been

in a situation that demanded great physical endurance? How were you changed by this challenge?

6. Despite Raphael Danton's attractiveness, Storm Syrrell initially finds him arrogant and manipulative. She later changes her mind and must look at him anew. Have you ever needed to reassess your first impression of someone? If so, why?

7. Toward the end of the story, Agent Emma Webb deliberately disobeys the orders of her superior. Have you ever been tempted by insubordination, and if so, for what reason?

8. Raphael Danton reacts to the tragedy of his wife's death by seeking revenge on the African tribe that was implicated in her murder. Can you recall a situation when you were filled with the desire for revenge? Would it have been possible to respond with forgiveness?

9. Two of the main characters in the novel—Harry Bennett and Emma Webb—clearly care for each other but are afraid to commit to a lasting relationship. What was the turning point that made the difference? Have

you ever found yourself at a romantic cross-roads?

10. *The Black Madonna* is written in the genre of a thriller and therefore includes many episodes of danger. Have you ever found yourself confronting danger? How did it make you feel, both physically and emotionally? What was the aftermath of the incident?

11. The Polish characters in the book demonstrate both a patriotic love of their country and a religious devotion to the Catholic church, and clearly see the two as mutually reinforcing. What is your view about the linkages between politics and religion?

Center Point Publishing
600 Brooks Road ● PO Box 1
Thorndike ME 04986-0001 USA

(207) 568-3717

US & Canada:
1 800 929-9108
www.centerpointlargeprint.com